MURDER BY SUGGESTION

Further Titles by Veronica Heley from Severn House

The Ellie Quicke Mysteries

MURDER AT THE ALTAR
MURDER BY SUICIDE
MURDER OF INNOCENCE
MURDER BY ACCIDENT
MURDER IN THE GARDEN
MURDER BY COMMITTEE
MURDER BY BICYCLE
MURDER OF IDENTITY
MURDER IN HOUSE
MURDER BY MISTAKE
MURDER MY NEIGHBOUR
MURDER IN MIND
MURDER WITH MERCY
MURDER IN TIME
MURDER BY SUSPICION
MURDER IN STYLE
MURDER FOR NOTHING

The Bea Abbot Agency Mysteries

FALSE CHARITY
FALSE PICTURE
FALSE STEP
FALSE PRETENCES
FALSE MONEY
FALSE REPORT
FALSE ALARM
FALSE DIAMOND
FALSE IMPRESSION
FALSE WALL
FALSE FIRE
FALSE PRIDE

MURDER BY SUGGESTION

Veronica Heley

This first world edition published 2018
in Great Britain and the USA by
SEVERN HOUSE PUBLISHERS LTD of
Eardley House, 4 Uxbridge Street, London W8 7SY.
Trade paperback edition first published
in Great Britain and the USA 2018 by
SEVERN HOUSE PUBLISHERS LTD.

British Library Cataloguing in Publication Data
A CIP catalogue record for this title is available from the British Library.

ISBN-13: 978-0-7278-8805-1 (cased)
ISBN-13: 978-1-84751-932-0 (trade paper)
ISBN-13: 978-1-78010-987-9 (e-book)

All Severn House titles are printed on acid-free paper.

Severn House Publishers support the Forest Stewardship Council™ [FSC™],
the leading international forest certification organisation. All our titles that
are printed on FSC certified paper carry the FSC logo.

Typeset by Palimpsest Book Production Ltd.,
Falkirk, Stirlingshire, Scotland.
Printed and bound in Great Britain by
TJ International, Padstow, Cornwall.

ONE

Monday morning, noon.

It had to be her daughter, Diana. No one else hung on to the front doorbell like that.

Ellie dropped her trowel and gardening gloves in her haste to answer the summons. What on earth was Diana doing, ringing Ellie's doorbell on a Monday morning when she should be at work?

Ellie opened the door and Diana pushed past her into the hall, tugging a large suitcase on wheels after her and thrusting a couple of coats in plastic covers into her mother's arms. 'You took your time, didn't you?'

'What . . .?'

Diana was already dragging in another suitcase and a folding travel bag for long dresses. Out in the drive a taxi driver was unloading a number of heavy plastic bags.

'Diana . . .?'

'You might help me!' Diana thrust a tote bag at her mother. 'I've got to get everything under cover before it rains.'

Ellie had been potting up geranium cuttings. Were her hands clean enough to touch Diana's precious things? Well, they'd have to be. Ellie slung the tote bag into the back of the hall and went back for another. What on earth was Diana doing, bringing her belongings here?

Surely the girl hadn't quarrelled with her husband and decided to move out? No, of course not. Yet the mounting piles of luggage seemed to suggest that was exactly what she had done.

Only, if Diana had left her husband, what had she done with her delightful if tiring small son? Ellie couldn't see any children's things among the piles of luggage on the floor.

Finally Diana dragged the last of her bundles inside and shut the front door. It did look as if it were going to rain. The panelled hall suddenly seemed very dark.

'Diana, what is this?'

Diana drew her hand across her forehead. 'He's thrown me out! I went off to work in the usual way. He wasn't up by that time – he likes a good lie-in nowadays – but the new nanny was bustling around, getting little Evan's breakfast, seeing him off to the nursery. Everything seemed normal. Nothing prepared me for the shock.' She sank down on to the hall chair.

Yes, she was in shock. Visibly trembling.

Ellie tried to grasp the situation, and failed.

'Don't just stand there gaping, Mother! Do something!'

'I don't understand. Why—?'

'I was in a meeting with a prospective buyer for the flats behind the cinema, a project I've been working on for months. He rang through and ordered me to drop everything and get back home. He ordered me . . . ordered *me*! *Me* who's kept him and the business going all these years – he ordered me to get back home! I said I couldn't leave just like that, and he said that if I didn't I'd find all my things out in the road. I couldn't believe it!'

Diana wrenched open her jacket with fingers that trembled. Yes, she really was in shock. As always, she was wearing a black suit over a white shirt. She kept her black hair cut short and her only make-up was a bright red lipstick, which today was slightly smudged.

If it had been anyone else in trouble but Diana, Ellie would by now have been giving them a cuddle and urging them to have a good cry, but Diana had always repelled physical contact. So instead Ellie asked, 'Why?'

A tinge of colour came into Diana's cheeks. 'It was a joke! If it went wrong, it wasn't my fault!'

Ellie blinked. Diana didn't *do* jokes.

Diana scrabbled at the neck of her blouse, tearing the collar open. 'He says I plotted the death of one of his friends – a golfing buddy, you know? It's ridiculous, and I'm going to sue him for . . .' A glitter of tears. 'Mother, I don't know what to do. He'd got the cleaner and the nanny to pack up all my things and put them in the hall. He wouldn't even let me go up to my bedroom to check if anything was left. He said that if I'd missed anything, he'd send it on. He grabbed my keys from me so I can't get back into the house and he said I couldn't take my car because it belongs to the business, and that's why I had to get a taxi to come here.'

Ellie would have subsided into a chair herself at that point, but there was only one in the hall and Diana was occupying it. So Ellie let herself down on to the next to bottom of the stairs. 'He can't do that. Can he?'

'He has. What's more, he's told that stupid Mrs Thing at work that she's being promoted and will be in charge in future and not to let me back in, so now I haven't even a job to go to and that big sale I was working on will fall through and I could . . . I could bite something!'

Ellie pinched herself. Was this really happening? 'But Diana, what about little Evan?'

Diana wept. Her face didn't distort, but tears ran down her cheeks unheeded. She was a hard, difficult woman in many ways, but she did love her little son who, somewhat confusingly, had been named after his father. 'My dear husband said he's going to court to get sole custody. He says he's rung the bank and told them I'd lost my handbag. He's cancelled all my credit cards and asked the bank to send replacements to him, so I won't get them. The taxi took the last of my cash. I can't believe this is happening!'

Neither could Ellie. 'Why, Diana? He can't just throw you out for . . . What did he say you'd done?'

Diana sniffed, found a hankie and blew her nose. 'He says I killed a friend of his. Bunny Brewster – dreadful little man. They called him Bunny because his nose twitched like a rabbit's when he ate. He died of an overdose a couple of weeks ago. No one's going to miss him. It was nothing to do with me, I swear it! I've not been near him.'

Yet there was something in her voice which told Ellie that Diana was not entirely without guilt or, perhaps, knowledge of the event? 'Why does Evan think that?'

'Oh, it's ridiculous! There was a group of us, wives of some of the men who are at the golf club every evening. We were looking at a brochure about a murder weekend at the club. We were joking, having fun, making up stories about how we'd murder someone, but it wasn't serious. How could it be? None of us meant it. It was just saying

"What if . . .?" You know? We'd all drunk a bit, we were bored, the men were off in a huddle as usual, and we were feeling neglected. What does it matter who said it? The fact is that the stupid man *did* get his pills muddled up and died, and Evan's saying that I was responsible and it's not *true*!'

Ellie believed her. 'No, of course not.'

'As if I would! What's Bunny Brewster to me? He was always around when we went to the club, not that I go much, but I don't think I've ever spoken to him except to say things like, "How are you doing?" Or, "Is Barbie not with you tonight?" Barbie is his wife. Was his wife. I told you that he'd died, didn't I? We all went to the funeral. It was sad, but these things happen. Now Evan says . . . I can't believe it! Why on earth would I want to kill Bunny? And did Evan really have to drag me away from work like that? Serve him right if we lost the sale of those flats. I can tell you this for nothing; it won't be him who closes that deal.'

She sniffed. 'He won't remember his dentist's appointment if I'm not there to remind him, or that he has to have his warfarin levels checked this week. He's lost the plot, know what I mean? And what will my poor little boy do without me to kiss him better when he falls down, and tell him bedtime stories?'

What, indeed? Diana's toddler son was another alpha male in the making but he was devoted to his mother. As for the estate agency, Ellie had heard Diana comment before on her husband's loss of interest in it of recent years, even though it kept them both in the manner to which they were accustomed. That big house and two sleek cars, the entertaining, the fees to the golf club; all that was paid for by some hard graft on the high street. Diana had a flair for business, and she worked hard. She might cut the occasional corner here or there, but . . . murder? No way. Had Evan really lost the plot?

Ellie said, 'You need a solicitor.'

Diana straightened up. 'That's what I thought. Can you get your man Gunnar on to it? He's the best, isn't he? I don't think Evan knows anyone of his calibre.' The businesswoman in her clicked into operation. 'I want a divorce, of course, and sole custody of my son. I know Evan rents our house and doesn't own it but I shall need alimony. It would best if . . . Yes, tell him I'll settle for his signing the estate agency over to me.

He's hardly ever there nowadays, anyway. Also, I'll need a sum to enable me to buy a decent flat somewhere. Right?'

Ellie reflected that her old friend Gunnar was indeed one of the best, and also one of the most expensive of solicitors. It didn't sound as if Diana was prepared to pay his fees. Ellie feared she knew who was going to have to do that, and who would have to find somewhere for Diana to live in the meantime. She went to the phone, found Gunnar's mobile number and dialled. The call went to voicemail. She left a message for him to ring her.

Diana was impatient. 'Trust you to ring the wrong number. Try his mobile, for heaven's sake, and leave him my mobile number to contact me direct.'

'I did try his mobile.' Ellie hadn't left Diana's number, because she was not at all sure yet what this affair was all about. Was it just a matrimonial spat? 'Diana, why exactly does Evan say you killed this man?'

'There was something on email . . . Someone must have rung Evan and told him where to look because he wouldn't personally know where to start. The girls email one another all the time. They copy me in, but I don't always reply. Someone must have shown them to Evan, and he thinks . . . I don't know what he thinks! As if I would try to murder someone by mixing up his pills! As if I've ever been in the Brewsters' place, except for the odd party and they only have those twice a year. Oh, I could wring his neck!'

Ellie could detect a note of panic in Diana's voice. She said, 'What is it you're not telling me?'

'Nothing! Absolutely nothing. I swear I haven't been inside their house since Easter, when he was made captain of the golf club. Was it Easter? I can't remember. Springtime, anyway. He had this huge trophy cup, which he filled with champagne. He would do that, wouldn't he? Horrid little man, throwing his weight about, pinching bottoms, making stupid jokes.'

'Did he pinch your bottom?'

'I'd like to have seen him try!'

No, a man would have to be pretty far gone to think that Diana's sleek, well-toned bottom would be pinchable. She gave the appearance of wearing chainmail inside her business suit.

Ellie tried Gunnar's chambers, and was told he was in court

that day. She left another message asking him to ring her back as soon as possible. This time she did give Diana's phone number.

'Right,' said Diana, buttoning herself up again. 'If you can get started with Gunnar when he surfaces, I'm going to go down to the bank and make sure they know I've separated from my husband but will continue to bank with them. Fortunately I've always paid my commissions into a separate account and he can't touch that. He probably doesn't even know about it, but even if he did find out and tried to cancel my card, the bank wouldn't play ball, would they? Now, I paid the taxi with the last of my cash and I'm going to need some more to be going on with. Fifty quid, if you've got it? A hundred would be better. And keys so that I can get back in here.'

Diana didn't explain why she had kept a separate bank account for the commissions she got from work and Ellie didn't ask her about it. Sometimes, however much you loved a daughter – and of course Ellie did love Diana – there were things you did not ask about. Besides, plenty of wives had separate accounts from their husbands, didn't they? Ellie herself did, for one.

Ellie fetched a spare front door key from the cupboard in the kitchen. She found her handbag, which luckily was where she first looked for it, and handed over sixty pounds in cash, which was all she had on her.

Diana pocketed both, stood up and flicked dust off her skirt. 'Have you still got that cook person living in the top flat here?'

Ellie started to say, 'Susan is not a "cook person". She's a student who rents . . .' But Diana wasn't listening. She was checking her make-up, flicking her hair back into its usual severe cut. She said, 'I suppose I'd better move into your big guest room for the time being. It is en suite, isn't it? Then, when I get my son back, you can shift the cook girl out and we can have the top floor to ourselves.'

Ellie said, 'No, I'm afraid that's not—'

'It's lucky you've no one else staying at the moment. I've never known anyone like you for taking in lame dogs. I'm surprised that new husband of yours allows you to spend so much of our family money on them. You'd better get him to say an extra prayer or two for me so that I can get a good settlement from Evan and move on with my life.'

Ellie gritted her teeth. She supposed that any child, however old, resented their widowed mother making a second marriage, but Reverend Thomas was a darling, a great big teddy bear of a man who was devoted to Ellie. He was also highly thought of by everyone who knew him . . . except Diana, who could not be brought to treat him with even common politeness. Diana maintained that Thomas was after Ellie's money, which he was not. It wasn't Ellie's money, anyway, but inherited wealth which was held in a charitable trust.

As usual when Diana made a snide remark about Thomas, Ellie told herself she had to make allowances, and said nothing.

Diana got out her mobile phone. 'At least Evan didn't take this off me. Taxi . . .? Yes, I'm at my mother's house, Mrs Quicke. She has an account with you, doesn't she? Yes. Well, charge it to her account. Her daughter needs to be collected from her house to go to the High Street. Yes, straight away.'

She clicked off that number and while trying another said, 'The taxi will be along in a minute. I'll wait outside for him. I suppose I'd better warn the others. Especially Trish and Russet. Though surely their husbands won't . . . No, that's ridiculous! Still, it wouldn't be a bad idea for us to get together and . . .' Still talking, she left the house.

Ellie took a deep breath to calm herself and went down the corridor to Thomas's study. This was a large room stretching from the front to the back of the house, which used to be a library. The walls were lined with bookcases holding heavy tomes, some of which dated back a hundred years or more. Ellie's Victorian ancestors considered a gentleman's library should hold runs of bound volumes of *Punch* for a start, but Thomas had added to the collection with his own choice of books, which overflowed the shelves and stood around on the floor in piles like stalagmites.

The library also held a huge table covered with papers and two computers; one for Thomas and a second for his part-time assistant, who didn't come in on a Monday.

Thomas had retired from the ministry some time ago but was still called on to take the occasional service for a colleague. He also edited a Christian quarterly magazine.

He looked up from his computer screen when Ellie came in and, seeing her worried expression, said, 'Something wrong?'

'Diana.'

'Ah.' He half-closed his eyes but gave no other sign of annoyance. However badly Diana chose to behave, he would not say anything because he loved Ellie and backed her up in everything she chose to do. His eyes strayed back to the screen and he lifted his hands to put them back on the keyboard. She wondered if something were troubling him, too.

She said, 'Can you spare a moment?'

He swivelled away from his screen. 'I'm all attention.'

Ellie moved some books off a chair, sat down and told him what had happened. He stroked his beard and nodded. She waited while he thought over what she'd told him.

He said, 'One thing sticks out a mile. That was a successful coup, planned with military precision. Evan had it all worked out; her things packed up, her cards cancelled, the instruction not to let her back into the office.'

Ellie sighed. 'Yes, that's what I thought. It's most unlike what I know of the man. He used to be a force to be reckoned with – they didn't call him the Great White Shark for nothing – but in recent years, and in particular after he had the accident which put him in a wheelchair for a while, well, he's not the man he was. I'm wondering if he had help?'

'Sounds like it.'

'Diana didn't see it coming.'

'Her reaction is interesting. She isn't fighting her banishment. She wants to cut her losses and get a divorce. She didn't take long to come to that conclusion, did she?'

'Agreed. I'd have thought she'd want to hang on to him. Marriage gave her a lifestyle many would envy. I'm not sure she ever really loved him as I understand love, but she wanted what he could give her. I suppose you could call it a marriage of convenience. She gave him a son. She looked after him and the house. And there's the boy. Poor little mite. I grieve for him. How is he going to cope? How can he possibly understand what's happening? I can't bear to think of what he must be going through.'

Thomas nodded. He was fond of his step-grandson, too.

Ellie and Thomas looked after little Evan for several sessions a week although they'd seen less of him of late because he'd started to attend a nursery school. He was part of their everyday life. Ellie in particular would miss him terribly if he were not allowed to visit as usual.

Thomas said, 'Evan's been married before, hasn't he? How many times? Three? He must know the ropes by now.'

'And the cost. Divorcing wives can be an expensive affair. I thought he and Diana were jogging along all right. I thought the marriage suited both parties.'

'Something sparked this off. Diana's not likely to have dallied in green fields outside the matrimonial home, is she? It's almost as if he engineered her dismissal. Do you think he has yet another youngish woman in his sights and has used the excuse of somebody else's unfortunate demise to get rid of his present wife? In other words, what has prompted him to do this now, today?'

As usual, Thomas had put his finger on the crux of the matter.

Ellie said, 'I would have thought he was a bit past it, wouldn't you? I mean, he's our age, near enough.'

They both smiled and Ellie went pink, because although she and Thomas were in their sixties, their marriage had been a love match and continued to be so.

'Right,' said Ellie, 'leaving that aside . . . I'm not on the gossip circuit, but I can certainly ask around to see if Evan has another wife in view. Diana may be this and that, but I don't think she broke her marriage vows and it's not right to separate her from her son. You agree we have a right to interfere?'

'Gunnar can tell you what the position is in law. I have a feeling that grandparents have no rights at all. Morally: yes, we can interfere. Legally: probably not.'

'Morally is good enough for me. I suppose I'd better go and see Evan.' She started to her feet. 'Heavens! I was potting up some geranium cuttings when Diana came, and I've left everything all over the place.'

'You clear up in the conservatory and I'll put a sandwich together for lunch. By the way, you're sure there wasn't anything suspicious about Bunny Brewster's death? You said Diana described her suggestion as a joke, but jokes don't usually lead to murder, do they?'

'Diana said that he'd muddled up his pills and that was that.' Ellie thought over what Diana had said and the way she'd said it. 'That's what she told me, and that's what she believes. I suppose

I could ask my policewoman friend if there is anything in it. After we've had lunch. Let's eat before we do anything else.'

Thomas left his desk with a lingering glance at the computer. It was approaching one of his busiest times of the year and this interruption was going to bite into his working hours, but he still had to eat, didn't he?

While Ellie sorted out her geranium cuttings, Thomas put some sandwiches together and they ate at the kitchen table, as they usually did. Midge, their marauding ginger tomcat, appeared, demanding sustenance. Midge did not care for Diana – the feeling was reciprocated – so he had waited till she'd gone before he arrived.

After they'd eaten, Thomas carried Diana's belongings up the stairs and along the corridor to the main guest room where Ellie tried to arrange them neatly. After that, Thomas retired to his study, saying there was a small problem he needed to sort out.

Ellie felt like a nap, but instead made herself go to the phone to ring her friend Lesley, who was doing well in the police force and who would have been doing even better if she didn't have to report to a man who thought the most appropriate job for women in the force was making the tea.

'Lesley, I'm glad to have caught up with you. How are you doing?'

'Not bad. I'm wondering if I'm getting that Sad Syndrome that they talk about. These dull autumn days get me down.'

Ellie had difficulty broaching the subject on her mind, so continued to go down the polite route. 'How's your husband?'

Lesley said, 'Cut the chat, Ellie. What's up?'

'Oh. Well. Brewster, nicknamed Bunny. Deceased. There's a rumour he got his pills mixed up and died of an overdose. Do you know anything about it?'

'No, I don't. That sort of thing happens.'

'I'm aware of that. It hasn't come to the attention of the police?'

Lesley was no fool. 'Ellie, what are you trying to say?'

'I'm not trying to say anything. I'm asking if the police are interested, that's all. I have no grounds, absolutely none, for thinking foul play is involved.'

Silence. Lesley waited.

Ellie said, 'Forget I asked. I'm sure it's nothing. You know how people make jokes about things and then they actually come true.'

'Jokes? What jokes? Ellie, are you involved in his death in some way?'

'No.'

'You rang me, Ellie. You asked about a particular death. You say you have no reason to believe there is anything wrong, but you haven't asked me to forget that you spoke.'

Now it was Ellie's turn to be silent. She didn't know what to say.

Lesley said, 'All right. I'll ask around and get back to you. Are you in this evening? I could drop in then. I think my husband's got a meeting somewhere so I'm free.'

'I'm in.' Diana would be in, too. Oh dear, Diana's advent was going to cause all sorts of problems. Diana despised people who ate in the kitchen for a start, and Ellie didn't use the big dining room for anything but committee meetings.

Ellie put the phone down. She couldn't decide whether she'd done the right thing or not. If Lesley thought there was nothing suspicious about Bunny Brewster's death, then Diana was in the clear.

On the other hand . . . Could you murder someone by mixing up their pills?

TWO

Monday afternoon.

Ellie didn't drive. She decided to walk rather than take a cab because it wasn't far to where Diana and Evan lived. They had a big, detached, red-brick house in good repair. There were two cars in the driveway: Diana's sleek black model, and another which was a tad sleeker and larger in every way. Someone with money was paying a call.

A name popped into Ellie's head. She rang the bell and wasn't surprised to find the door opened by a woman in her early seventies with the head of a Roman emperor. Her figure was thickset but she was beautifully turned out. She was leaning on a stick. Really leaning on it. It was not a fashion accessory, but a necessity.

Enter Monique, Evan's first, long-divorced wife.

Monique had been some ten years older than Evan when they'd had a one-night fling leading to a short-lived marriage. Between them they'd produced a boy who had never been quite the thing and who had ended up in a locked ward in a psychiatric hospital. Monique had divorced Evan when his fancy strayed to another woman . . . and then another.

Monique had not been the loser by the divorce as she herself owned an estate agency even more upmarket than Evan's. She had remained on good terms with her ex-husband throughout all his matrimonial ups and downs but had only encountered Ellie a couple of years ago, after Diana had strayed into his orbit.

Monique was a formidable, practical and intelligent woman. Ellie liked and respected her. It was now clear to Ellie that it was Monique who had helped to mastermind Diana's eviction and, if Monique had taken a hand in the game, there was no way that Diana's broken marriage could be mended.

Monique said, 'I thought it might be you. Come on in.'

The house seemed unusually quiet. No scampering sounds of a small boy playing. Ellie looked for the little boy's favourite toy, which was a pink velvet hippo, but it was nowhere to be seen. He wasn't at home, was he?

Monique led the way to the big front room where Evan was usually to be found, watching television. As he was now. With a cut-glass tumbler of whisky and water in his hand.

Evan had been known as the Great White Shark in the old days when he was captain of the golf club and ran his agency, but now, although he was younger than Monique, he looked older. He lifted his glass towards Ellie. 'Welcome, Mother-in-law. We were wondering when you'd be round.'

Ellie took a seat, looking around her. She remembered the transformations which had attended this house as first one wife and then another had redecorated the place to their own taste. Diana had gone in for the leather-and-glass Harrods look, which wasn't particularly comfortable to sit on. Evan, of course, had his own reclining chair near the built-in bar with its constantly renewed supply of whisky and soda.

Ellie was shocked by Evan's appearance. He'd lost weight and become even more beaky than when she'd last seen him. Did the hand holding the glass tremble? Yes, it did. Early Parkinson's disease?

Diana had said that Evan rarely turned up at the agency any more. Not wanting to be outshone by the hired help, Diana had appointed a woman of limited ability as her second-in-command. The agency was going to go downhill if Diana were not allowed back. Who would run it in future? Ellie recalled that Evan had a grown-up daughter who seemed to have some business sense, but Ellie hadn't heard anything about her for ages. Diana had eased her out of the house. To university, perhaps?

Evan said, 'Have one?' and lifted his glass suggestively.

Ellie shook her head.

Monique said, 'Tea would be more your thing, Mrs Quicke, but the nanny's out and I can't carry a tray around.' She tapped her stick on the wood-block floor in a meaningful fashion.

Ellie recognized this as a ploy. She was supposed to offer to make the tea and bring it in like a servant, which would put Monique in top dog position. So, no thank you.

'Monique, I haven't seen you for ages. You were due for an operation on your back when we last met. It didn't go to plan?'

Monique snorted. Diamond drops shimmered in her ears. 'No, it didn't. Keep away from doctors if you can. That's what I say.'

Evan wafted his empty glass. 'I could do with another.'

Monique wasn't playing. 'Get it yourself, you lazy lump.'

Yes, Monique was definitely top dog here.

Monique and Evan looked at Ellie with slight smiles on their faces. They thought she'd come on a fool's errand and maybe she had. Did they expect her to plead Diana's cause? Yes, they probably did. But Ellie was not going to do that.

Ellie eased forward on her chair. Like its predecessors, it was too deep for a small woman's feet to reach the floor. 'Diana wants a divorce and I suppose you do, too, Evan?'

'I have already instructed a solicitor.'

'I see. Well, Diana has been a good wife to you, Evan, so—'

'Tchah!' said Evan.

'She has,' said Ellie, refusing to show annoyance. 'She has done the best she could. She has been faithful. She has looked after you well. She is fond of you. I can't see any good reason for a divorce myself, but I do understand that if you think the marriage is over, you would want it tidied away. The boy, though. You've been a trifle high-handed there, haven't you? You can hardly expect to get sole custody. Diana is a good mother and she loves the boy dearly. The courts will, I am sure, give her custody and you – if you want them – visitation rights.'

'Not with what we have on her,' said Evan, grinning like the Great White Shark which he used to be. It reminded Ellie that even in his decline, he was still a force to be reckoned with.

Now they'd come to the point, hadn't they?

Monique said, 'I've made copies of the evidence for you and for our solicitor.' She handed over some sheets of paper.

Ellie looked at them in bewilderment. 'What are these? You've printed off some emails from the Internet? Who are these people? I don't know them, do I?'

Evan snorted. 'So-called friends of Diana's. They email one another every day. Busy, busy, tattling away. Did they think we'd never find out?'

Ellie scanned the papers. 'None of these are from Diana. I don't understand.'

Monique sighed. 'Try the one from someone called Russet, who is married to one of Evan's oldest friends. Read what she says there and tell me Diana doesn't deserve everything that's coming to her.'

Russet was into emojis. Funny faces appeared on almost every line.

'*. . . I thought it was a good evening, on the whole. We had some fun, didn't we? If only the men knew! Was it Dinky Di who said the best way to kill your husband off was to mix up his pills? I can't remember if it was her or Barbie. I know it was something about using one of those boxes from the pharmacist with a compartment for each day of the week. My beloved doesn't need one of those yet, but if he did I now know what to do. I tip all the pills for a week out on to the table and mix them up so* *that all the ones for high blood pressure end up in one compartment. It only takes four or five, is that right? And then all you have to do is wait till he takes the lot! I'd worry about that, if I were Evan . . . or Bunny, come to think of it! By the way . . .'*

Ellie stared at the paper. Read the text again. *Dinky Di* was Diana? Diana had suggested a neat way of killing her husband and it had been put in an email which could be read by anyone, and forwarded to any number of people?

No way! She couldn't believe it! Ellie supposed it was just possible that Diana might have suggested it if she was caught in the wrong mood, but she would never admit to it on an email. Foolish in some respects she might be, but not insane.

Diana had told Ellie that the whole thing had been a joke.

A *joke*?

'You see?' said Evan.

'No, I don't see.'

'Read on.'

The next email was from someone who signed herself 'Trish', who said that yes, it had been Diana who had suggested mixing up the pills, but she herself had suggested pushing someone down the stairs, ha ha!

Ellie put the papers down for a moment and closed her eyes. When Diana had been about to leave that morning, she'd ordered a taxi – which Ellie would have to pay for – and said she was going to warn two people about what had happened to her. Their names? Ellie tried to recall. Yes, they were Trish and Russet.

Trish and Russet were two of the people to whom the emails had been addressed. Among others. There were five names in all.

None of them were known to Ellie. Five women in an email group. Copies went to all five. Their names were Diana, Russet, Trish, Barbie and Kat.

Barbie had written the next one on the list. Barbie didn't go in for smiley faces but went straight to the point.

No, I didn't suggest mixing up the pills. My method was to have been much more pleasurable. Shag him senseless. Give him a heart attack. Trish, how like you to suggest something physical! I can't remember what Kat suggested. Something straightforward, wasn't it?

Another email. Ellie turned to the next page. Kat hadn't replied, but Russet had, with more smiley faces. *I've had another think. Suppose we turn ourselves into mermaids and hold them under the water in our very own swimming pools? LOL again. Not that we have a swimming pool! He's far too mean to spend money on something that I'd like. Perhaps we should just set fire to their pants? I think they all need a shot in the arm, they're so . . . well, of course we love them dearly, but . . . well, you know!*

And so on. Kat had joined in the fun eventually. She'd advocated rat poison, which Ellie thought was rather old fashioned. Perhaps Kat hadn't much imagination?

Diana had not replied to any of the emails. She didn't appear to have taken part in the conspiracy, if that was what it was. Her only involvement was that she'd been copied in to what the others – and she herself – had suggested.

Ellie went back to the beginning and reread the lot. She spotted the date. She lowered the papers, thinking hard. The emails weren't recent. No. They were ancient in email terms, dating back nine or ten weeks. During those nine or ten weeks no one had died, had they? Until Bunny had popped his clogs a couple of weeks ago.

'You see?' said Evan. 'Diana was planning to kill me.'

Ellie slapped the papers down. 'No, she wasn't. I don't know how you got hold of these emails—'

'Kat's husband brought them to me after Bunny died. He'd found them on his laptop and thought I ought to know what was going on.'

Ellie looked from one to the other. 'I can't believe you're taking this seriously! Your reaction is out of all proportion to what happened. The first thing that occurs to me is that this is the sort of thing women usually text one another about. Surely these intimate exchanges are usually made on smartphones, not on computers?'

Monique said, 'Apparently one of the group didn't have a smartphone till recently.'

'Really? How odd. The other thing that strikes me is that these emails were written over two months ago. Am I to understand that someone brought them to you ages ago and you didn't think anything of them until now?'

'No, no. He only brought them to us last week, after Bunny's funeral. We saw that it was a conspiracy straight away.'

'No conspiracy. I understand there was some joking about murder among a group of women, of whom Diana was one. Only joking, mind! The presence of the emojis proves that. As to claiming that Diana was seriously trying to kill you, that's ridiculous. If you brought these papers into court, you'd be told to get lost. In the first place, anyone could make up and print off some suggestive emails. You'd have to produce the laptop for them to be admitted as evidence.'

'That's true,' said Monique, not a whit disturbed. 'We have that.'

'Even if you did,' said Ellie, 'it doesn't prove anything against Diana. None of these emails are from her. The "evidence" against her is hearsay, which is not admissible in court.'

'Oh, yes, it is,' said Monique. 'Because Bunny upped and died.'

'Diana didn't kill him.'

'She supplied the method. She told the killer what to do. She is as guilty as his wife.'

Ellie blinked. This was serious. 'If you think that, then you must take these emails to the police and get Bunny's wife charged with murder.' *And Diana as an accomplice?*

Evan grinned. 'No, no. You don't understand the beauty of the situation. When Rupert – that's Kat's husband – brought me the laptop, I phoned Monique, because she always keeps a cool head, and arranged for us men to meet at Rupert's place. Kat went out to do the shopping as usual, and we worked out what to do.'

'With Monique as chief strategist?'

'If you like, yes. She helped us work out a timetable. We realized we must take action simultaneously. She wrote out a list of what had to be done. First, we had to choose a time when our wives would all be out of the house at the same time, so they couldn't warn one another what was going to happen. Then we got cleaners in to pack up their stuff while our secretaries phoned the banks and cancelled any direct debits that were in operation. Bunny's widow might have been a problem but fortunately his first wife and son have never liked her and were delighted to get her out of the house.'

'You take my breath away.'

Evan grinned. 'We got five out of five. They didn't know what had hit them. All they ever thought about was how to spend our money. They didn't care for us, so why should we care for them? Once we understood that they were planning to murder us, we had every right to protect ourselves.'

Ellie protested, 'They weren't serious threats.'

'Bunny died, didn't he? As per Diana's suggestion. It's true he'd been drinking heavily of late and, to be frank, was in danger of losing the plot. Alzheimer's, here I come. To be honest, no one will miss him. His widow certainly won't. But what would be the point of charging her with murder? She's personable enough, I suppose, if you like that sort of thing, and will no doubt be able to find another sucker to marry. If we go to the police with what we've got she might well find a good solicitor to get her out from under a murder charge.'

With Diana to be charged as accessory.

Ellie looked at Monique. She felt chilled to the bone. 'I'm shocked. This is not about Bunny's death at all. Evan has got tired of Diana and wants to get rid of her without her making a fuss!'

Monique nodded. 'Exactly.'

'So you devised a strategy to sweep her out of the house and threaten her with a murder charge if she resisted. How could you!'

'That's what he wants.'

'And the children?'

'Evan's the only one who's got a child of school age. The other children are much older and have left the nest.'

Ellie objected. 'That is so cold-blooded.'

Monique said, 'Ellie, I respect you and I respect your judgement in the main, but you have always been weak where your daughter is concerned. She's a cold, ambitious woman who married Evan for his money. Evan doesn't have to put up with her now she's made plans to murder him.'

'She didn't!'

'Are you sure? See how quietly she's accepted her dismissal. Her response is not to proclaim her innocence, but to ask for a divorce. You've accepted it, too, or you'd be going down on your knees to beg him to take her back.'

That was true. But. 'Diana is in shock at the moment. She may or may not decide to fight—'

'She's not going to fight to stay married to Evan, is she? I daresay something suitable can be arranged about the boy and alimony agreed, provided she accepts a divorce without making a fuss.'

Ellie abandoned that line of attack to say, 'Diana is a good businesswoman. You've deprived her of her means of earning a living by barring her return to work.'

'She'll find something else.'

'She's been running that agency for years. What will happen to it if she goes?'

'I've promoted her assistant. You accept the inevitable?'

Ellie didn't know what to say. 'I can't answer for her.'

Monique got to her feet with an effort. 'Let me show you out. The nanny should be bringing the boy back from nursery soon. I don't want him upset so I suggest you leave before he returns.'

Ellie felt tears come to her eyes. 'I'm told that grandparents don't have any rights in questions of custody arrangements. Is that true? Thomas and I are very fond of the boy. We're accustomed to seeing him at least once a week.'

Monique patted Ellie's arm. 'I'll see what I can do.'

She showed Ellie out into the hall and shut the door behind her. So now they were to have a tête-à-tête, were they? Two women having a private word without Evan overhearing what they had to say?

Ellie got out her hankie – it was lucky she had one on her as she often forgot – and blew her nose. She understood very well what Monique had meant: Ellie and Thomas could see the boy if they agreed not to help Diana make a fuss.

Game, set and match.

Monique said, 'Now we're alone, I must tell you that Evan is not well.'

Ah, so that was it! Subtext noted. Evan didn't have long to live?

Monique said, 'He's afraid of all sorts of things. Starts at his own shadow. He's been a lot worse since Bunny died. Wants someone to taste his food first, and so on.'

Ellie argued, 'I can't see what he's so worried about. You say

Bunny Brewster was losing the plot. He mixed up his pills and died. It's a coincidence that Diana may have suggested, in jest, that this would be a good way to kill off a husband. Diana didn't try to kill Evan, did she? Another thing: Diana would have stuck by Evan in sickness and in health. She may be a cold fish as you say, but she has a strong sense of duty. She'd nurse him to the end.'

'I daresay, but that's not what he wants now.'

Ellie thought that through. 'You mean, Evan's got his eye on a buxom young girl who'll pillow his head on her breast and soothe his troubled brow and all that stuff? A girl with no brains but a warm bedfellow?' She put her hand over her mouth. 'Oh, I'm sorry. I shouldn't have said that. It wasn't nice.'

'It's accurate. Mrs Quicke, you must realize this situation is not of my making. I've known Evan for twenty-odd years. We had a child together. It makes a bond. I am not influenced by any sentimental nonsense but I'm trying to do the best I can for Evan for old times' sake. He's all the family I have left now.'

Ellie thought of asking if Evan and Monique's only son had died. It might well be so. She didn't enquire. It must be an open sore for Monique that her only child had never been any good. So, Ellie blew her nose again and said she really must be on her way.

Monique opened the front door for her. 'Let's keep in touch, shall we?'

Ellie was reluctant to leave things like this. And yet, she didn't know what to say to Monique except, 'This is all wrong!'

Monique smiled, waved Ellie through the door and shut it behind her.

Dear Lord above! Help! I don't know what is real and what has been twisted, or invented or . . . Why on earth was Diana so stupid as to be drawn into a game of How to Murder your Husband?

If that is what it was.

Monique has a point. Diana's accepted her exile far too easily for someone who is totally innocent, but she can't have gone as far as to collude with someone to murder their husband. That I do not believe.

Dear Lord, if you could spare a minute to help me out here? Tell me what to do?

She made her way home. It was beginning to drizzle, and she hadn't an umbrella or a waterproof jacket with her.

A taxi came out of her drive as she turned the corner of the road. Had Diana returned? Two other vehicles had been parked right up to the porch: a swish-looking affair with tinted windows and an expensive estate car. Visitors?

Ellie put her key in the lock of her front door and immediately knew something was wrong. The door had not been properly shut and there was a babble of noise inside. What was going on?

She pushed the door open and recoiled.

'Move your stuff over! I can't shift—'

'Where's the toilet?'

'But what I want to know is—'

'Where's Diana!'

'Oooh! How could he!'

'That's exactly what happened to me when—'

The hall was full of noise, and luggage. Two matching sets of cases with designer logos on them, a third displaying a monogram, multiple carry-on bags, a mountain of plastic bags containing expensive dresses and coats, make-up boxes, hand luggage of every type under the sun, some cardboard boxes, hat boxes galore . . .

And three . . . no, four! . . . women aged thirty-five and upwards, all competing for attention. Two women with blonde hair of varying authenticity, a redhead and a brunette. But no Diana!

THREE

Monday afternoon.

What was this? A refugee camp?

The nearest woman was a fake blonde who probably thought she looked like Lauren Bacall, which she did if Lauren Bacall had turned to stone. She had good bone structure but had indulged in too much Botox. 'Are you the cook person? About time, too. I need—'

'Oh, there she is!' said the redhead, who was smoking a cigarette. 'Which is my—'

'Where have you been! Where's Diana? She said to come here and you'd—'

'I was first!' The Lauren Bacall lookalike. 'Here, you! Whatever your name is. Where can I—?'

'Hold on! I need the toilet!'

Ellie blinked. Four intruders? FOUR?

There was no sign of Diana, and they thought Ellie was a servant?

Four women, plus luggage! Yes, this must be the rest of the conspirators. Why had they come here?

For two pins Ellie would have stepped backwards out of the front door and left them to it. Except that this was *her* house and she was going to have to deal with the invasion at some point.

She needed back-up. Ignoring the women's various calls for attention, Ellie slid sideways between mounds of luggage and fled down the corridor to the library . . . only to find it empty. What? Where was Thomas?

Ah, but he'd left a note on his keyboard for her.

Ellie. I suspected something was wrong this morning, but it's taken me a while to sort out. The printers seem to have gone bust. I'm off to see them, to find out what can be salvaged. Back soon. Thomas. xxx

So, no back-up. She was going to have to deal with the problem herself.

The women turned on Ellie as she re-entered the hall, all shouting instructions at her. One wanted the toilet, another demanded help with her luggage, a third asked for Diana, and another sobbed aloud that she didn't know what to do.

Ellie felt like Alice in Wonderland when the pack of cards fell on her.

Presumably these were the other rejected wives. Why were they here? Had Diana invited them? *How dare she!* Had Diana given them her key to the front door to get in with? And where was Diana herself?

Lauren Bacall got in Ellie's face. 'Look, if you are the cook person, can you please tell me—'

'What I want to know is, where—'

Ellie said, 'If you please . . .!' and was drowned out by the complaints of the refugees. The woman who was rocking to and fro raised her voice in a wail. 'Oh, oh!'

The redheaded smoker threaded her way through the luggage to address Ellie. 'Look, where's the toilet?'

'*If* you please!'

Ellie yelled, 'Quiet!'

And there was quiet. Everyone looked at Ellie. Even the sobbing woman suspended operations for a moment.

'What . . .!' said the redheaded smoker. 'Who . . .?'

'Quiet!' said Ellie, not as loudly or as forcefully as before, but loudly enough to gain their attention. 'May I have your attention, please?'

A rustle of discontent, a pouting of lips, but they did simmer down.

'Now,' said Ellie, collecting eyes. 'Let me introduce myself. My name is Mrs Quicke, and this is my house. I own it.' She let that fact sink into their minds.

The hall seemed very dark, and the faces turned to her were strained and anxious. It was definitely going to rain. Ellie reached for the light switch by the door and turned it on. One or two of the women blinked. One put up a hand to shade her eyes. At least they'd all shut up for the moment.

Ellie said, 'I was not expecting visitors. Who are you and why are you here? Above all, how did you get in?'

The redheaded smoker flicked ash. 'Diana invited us. Said we must have a council of war. She said we could stay here till we could decide what to do. Some man or other let me in when I explained that Diana had asked me to meet her here. He didn't like it, but he said he had to go out on some matter of importance. Then the others arrived and I let them in.'

So that was it. Ellie kept her voice steady. 'As you can see, my daughter Diana isn't here, and I certainly didn't give her permission to invite you into my house. This is not a hotel. Understand?'

'But she said we should all . . . she p-promised . . .' The pudding-shaped woman who'd been rocking to and fro stammered to a halt. Tears brimmed. 'Where can I go? I don't know what to do!'

'I need the toilet. For heaven's sake, where is the toilet?'

Ellie took a good look at them. Shifting from one foot to the other. Miserable. Not knowing where to turn. They'd followed Diana's lead and now Diana wasn't here. They'd been thrown out of their homes, hadn't been to the toilet for hours and could really do with a cup of tea and a biscuit, although some of them would probably prefer a stiff drink.

Ellie said, 'This situation is none of my making but, as you're here, you'd probably like a cup of tea before you decide what to do next. In a few minutes I'll serve some tea in the sitting room at the back of the hall over there, but before that I expect you'd like to freshen up.'

She gestured to her left. 'That door leads to the kitchen quarters. There's a toilet off that corridor. Two of you, use that one.' The two nearest the kitchen made a beeline for it.

Ellie gestured to the other two. 'Upstairs. Take the corridor almost to the end. There's a bathroom there you can use.'

They didn't argue, but disappeared, racing one another to get to the loo first.

In a couple of seconds Ellie was alone in the hall, standing amid piles of luggage.

Poor things. How dare Diana bring them here and abandon them!

Ellie set herself in motion down the corridor to the kitchen, taking her mobile phone out of her handbag as she went. She had Diana on speed dial. *Brr, brr. Brr, brr.*

Her guests were going to need strong tea with plenty of sugar for shock. And carbohydrates. Had she enough biscuits to go round?

The call to Diana went to voicemail. Bother.

There was no sign of the cat, Midge. He wouldn't have enjoyed the invasion of all those frightened women and had probably retreated to the master bedroom upstairs.

Ellie tried her policewoman friend Lesley next and, by great good fortune, got through to her straight away. 'Lesley, a bit of a crisis here. Did you get a chance to look at the file on Bunny Brewster's death?' Tucking the phone into the angle of shoulder and jaw, Ellie filled the kettle and switched it on.

'I've had a word with the officer in charge. The man spent the evening out, had several drinks before he retired for the night, then a shower, put on his pyjamas and took his pills. He got into bed, fell asleep and died in the night. The box was found on the floor the next morning with all seven sections empty and pills everywhere on the carpet. The autopsy revealed he'd taken five times the recommended dose of the pills to treat his high blood pressure. If I've got it right, one pill calms you down, two makes you drowsy, three or four render you unconscious. Five or six and you flatline. He'd been prescribed a cocktail of pills: statins and high blood pressure tablets, something for his gout and his prostate, and his hay fever and Lord alone knows what else. He was supposed to take some in the morning, some before meals, some after food and some at night. According to his wife, he simplified this regime by taking the whole day's allocation with a glass of whisky when he went to bed in the evening. And no, he wasn't supposed to take more than one high blood pressure pill at a time.'

Ellie decided her guests should have the best china cups and saucers and not any of her collection of mugs. She started to lay the crockery out on a tray. 'So, in a drunken haze, he might well have upset the lot on to the floor, picked up what he thought were the right ones – only they weren't – and his death was accidental.'

'True. That's the official verdict as of this moment.'

'Bunny slept alone and his wife heard nothing, saw nothing, and said she knew nothing about it?' Ellie rummaged in a bottom cupboard for her largest teapot.

'Correct.'

Ellie looked in the biscuit tin. Half full. It would have to do. 'I've seen those pill boxes. You get them from the chemist under doctor's orders. Some people take five or six pills every day. I've often wondered how people can remember what they have to take, and when. Does the chemist fill the boxes for you, or are you allowed to do it yourself? In other words, who put the pills in his box each week?'

'His wife did. She said she couldn't trust him to do it. The officer sent to take her statement believed her.'

'Is it possible that his wife put all his high blood pressure pills into one compartment to make sure he took an overdose? Then, in the morning, she emptied all the other compartments out on to the floor and claimed he was so drunk he did it himself?'

'Mm. Possibly. No one's suggested foul play. The widow made a good impression. Unless we can prove a motive . . . Even then, it's doubtful we could get a conviction.'

Ellie opened the cutlery drawer. Did they need teaspoons? Yes. Where was the sugar bowl? 'I think I'd better put another packet of biscuits in the tin. They're going to need more than one chocolate biscuit apiece to get them through this. Sorry, Lesley; thinking aloud. I have four visitors for tea and, if I'm right, one of them must be Bunny's widow. So the police aren't going to take it any further?'

'They weren't. No. Not until you rang me and pressed the alarm button.'

Ellie poured boiling water into her largest teapot to warm it. 'I'm not sure there is anything suspicious about his death.'

'Then why did you ask about him? Do you know of a motive the widow might have had for getting rid of him?'

Now Ellie had a choice. Lesley didn't know about the group eviction of the wives, or the emails. Was it relevant? Ellie really didn't know what to think.

When in doubt, tell the police what you know and let them decide what to do about it. Yes, but that would mean bringing Diana into it, and it was Diana who was supposed to have come up with the idea of muddling the pills so that someone would die.

Oh, there was no need to mention Diana, surely!

But, suppose someone had acted on Diana's suggestion and Bunny's death was murder, then . . .? No, Ellie had to tell.

She emptied the hot water out of the teapot and reached for the teabags. How many should she use? Three or four?

'I can give you some background which might help you decide what to do. There were five married men who were members of the golf club and spent a lot of time there, socializing. Their wives went along for the ride. The women were thrown into one another's company because the men were only interested in drinking and their own concerns. The wives began to exchange confidences. The men were all wealthy and most if not all were on their second or third wives. None of their current marriages were very stable because the men have so little sense they think that as their current wives age, money can buy them a prettier piece of arm candy or a nice little woman who will nurse them in their dotage.'

'I'm familiar with the syndrome,' said Lesley. 'It usually ends in tears.'

A woman's voice called out from the corridor, 'Mrs . . .? Can you find us some more toilet paper?'

'Hold on a moment, Lesley.' Ellie fished a loo roll out of a cupboard and took it along to the downstairs loo. Once she was back in the kitchen, she resumed her conversation. 'So, Lesley; what do you think?'

Lesley said, 'How do you know all this?'

'Evan, my son-in-law, threw Diana out this morning. She came straight to me. She was in shock. She said he was planning to keep their little boy and not let her have custody. Thomas and I are fond of the boy, so I went to see Evan and was given chapter and verse. I fear he has yet another, younger wife in view.'

'That'll cost him something in alimony.'

'Men never seem to realize what divorce is going to do to their income. In this particular case, the women played into their hands. They were all joking one evening, talking about how they might make away with their husbands. Diana's suggestion was, apparently, to muddle up his pills. I'm pretty sure she didn't mean anything by it. The other women were accustomed to emailing one another about the trivia of their lives, and a couple of them were stupid enough to include their suggestions for murder into the said emails. Evan told me that when Bunny died these emails came to light, and the men used them as an excuse to get rid of the women. Wholesale. In one clean sweep. Diana seems to have invited the discarded wives to dump themselves on me. Here. In my hall. With all their belongings.' She poured boiling water on to the teabags in the pot.

'What! You mean—?'

'Four of them. Plus impedimenta. Weeping and wailing and needing the toilet. And no sign of Diana.'

'Your daughter has always taken you for granted, I know, but—'

'Yes, this is one demand too far. By the way, she didn't

write any of the emails about how to dispose of a husband. One of the other women quoted her as having said it, that's all. The husbands have got those emails and printed them out. Even if Mrs Brewster did muddle up her husband's pills and caused his death, I suppose it would be very difficult to prove murder.'

'Unless . . . Haven't you just handed me a motive for murder? Did Diana realize she was about to be superseded in her husband's bed?'

'I'll check it out, if you like. All I've seen so far is four women in a state of shock.' Ellie surveyed the laden tea tray. 'What I need is one of those old-fashioned trolleys to save me carrying heavy things around. Look, I'm about to give these women tea and biscuits. Care to join us?'

Milk! She'd forgotten the milk. She'd have to use a milk jug. She couldn't put the milk bottle on the tray for this lot.

Lesley hesitated. 'Not immediately, no. I have a report to write. When I finish work, maybe. Do you think it could have been murder?'

'I'm not sure. I can't think straight. I'll have a quiet chat with them over a cuppa and see if I can pick up anything concrete. I could ask, for instance, if any of them knew or suspected that they were about to be discarded. If not, you can mark the case closed and let them move on with their lives.'

'Don't be so hasty. You mentioned emails. Who's got them? I need to see them.'

'Evan says he's got the laptop which contains the emails but he gave me a copy of some of the messages which do seem to prove his point that the women were conspiring against their husbands. Or rather not conspiring, exactly. Looking on the bright side, I suppose the most you can convict them of is disloyalty and a misplaced sense of humour. The men think they have enough evidence to force the women to accept a divorce without complaining and so far, they've pitched it right.'

'I think I'd better see those emails.'

'Drop round after work and I'll let you have my copies.'

'Can you keep the women with you till I come? Or else, find out where they're planning to go? I may need to interview them later.'

Ellie sighed. 'I do hope it won't be necessary. I feel sorry for them.'

'You don't feel sorry for the one who could have killed her husband?'

'Come on, Lesley – there's no proof.' She clicked off the phone and pushed it into her pocket as one of wives – the brunette with the boyish, feathery haircut – appeared in the doorway asking if she could help. Big-boned and tall with it. Not an obvious beauty but a healthy, milkmaid type.

The newcomer had a nervous smile. 'Can I do anything?'

Was that a bruise on her jaw? No, probably not. The light in the kitchen was not marvellous. At least this girl had the good manners to offer to help.

'Thank you, yes. If you could carry that tray, I'll manage this one.'

Together they ferried the tea things along the corridor and into the big sitting room which overlooked the garden at the back of the house. It was definitely raining now. Ellie switched on the lamps that threw the centre of the room and the settee into the light but left shadows at the edges. One by one, the guests arrived to look around and find themselves a seat. Ellie dispensed tea and biscuits.

The hard-faced blonde who looked like Lauren Bacall with a hangover said, 'Haven't you any Earl Grey?' She was so tense she looked as if she'd take a bite out of her cup rather than drink from it. Ellie took a good look at her. Yes, the woman was so angry she didn't know what to do with herself.

Ellie was soothing. 'No. It's builders' tea. Strong. Better for you at the moment. Take it with lots of sugar as medicine.'

No one took sugar. They were probably all on a diet. Except for the pudding-shaped one, who looked as if she wouldn't even know how to spell the word.

'Still no sign of Diana? Where is she?' The pseudo redhead took out another cigarette and lit up. 'She said she was on her way to her solicitor's but would meet me here.'

Ellie said, 'Please, no smoking.' Ellie thought the woman was going to refuse, but she did grind the cancer stick out in her saucer. Ellie winced. But still, the dirty mark should come out with a careful wash.

'I've no idea where she is,' said Ellie, pouring out a cup for herself. 'My call to her went to voicemail.' Ellie addressed the redhead. 'May I ask your name?'

The redhead crossed her arms. She was, perhaps, forty years of age, attempting by way of Botox and the assistance of a good hairdresser to look thirty and almost succeeding. She had probably been a natural redhead in her youth but now she'd touched up her fading tresses with a rich auburn dye. She wore an expensive green tweed suit with asymmetric fastenings.

'They call me "Russet".'

Russet had been the one who'd larded her emails with emojis.

Ellie said, 'What happened to you?'

Russet took out another cigarette until a stare from Ellie made her think again. 'What happened to me? I don't know. I can't make sense of it. Why? Why now? Why didn't I see it coming?'

'Tell me,' said Ellie.

'Well, I had an early appointment for a manicure. Hubby and I were supposed to be going out tonight to . . .' She bit her lip. 'Is he going to go by himself? What excuse is he going to make that I'm not with him? It's . . . The world's gone mad. I got back about eleven, I suppose. I parked in the drive because I was supposed to be playing bridge this afternoon.' She hit her forehead. 'Heavens! My name must be mud. I haven't thought to ring them to say I can't come.'

'Go on. You got back about eleven.'

'Yes. About. I didn't look at my watch. There were these women, I've never seen them before in my life, carrying my belongings out of the house!'

'What women?' asked Ellie, with a prickling feeling at the back of her neck. Both she and Diana employed cleaners twice a week from a local firm. Was it possible that they might have been the ones instructed to pack the women's things up?

'Who were they? How should I know? Cleaning contractors or something. Not the woman I've been using for years. Strangers. So I storm in and there's my husband waiting for me, saying our marriage was over and I should find some other fool to bankroll me in future. He was sitting on my mink coat! Not that I've worn it for ever, fashion being what it is. So I said, "What do you mean?" and he said I knew jolly well what he meant and that if

I didn't go quietly he'd lay information against me to the police that I'd been plotting to kill him. I couldn't believe what he was saying! All the time those women were traipsing up and down the stairs, putting my stuff outside and it was beginning to rain. I just gaped at him.

'He said he wanted my house keys. He tried to pull my handbag off my shoulder. I hung on to it like mad. My phone rang. He let go and I almost fell. He said I should hand over the phone as well because he was paying for it. I saw he meant it and I thought I was going to have hysterics, but the phone went on ringing, so I ran out of the house with it in my hand, and it was Diana on the other end. She said, "Are you in trouble?" And I said, "How did you know?" She said to bring my stuff here and we'd have a council of war. So I piled everything into my car and left, though I had to leave my mink coat behind. I just don't get it! What's got into the man? I thought Diana must know, but here I am and Diana is nowhere to be seen.'

Ellie said, 'So you were planning to get rid of your husband, only he got in first?'

'No, of course not!' An affronted stare. 'Honestly . . .!'

'He was given proof that you were planning to knock him off. You were the one who suggested drowning him in a swimming pool, weren't you?'

The woman's eyes narrowed. 'What? But that was ages ago. You don't believe . . . No, that's ridiculous! That wasn't serious. I mean . . . Totally not! Anyway, we don't have a swimming pool.'

Ellie was pleased with herself. She'd connected the woman with the right husband! 'No, I gather it was a source of considerable annoyance to you that your husband wouldn't stump up for a swimming pool.'

'What . . .? Well, yes, I did think we might have a swimming pool because so many of our friends have them. He said, he promised, he had some big deal or other going on, and he told me that maybe next year . . . Next year isn't going to come, is it? I just don't get it!'

The Lauren Bacall lookalike said, 'You think that this is all about money? But . . . Mrs Quicke, is it? Is that your name? How did you get to hear about the pool?'

'I was given copies of your emails this morning.' Ellie looked round at the others. 'Somebody's husband found the emails and now the other men in your group have seen them. They intend to use them to obtain a divorce which they don't think you will dare to contest because each of you made suggestions as to how you might kill off your husband.'

'Is that really what this is all about?' Russet almost laughed. 'The world really *has* gone mad.'

'I suppose I can see how they might take it the wrong way,' said the brown-haired girl with the feathery haircut, the one who had helped Ellie to carry the tea things through. She was the youngest of the bunch and perhaps a trifle on the thin side. Her collar bones stuck out. She had big brown eyes and excellent quality casual clothes. She said, 'But honestly, Mrs Quicke, there was nothing in it. Look, we were all at the golf club one evening, bored out of our minds because the men were in a huddle when one of them started to choke. He'd drunk too much and had been eating too many salted peanuts. He almost croaked, there and then. Only the bar manager gave him that hug thing . . . what do they call it? Himmel-something. He threw the lot up, wine and food and everything. All over his trousers and the carpet and everywhere. It was disgusting. So embarrassing. Ugh!'

She refrained from looking at any of the other wives, but Barbie and Russet both looked at the pudding-shaped one, who sniffled into her hankie and said, 'Yes, it was Rupert. He's not usually like that.' Her voice was thick with catarrh.

The others turned a 'look' on her. It was clear to Ellie that Rupert was indeed *like that*!

Russet, the smoker, said to Ellie, 'You know how it is with these men – they want us to appear beautifully dressed at all times and to warm the bed for them and pander to their every whim, but they don't care what they look like themselves, and boy – can they put the drink away! That night at the golf club was particularly bad. They were making rude jokes at our expense, saying, oh, the usual—'

The Lauren Bacall lookalike said, 'Talking dirty, you mean. Saying what they'd like to do to the barmaid. Embarrassing! Talk about porn – they've got the filthiest minds imaginable. It was most uncomfortable.'

Russet said, 'That's when we saw the brochures advertising a murder mystery weekend at the club. It was that weekend, wasn't it? So we started talking about it among ourselves, just joking, saying how we'd kill people off. It was fun. We laughed a lot. We did wonder about going to the actual event, but the men said they had some kind of meeting and that it was all nonsense, anyway.'

'What kind of meeting?' said Ellie.

Russet shrugged. 'Dunno. They like to think of themselves as movers and shakers. They talk big, trying to make out they've still got what it takes in bed and out of it. Which we know very well they haven't, which is why they drink so much.'

Ellie shook her head. 'It wasn't a joke when Bunny died though, was it? Which of you is his widow?'

'I am,' said the Lauren Bacall lookalike. Her hand trembled as she rattled her empty cup into the saucer. She was so tense she practically twanged. 'I'm Barbie. Short for Barbara.' She bit the words off as she spoke.

Ellie ironed out a smile, because the image that rose to her mind was one of barbed wire. This was no pretty doll. Fifty trying to look forty. Beautifully dressed, wonderful shoes, designer handbag. And brains. Ellie's first impression was that if this woman had decided to kill off her husband, she'd have succeeded in such a way that she'd never be suspected of the crime. On the other hand, the woman was in enough of a rage at that moment to speak her mind without remembering to guard her tongue.

Ellie said, 'They tell me you filled your husband's pill box every week?'

'What is this?' A sharp note in her voice. 'Are you daring to question me?'

Ellie produced her meekest tone of voice. 'Diana didn't tell me she'd invited you all to come here, but she did tell me something of what has been going on. I'd really like to hear your side of the story, too.'

Barbie tossed her blonde mane of hair back, considering whether or not to talk. Finally, she shrugged. 'Oh, well, I've been through all this with the police. Yes, I did fill his pill box for him every week. He'd have killed himself a lot sooner if he'd been allowed to do it himself.' She looked away, down to the floor. 'It was hard to watch him deteriorate, it really was. Every week I could see that he'd lost the ability to do this or that.' She braced herself. 'Well, no point in going on about it. He knew he'd got Alzheimer's and his remedy was to get pie-eyed every night. By nine every evening he was slurring his words, having difficulty working out how to operate the stair lift. To be frank, I was almost relieved when he went.'

'If you're innocent of his death—'

'Don't be ridiculous!' Barbie picked up her cup, found it empty, and slammed it back down on to its saucer.

'Then why aren't you at home, checking over his insurance policies and preparing his will for probate?'

'Because the fool never changed his will after we got together. He told me he was going to do it. He swore to me that I'd never want for anything, but when I went to see his solicitor' – and here she ground her teeth – 'he told me Bunny hadn't signed a new will. The one he made when he got married to his first wife was cancelled out by the divorce, but he made another one a couple of years after, leaving everything to his son. So the second will stands and his son gets everything, despite his turning out so badly. His first wife doesn't get anything from the second will, thank the Lord . . . not that she didn't get more than her share of his worldly goods when they parted . . . but his son now cops the lot – the paintings, his portfolio, the house and cars, the flat in France. Everything.'

'You can sue them for a decent pay-off?' suggested Ellie.

'The solicitor says I can probably make a case out for something from the estate, but he doesn't hold out much hope. And how am I to pay a solicitor? By selling my diamond watch and rings? They've stripped me of everything else.'

'How about an appeal to your stepson?'

Barbie shuddered. 'I wouldn't waste my time. His mother spoiled him rotten and he's not turned out well. I've heard that he enjoys getting young girls into bed and then . . . well, he's lucky not to have been prosecuted, I'd say. He's into drugs, even offered some to me, once!'

Ellie had some sympathy for the woman. 'What are you going to do?'

Barbie pulled a face. 'I can't think straight. This morning when I woke up I thought I had enough to see me through with what I'd put in the safe, but now . . . Well, I've got a few shares in this and that, but not enough to last till it's Old Age Pension time. I suppose I'll have to go home to look after Daddy in Worcester and put up with his funny little ways until he passes on. He likes everything "just so". I'm fond of him, and we get on well enough if we don't see one another too often, but . . . I can't see any alternative. When he dies I'll get his flat but who wants to live in Worcester? I like London. I'm a Londoner. Selling that flat won't bring in enough to get back into the housing market here. I tell you, I could spit!'

'You don't have a job?'

'I used to. I worked in an art gallery for a friend. That's how we met. Bunny liked to buy the odd picture, keep it awhile, and then sell it again, usually at a good profit. I had a good eye and we became partners in buying and selling pictures. We made a good team though I say it myself. We had a lot of fun, too. And now, what can I do? Without access to my capital, I doubt if I can get started again in that line, and the galleries all want curvy twenty-year-old receptionists now. I'm too old to retrain for anything else. Fifteen years I've spent working with him to locate, buy and sell pictures. I drove him to and from auctions and placed bids for him. I've organized his cosy little dinner parties, been at his side to prompt him when his memory failed him, ferried him to and from the doctors and the hospitals . . . and everything's gone, overnight. I could murder him, I really could.'

The others didn't react, which told Ellie that Barbie had said such things before and they hadn't taken her seriously. So neither did Ellie. She said, 'Tell me what happened this morning.'

'I went to the gym as usual. On my return I found a pile of my belongings in the driveway, where that cow, his first wife had thrown them. She and her son stood there, gloating over my downfall. I'd known for several days that I was going to have to move out but the solicitor had said I had a month's grace, time to find somewhere else to live and remove my belongings from the safe. They didn't even let me go back indoors, can you believe it? I told them I had some personal property in the safe, and I told them what it was. Not only did I have some diamonds – Bunny was generous with diamonds, said they suited me – but I'd invested my share of what we'd made in the art market in some rather good miniatures. They asked if I could prove ownership and I said yes, the paperwork was in my desk. They looked at one another and said there was no paperwork in the desk, and without proof I couldn't claim ownership. I bet the first thing they did after I left was to find that paperwork and destroy it.'

Russet said, 'But darling, you should have stood your ground, got the police to get you back into the house to get your things from the safe. They had no right to throw you out before the month is up.'

Barbie grimaced. 'I realize that, now. It was shock, I suppose. They knocked me off balance and I'm only just starting to process what's happened. It's too late now. Bunny always left the combination for the safe in his diary, so they won't have lost any time in getting in and removing the evidence. If only I'd put the stuff in the bank! I thought I had plenty of time to do that. I feel such a fool! All I've got left is what I put on this morning. If Bunny were still alive . . . But he isn't. I miss him, you know. I really do.'

Barbie looked as if she were going to break down and cry, so Ellie changed the subject. 'When did Diana ring you?'

'While I was picking up my stuff in the drive. She said Evan had thrown her out and asked if the police had been round to see me. I said, "Why would they?" Because I'd had them round asking questions when Bunny kicked the bucket, and I'd told them then exactly how stupid my beloved had been about drink and taking his pills. They'd understood how it was then, so I asked Diana why they should come again, and she said it was complicated. I said I couldn't stop on the phone because Bunny's first wife had just thrown me out and I had to find somewhere else to go. That was when Diana said to come round here and we'd talk. Here I am and here she is not!'

Barbie passed her cup over for a refill. Ellie looked in the teapot. Empty. So was the biscuit tin. She said, 'I'll make another pot of tea, shall I? And see if I can find some more biscuits. There may be some in the freezer.'

Back in the kitchen, Ellie refilled the kettle and switched it on.

Then dived into the freezer. She'd just found a box of something that was labelled 'ginger snaps' when her phone rang.

It was Lesley. 'Ellie, I've been thinking. I could be round in about an hour. Have you found out anything yet?'

Ellie said, 'Mrs Brewster, aka Barbie doll, is in the clear. She had nothing to gain by her husband's death.'

'Agreed. I've been looking at her statement. Instead of gaining by his death, she lost her meal ticket.'

'She's no fool. If she'd done him in, she'd have made sure he changed his will in her favour and put some insurance in place first.' Ellie pried open the plastic box and looked inside. Ranks of ginger snaps plus some chocolate brownies. Hurray! She would give them a blast in the microwave to defrost them. Ellie emptied the teapot and put in some more tea bags. 'So, Lesley – would anyone else have had the opportunity to mix up the pills?'

They thought about that while the kettle boiled, the microwave churned and Ellie made more tea. Midge the cat bravely made an appearance through the cat flap. He knew the house had been invaded by strangers but wanted food. Ellie obliged.

'It's a possibility,' said Lesley. 'A cleaner, say, might have spilled the lot out by accident and put them back in the wrong compartments, hoping no one would notice. Husband and wife slept in different rooms. She'd not bother to check. Why should she? In which case—'

'The verdict is still accidental death, or misadventure.'

'If it wasn't for those emails, I'd agree. I ought to see them before I decide that no further action should be taken.'

Ellie sighed. Where was Diana? Why wasn't she here, helping her friends through this traumatic event? 'Agreed. But I think they're a red herring. I've only heard from Mrs Brewster and her friend Russet so far. I'll try to find out what the others have to say, for form's sake. Then, if you still think they're important, I'll give you the copies of the emails.'

'I'll be there as soon as I can.'

The brown-haired girl appeared in the doorway. 'How can I help?'

She was the only one who had offered to help. It might be interesting to find out why.

FOUR

Back in the sitting room with fresh supplies, Ellie found Russet smoking again.

Ellie gave her a look.

Russet shrugged but stubbed out the cigarette and ran her fingers back through her hair, which might have been touched up colour-wise but was still a satisfying auburn and of a good length, too.

Ellie refilled cups and watched the box of biscuits go the rounds. Most took one, if not two.

Ellie looked at the brown-haired girl who had remembered her manners even under stress. Even now she was passing the biscuit tin over to the pudding-shaped one, but she didn't take one for herself. She was the only one on a diet, perhaps?

Ellie said, 'Thank you for helping me. What is your name?'

'Trish. Short for Patricia.'

'And your husband's name?'

'Terry. Terry and Trish. Big man, little woman.' Her smile wobbled. Was she on the verge of tears? And why did she refer to herself as 'little woman' when she was a strapping wench, taller and bigger than Ellie in every way?

'Big man, bad temper,' said Barbie, and Russet nodded in agreement.

Trish reddened. 'Oh, no. Not really.'

Ellie said, 'Well, Trish; was it you who suggested making love to a husband until his heart gave out under the strain?'

Russet shook her head. 'No, that was me. As if . . .!'

Trish produced a painful smile. 'That wasn't me. I would never have thought of that. Russet did suggest Viagra might help my husband some time ago, but it turned out it was all my fault he couldn't . . .' She bit her lip and stopped.

Russet swung her bright mane of hair forward and back, and grimaced. 'We've all thought about getting our men on Viagra at one time or another, haven't we? I got as far as mentioning it to mine but he acted so insulted . . .' She tried to laugh, bit her lip and looked away into the distance. 'Anyway, I reckon it would have taken a double dose even to get him to started, and as for finishing . . .!'

Trish reddened. Was she really such an innocent as to blush at the thought of giving her husband Viagra? Perhaps she was. She had a round, white-skinned column of a neck. And a yellowing bruise on the left side of her face. She hadn't gone in for a tan, unlike Barbie.

Trish said, 'You want to know how I came to be here? Terry punched me, really hard. Not like the occasional slap he's given me before when I've been stupid. My friends here had warned me he would do it again and I hadn't believed them. Then, when he actually knocked me down, I remembered what they'd said, that I should get out of the house and give him time to calm down. I know he'll be feeling terrible about it now. He thinks before he acts, you know. He hears something, twists something. He's always sorry, afterwards.'

The others reacted to this statement as if they'd long expected it. Raised eyebrows and shoulders.

Barbie moved over to put her arm around Trish. 'You can't go on making excuses for him. It's about time you got out from under.'

Russet said, 'We did warn you.'

'Oh, poor Trish,' said the pudding-shaped one.

Trish was on the verge of tears but fighting them back. She did not wear the haunted, defeated air of Barbie and Russet but she was certainly undergoing considerable stress. She was dressed in an expensive blue sweater over jeans and boots. She was not a pretty woman, but in the old days she'd have been termed 'handsome'.

That was a bad bruise developing on her jaw.

Trish spoke to her friends rather than to Ellie. 'I'd taken the dogs out after breakfast as usual. I don't know what he'll do about them now. I mean, they're his dogs, but it's always me who takes them out. Will he remember to walk them? Oh dear! I ought to have taken them with me, except that they're not mine. He *is* fond of them. He loves to have them around. He's always telling people about their pedigrees and that, but . . .'

Barbie gave Trish a little shake. 'Trish, they're his dogs. He'll have to get someone else to walk and feed and groom them, right?'

Barbie looked at Ellie. 'He's slapped her a couple of times before. We've been trying to tell her that he's no right to do that, but she's one soft-hearted creature, aren't you, Trish?'

Trish was wringing her hands. 'He got this idea in his head that I've been sleeping around. I don't understand why, I really don't.'

Barbie said, 'I do. Those men and their gossip! They're living in a time warp, thinking a man has to show the Little Woman how to behave and all that rot.'

Trish said, 'It is partly my fault. When he says these things I'm slow to react and he doesn't believe me when I say they're not true. I'm not clever, I don't think things through as quickly as he does, and it does irritate him. I have tried to be the kind of wife he needs, I really have.'

'Yes, yes,' said Barbie. 'Three choruses of hearts and flowers. He's a bully, and that's the beginning and end of it.'

'Oh, no. Not really. He loves me, he really does. It's just that when I do something stupid, he has to try to set me right. I know he ought not to hit me, and he hasn't, honest, not for weeks. I have listened to what you've all said about the way he reacts, and I do understand he needs to stop and yes, I was afraid but underneath that I was angry with him, but I shouldn't have, really, I know I shouldn't. I didn't mean to hurt him.'

Barbie was surprised. 'You mean you actually landed one on him in return?'

Trish bit her lip. 'I didn't mean to, but somehow, yes, I did. I do hope he's all right.'

Barbie laughed. 'I hope not. Go on, girl! Tell us!'

'Well, when I got back with the dogs he was in the drive, saying our marriage was over and that he didn't want me going back in the house after what I'd done. I couldn't think what he was on about. The dogs started barking as they do when he raises his voice, and he was calling me all the names under the sun, and I just stood there like a dumb cluck with my mouth stuck open.'

'What names did he call you?' Barbie was interested.

'Whore. That sort of thing. I'm not, honest! He said I'd been flirting, making an exhibition of myself with men. It's not true!'

'No, no,' said Barbie. 'We can all bear witness to the fact that you're a real innocent.'

Trish said, 'I suppose I must be. Anyway, he woke up to the noise the dogs were making and took them into the house and slammed the front door in my face, and before I'd got my keys out, some woman I'd never seen before came out with a couple of my travel bags and dumped them in the porch.

'I asked her what she thought she was doing, and she said it was orders and when she went back in I followed her and found him in the kitchen, and I asked him what was going on and he shut the inside door and started calling me filthy names again, saying I'd broken my marriage vows and he was divorcing me because I was a slut and had plotted to murder him, and I could consider myself lucky he'd allow me to take some of my clothes with me. I couldn't believe what was happening. I must have laughed because . . .'

She gulped. 'That was probably a mistake. I started to say that I'd better go out for a while, but he was beyond listening and he walloped me one. I half saw it coming and I tried to duck, but . . .' She rubbed her jaw, where indeed the yellowing bruise was beginning to deepen and darken in colour.

Barbie made a clucking noise. 'We did warn you, my sweet! We told you he'd put his first wife in hospital several times, but you didn't want to know.'

'He swore to me she'd made it all up so that she'd get a decent sum of alimony when they divorced. Of course I believed him. He really, really loves me. Truly. I know you'd said he was working up to hitting me again, but I never thought he would. When he did, I came over all dizzy, sitting there on the floor. Honest, I was just so surprised!'

'Trish, this is the third time he's hit you,' said Russet.

Trish winced. 'Yes, I know. But not like that. Not to knock me down. Just a couple of slaps when I've been extra stupid. They didn't really hurt. But when he hit me so hard today, I realized you were right and that he doesn't know his own strength. I remembered what you said, that if I didn't fight back, I was going to end up in hospital like his first wife. I got angry, and somehow, I don't know how, I got to my feet, and I balanced against the counter and when he took another step towards me . . . The dogs were barking, and my head was spinning, and I could hear you all saying I must not let him get away with it . . . So I kicked him where it hurt and he folded up on to the floor, making a noise like a cat, yeow!'

She smiled, a hurting smile. But a smile, nevertheless. And rubbed her jaw.

Barbie said, 'Good for you!'

Russet clapped her hands.

The pudding-shaped one put her hand over her mouth and said, 'You didn't!'

'I did,' said Trish, tears standing out in her eyes, but pleased with herself. 'Only then, of course, I felt awful. For two pins I'd have joined him on the floor and given him a cuddle and apologized, but then I remembered Barbie saying that once he'd started, he'd do it again and again unless he agreed to see a therapist. And, Russet, you said that if I let him hit me again, it would be because I'd let him. So I held on to the counter and managed to get myself out into the hall.'

Russet said, 'Great. So that's when he threw you out?'

'Not exactly, no. I saw one of the strange women – there were two of them, never seen them before in my life! – bringing my winter coats down the stairs. I wasn't sure I could climb the stairs, but I made it. Slowly. The women had cleared out my walk-in wardrobe and cupboards. I tried to think. I love Terry so much! He's really a lost little boy and he needs me. I just have to give him time, and he'll apologize. I do know you said he's got to learn to respect me. It's just that when he gets in a state, he doesn't think straight. He says I'm always laughing too much and that it shows I'm a slut at heart. If I so much as speak to or smile at another man, he asks me where I met him and . . . Oh, it's all so stupid! So unnecessary!

'I stood there on the landing and told myself that this was a crisis. I had to do something to stop him hitting me. He'd said he wanted me out and I decided to be brave and take him at his word. I would go and not return till he'd promised to see a therapist. So I helped the women take my stuff from the bathroom, which they'd forgotten to do. Then I went back downstairs and he was sitting up and taking notice again. I said I didn't know what bee he had in his bonnet, but he was quite wrong about me wanting him dead, because we did have a good thing going, didn't we? He'd even got tickets for the Orient Express for our fourth wedding anniversary next month. I said I was going to leave him to stay with my parents for a few days to think things over and he could phone me on my mobile when he wanted to talk. I got those two women to help me pack up the car with everything and was just fitting the last bundle into my car when Russet rang to say she and Barbie had been thrown out, too, and that they were at Diana's mother's house and would I like to join them, because it's a long drive to my parents and it's true, I didn't feel like facing the motorway. So I came here instead. Did I do the right thing? I shouldn't have left him, should I? I'm in such a muddle!'

So the cars outside were Trish's and Russet's?

'You did the right thing,' said Barbie. 'If you'll take my advice, you'll not answer his calls for a few days. Give him time to calm down. Don't agree to meet him on your own, either. Perhaps have your solicitor with you? Get him to agree to see a therapist before you'll even think of returning to him. That is, if you think he's worth it.'

'Of course he's worth it,' said Trish.

The others looked unconvinced that Terry was worth a cough or a sneeze but nodded to show solidarity.

Russet said, 'Trish, I'm thrilled you got out from under, but can you keep it up if he refuses to see a therapist and comes crawling back to you tomorrow, weeping salt tears and declaring eternal love?'

A wriggle of the shoulders. A moment of doubt. 'I don't know. It shook me when he swiped at me like that. I didn't recognize him for a moment. He'd gone all red and horrible. It crossed my mind that he ought to have a check on his blood pressure, but . . . Oh, I don't know. If he can learn to curb his temper, but . . .' She braced herself. 'I'm not going to be anybody's victim. If we divorce, not that I want to, but if we do then I'm young enough to start again. Thank the Lord we never had any children. But let me make it quite clear: I was not plotting to kill him.'

Barbie said, 'I'm sure you're right. Give it time. Your family has money. They won't let you starve.'

Trish managed her painful smile again. 'I'll be all right. What about you lot?'

There was a new sharp note in Russet's voice. 'I'm not going to put up with being thrown on the rubbish heap at my time of life.'

Ellie raised her hands. 'Girls, girls! Now,' she turned to the pudding-shaped one, 'what's your name, and who is your husband?'

The last one of the four had been sobbing her heart out when Ellie arrived, and hadn't stopped for long since. Or repaired her make-up. Correction: she didn't wear make-up. She'd washed her face and had stopped crying but looked as if she might start again at any minute.

'I'm Kat, short for Katarina.' A whispery voice. She was not like the others, who all showed evidence of careful and expensive grooming. Kat's figure was sinking into middle-aged spread without being checked by diet or corsetry. Her hair was naturally fair, almost ash-blonde though turning grey. She had not visited the hairdressers recently and her dense mop was tied back in a scrunchy at the nape of her neck. She was so unlike the others in presentation that it was almost laughable, and it seemed she was the only one who'd cried that day. Also, that thick quality in the voice wasn't catarrh, it was the trace of a mid-European accent.

Kat blew her nose. 'Is it possible, my hankie is finished. A tissue?' She was helplessness itself.

Ellie said, 'There's a box on the table by the window.'

It didn't surprise Ellie that Trish went to get it for her friend, but it was surprising that Russet put her arm around Kat and gave her a hug. 'You'll be all right.'

Barbie said, 'Yes, buck up, Kat. We'll sort this and find somewhere for you to go.'

So those three well-groomed, expensive women were rallying around Kat? Perhaps because she was so helpless and they were so obviously not? There was a certain irritation in their care for her, but Ellie thought all the better of them for troubling themselves to look after Kat when they were in such a difficult position themselves.

Ellie had seen women using their weakness to get their own way before but, observing Kat now trying to smile and to thank her friends, Ellie acquitted her of doing so with intent. The woman was just what she seemed: a nice enough creature without much gumption. If she'd been the one to muddle up her husband's pills and cause him to meet an untimely death, no one would have been surprised. But it wasn't her husband who'd died, was it?

'So, which is your husband, Kat?'

'Rupert. Oh, dear, I always cut his toenails on Monday evenings. Who's going to look after him now? It is not possible for him to get down to his feet.'

'He'll manage,' said Barbie, with a bracing air and the tiniest roll of her eyes. 'He managed before you came, didn't he?'

Barbie had no illusions about Rupert, did she? She probably didn't have an optimistic view of the human race as a whole, either.

Ellie said, 'I must ask, Kat. Was it your laptop which revealed the emails?'

'It was Rupert's old one. When I came to this country I knew nothing, but my friends teach me to use Internet and Rupert gave me his old laptop that he did not use any more.' She beamed at her friends, and they all smiled and nodded back.

Kat said, 'I have skills now. I can get another job to look after house. I can search online for a gardener. I know about electric meter, and gas and everything. Barbie and Russet are so kind, and Trish, too. They help me learn first on laptop and only one month ago they gave me smartphone. Now I text just like other people, and I Skype my family in Bosnia every Sunday. My brother and sister, they wish to visit, but my husband says "No", so I tell them, "Not this year, but maybe next".'

'Maybe.' Russet patted Kat's shoulder and explained what had happened to Ellie. 'Rupert's first wife went off with the milkman or the insurance agent or some such. Kat was his housekeeper while he dillied and dallied semi-romantically with a couple of expensive young women. When he realized how much they would cost to keep, he decided to save himself a packet by marrying Kat and saving her wages.'

'No, no!' Kat sobbed again. 'He is good man and much worried with his health. What will he do if I am not there to make his special diet?'

'He should have thought of that,' said Russet with a grim smile. 'I'll bet mine won't remember his chiropody appointment, either.'

Ellie said, 'What happened to you today, Kat?'

'The same. Like the others. He sent me to the shops for some special laces for his new boots and when I got back, my bag that I brought from home was in the drive, with another I do not know. He say, I am bad wife, and he has packed up my bag and he lends me another on wheels to take all that I have in the world. I cry, and he give me fifty pounds to go away. Then Diana ring and say to come here to this address. So I come by bus, and then I ask where is it, and I walk and walk and I get here.'

Russet patted Kat's knee. 'I don't know why you put up with Rupert for so long. He paws everything in sight after he's had a couple.'

Barbie exchanged glances with Russet. 'You, too?'

Russet pulled a face. 'Hands everywhere. Ugh.'

Trish said, 'If you don't smile as if you like it, he pinches you.'

Barbie tapped the table. 'I don't believe in coincidences. Someone with a good brain masterminded today's little coup. Knowing our beloved husbands, I can't imagine any of them being responsible. What do you think, girls?'

'What!' Trish's mouth fell open. 'Oh. But . . . what do you mean?'

Barbie's fingers, dark red-tipped, drummed a rhythm on the table. 'It was like a military operation. We were all absent from the house for a while this morning. It's no secret that I always go to the gym on a Monday morning, or that Trish walks the dogs at that time of day. Russet and Kat went shopping. My husband's first wife and his son arrived to clear out my stuff when I was out, at the same time as a team of cleaners do the same to you, Russet, and to Trish and to Kat. What I want to know is who contacted my husband's ex, and who arranged for the women to pack up our things in our absence? Which of the men do you think hated us all so much to do that? And how did they know we'd been exchanging emails? I mean, we haven't used laptops to keep in touch for a while now.'

Ellie gave a little cough. 'Actually, I may know part of the answer to that. Diana's husband, Evan, told me what happened. Rupert found the emails on his old laptop and took it to Evan. I don't know why he looked there, but he did.'

'Oh, that's easy,' said Trish. 'He knew she was Skyping her family every week, and he was dead scared some of them might come over to visit and he'd have to put them up or – horrors! – actually feed them for a couple of nights. So every now and then he used to check what she'd been up to on his old laptop. Isn't that right, Kat?'

'Yes, yes. That is true. My family think I am very rich now, living in London. They do not understand I have no money except for housekeeping. I say to Rupert, maybe when my brother come he pay for his food and service the car, because he is very good mechanic, but Rupert, he say, "No way". Yes, Rupert take laptop and I say, "Where is it?" and he say, "It is gone for repair".'

Ellie said, 'He took it to Evan when he found those silly emails suggesting how to kill someone.'

Barbie was doubtful. 'You think Evan has the brains to plan all this? I wouldn't have thought so.'

Russet shook her head. 'I don't think Walt has, either. He's a brilliant businessman in many ways, but he's not that good with detail.'

Trish said, 'Terry might, I suppose. He was, like, crazy mad this morning.' She shivered. 'Do you know, I wasn't frightened at the time because it came out of the blue, but now I . . .' She had seated herself at one end of the settee. Now she put her head down on her knees and folded her arms above her head. Gasping. Shuddering.

Delayed shock.

Barbie shifted to sit close to Trish and put her arm around her. Russet hastened to the other side of Trish and did the same, the two of them enclosing her in their arms.

'There, there. There, there.'

Russet said, 'You've been so brave . . .!'

Kat hauled herself to her feet. Her face was blotchy with crying, but her practical nature was beginning to reassert itself. 'Have we blanket to keep her warm? Or strong drink, maybe?'

'No, no.' Trish tried to sit upright. Attempted a smile. 'I'm all right, really.' She was still shaking.

Ellie found the throw which was kept behind Thomas's reclining chair and swathed Trish in it.

'Thank you,' said Trish. There were tears in her eyes. 'You are very kind.'

And you are a good girl.

Ellie returned to her chair. 'Well, ladies; I think I can answer your question as to who was responsible for today's events – in part, anyway. My daughter Diana is Evan's fourth wife. His second wife is dead, and his third has gone on to have a successful modelling career for underwear and is no longer in touch with him. His first wife, however, is another matter. She was older than him when they met and a lot brighter. They had a one-night stand, during which she got pregnant. They married and produced a child. They had nothing else in common and eventually divorced. The child is out of it, but Evan and his first wife have stayed in touch over the years. Her name is Monique, she has a first-class brain and retains some fondness for him.

'I went to see Evan at his house this morning and she was there. When Rupert took the laptop to Evan, he learned that Diana had suggested a way to kill someone. He panicked and asked Monique to advise him what to do. You've seen the result. Monique admitted it was she who masterminded the expulsion of the wives.'

Russet stared at Ellie. 'It's a lot of codswallop! We're not trying to kill them. None of us.'

Ellie nodded. 'I believe you, but the men have chosen to think otherwise.'

'It's not true, so we can fight this,' said Russet. 'Can't we?'

Ellie said, 'If you can get hold of good solicitors. If you have enough money to pay them well and if those emails are not produced in evidence. If they are, the judge might think they showed intent. That might make it tough.'

'We didn't mean it, any of it!'

'Be realistic,' said Ellie. 'The fact is that Bunny died in the way that Diana suggested. That slants the evidence a different way.'

Barbie fidgeted with her rings. 'I didn't kill him.'

'No, but according to your own words, you were not madly in love with him, either.' Ellie looked around at the women.

'Look, I've been married twice, and I cried when my first husband died, and I'd be devastated if anything were to happen to my dear Thomas. I know that, over the years, the first wild flush of love can change into affection and tolerance. Apart from Trish, you were all moving into that state. You were not unhappy, but you were not wearing rose-coloured spectacles, either. I don't think any of you would have chosen to break-up, but now that it has happened, are you clear in your minds that you want to go back to men who have taken such drastic action to get rid of you?'

'There is that.' Russet bit her lip. 'But . . .'

Trish huddled into the folds of the throw. Her colour was poor. She said, 'I believe in marriage, too. I'd go back if only . . .' She rubbed jaw and said, 'Ow! If only if I can be sure he'd tackle his temper.'

'If he doesn't?'

Trish was exhausted. Deep shadows were forming around her eyes. Even her voice faded. 'Surely, we can talk it through? You're right, of course. Now he's hit me so hard, I'm afraid that he might do it again. I'm trying to think positively, but where do we go from here?'

Kat's eyes were huge. 'You are thinking Rupert will take me back? I'd like that. I mean, yes, he is not always kind, but I do not marry thinking to divorce. No. That I do not believe in. It was registry office wedding, but I am still a Catholic.'

Russet pushed her hands back through her hair. 'The thing is, if we go to law, it's going to take ages—'

'And what are we going to live on in the meantime?' That was Barbie. But her eyes flickered here and there. 'I admit, I do have a little nest egg but without the diamonds and the miniatures I'd put in the safe, I don't have enough to buy another place in London.'

Russet held her head in her hands. 'Suppose we say we'll accept being divorced, but that we'll make one hell of a stink if they don't give us a proper division of property? They won't go to the press with what they've got. Will they?'

'I'd be happy with a decent pay-off from Bunny's estate,' said Barbie. 'I'm not risking another venture into matrimony at my time of life.'

There was a general looking-at-watches and settling of hair, except for Trish, who had closed her eyes. Russet took out her phone, frowned at it and sat with it in her hand, considering what to do next.

In a minute they'd all be trying to make plans for the next phase of their lives.

Ellie debated with herself. She had not learned anything to feed the suspicion that Barbie had killed off her husband. In fact, the reverse. She could definitely say, hand on heart, that Barbie had not done so.

Ellie could now see the whole picture of who had done what, to whom, and by what means. Could criminal charges be brought against any of the women on the evidence of the emails? Unlikely. The only crime committed, as far as Ellie could see, was that Terry had hit Trish. But then, she'd given him what for in return . . .

Ellie could wave them on their way and wipe the whole episode from her mind, except that she'd still have to help Diana . . . and Diana was still missing.

And the whole thing was *wrong*!

Every feeling revolted, and so on.

There was no real villain. There really wasn't. A lack of romantic love was not a notifiable offence in legal terms. What would Lesley say if Ellie let the women go? What *could* she say? There was nothing for the police to work on.

Except for the emails. But no, they were rubbish. Any half-good barrister would laugh those out of court. Lesley had said she wanted to see them, but what good would that do?

Ellie had enough to worry about, with Thomas having gone out in a state, and her little grandson having been whisked away by Evan and Monique. Let sleeping dogs lie.

She stood up and collected eyes. 'We are all waiting for Diana, who has gone, as you've guessed, to see if a solicitor can help you all. I expect you will like to hear from her before you make plans for the future. Meanwhile, I don't have unlimited accommodation here, but I think I can find beds for you for tonight.'

FIVE

Drooping heads revived, except for Trish's, which sank even lower. Trish was falling asleep? With a sigh, she put her head down and curled up on the settee. She was worn out. Barbie and Russet made room for her.

Ellie said, 'Yes, leave her be. She's had a rough day.'

Barbie was frowning. 'Do you really mean you can put us up tonight? I mean, it would be wonderful, but won't it be a lot of work?'

Ellie said, 'Some of the beds are not made-up. I'll have to find sheets and some of you may have to have old-fashioned blankets instead of duvets, but if you don't mind roughing it for a night?'

'That is very good of you. We're very grateful,' said Russet, and sounded as if she meant it.

Kat said, 'I will help. I make beds good.'

'Thank you, Kat,' said Ellie. 'Now, it's going to be a problem to fit you all in. Diana is in my big guest room on the left after the master bedroom, but there are two more bedrooms at the end of the corridor which I suggest Barbie and Russet might like to occupy tonight. The big room at the end has a double bed in it but has not been made-up. The smaller room at the side is the one used by my grandson for sleepovers, and if you don't mind using his sheets, one of you can move in there straight away. On the other side of the house there's a bedroom which can be reached by the stairs off the corridor to the kitchen. I suggest Trish has that, and I'll see what I can do for Kat in a minute.'

Barbie revived enough to stand up. 'You have some kind of cook person who could help us carry our stuff upstairs?'

'No,' said Ellie. 'She is not a cook person. She is a student at the university who rents the top-floor flat from me. I suggest you take what you need for tonight upstairs with you and leave the remainder in the hall. Right? Get yourselves settled in, and then perhaps you'd like a short rest while I see if I can find something in the freezer for supper.'

'You are very good,' said Barbie. 'Thank you.'

Barbie and Russet went off together, arguing in friendly terms about who should have the big room at the end of the corridor.

Ellie guessed it would be Barbie. She began collecting the dirty cups and saucers and rescued the empty biscuit tin from under a chair.

Kat stood up. 'I help you, no? Or I look after Trish?'

Trish was asleep, tears on her cheeks and her bruise darkening.

'You look after Trish,' said Ellie. 'Do you think she has concussion?'

Kat felt Trish's forehead and checked her pulse. Kat knew what she was doing. 'No fever. Pulse normal.'

Ellie paused, loaded tray in her hands. 'Might she be pregnant?'

Kat sighed deeply. 'No. She wished for children so much. When they marry, he say she can have one baby, but then he make excuses, all the time excuses. She hopes he will change his mind, but it does not happen. He has two grown-up children who have nothing to do with him. He is older than Trish, you understand.'

'Poor thing.' Ellie took her laden tray out to the kitchen and dumped it on the table. Then went back for the other. Her mobile rang and she answered . . . only to find it wasn't her mobile making that noise, but the front door. A long ring and a short buzz, repeated. Lesley?

Ellie opened the door to let her friend in and signalled silence by putting her finger to her lips. 'Someone's asleep. Go through to the kitchen, and I'll join you there.'

Lesley's eyebrows rose but she did as Ellie suggested.

Ellie took a moment to phone Diana. *Ring, ring*. The call went to voicemail again. What was Diana up to?

Ellie peeped into the sitting room and noted that Kat had sunk into a chair and joined Trish in having a nap. Sensible woman. Ellie followed Lesley down the corridor and into the kitchen. With the familiarity of old friends, Lesley helped to pile the dirty dishes into the dishwasher while Ellie reported on the doings of the day: Diana's arrival, Ellie's visit to Evan and Monique, and the four women's stories.

When Ellie had finished, Lesley said, 'So, in your opinion Mrs Brewster didn't kill her husband, and though the men have acted precipitously by dumping their wives en masse, there is no need for the police to get involved. I'd agree except that, as a policewoman, I have a suspicious mind and need to see those emails.'

'You shall. One thing strikes me: they were written weeks ago so I'm wondering why they've only come to light now. I've arranged for all the women to stay here tonight so you can have a word with them if you wish. Now, what can I find in the freezer that will feed five or six people for supper? Presuming that Thomas returns in one piece.'

Lesley put her hands on her hips. 'I know you, Ellie Quicke. Something's bothering you or you'd have told those women to get lost instead of taking them under your wing.'

Ellie measured her words. 'There is no reason I can think of to involve the police, but yes, you're right: I'm not happy about the situation. However, unless you count the fact that Trish's husband took a swing at her and she swung back, there's nothing to report in the way of a crime.'

'Set reason aside. Think blue sky. Or rather, don't think. Just blurt out whatever comes to mind.'

Ellie sat down and closed her eyes. She needed a quiet moment for this. She'd been so stirred up by what had happened . . . Those poor women, some more able to look after themselves than others . . . Thomas was late, oh dear, that business of the printer going bankrupt sounded serious. What had happened to Diana . . .? Then, what about the geraniums she'd been potting up this morning when everything began? She hadn't finished dealing with them, had she? She'd left some on the side, and not in water? Water would keep them going till she could get round to dealing with them again. And her poor little grandson – he must be so bewildered, wanting his mother . . .

Dear Lord above. What a mess. I know you are here as well as in church. I haven't time to tell you all that's been happening. Oh, how stupid I am. You know, anyway, don't you? Any words of wisdom for me?

She quietened herself down. Then, with her eyes still closed, she said, 'The only thing that bothers me, the only discrepancy that I've come across apart from the time lapse . . . Could this really be all about money?'

She opened her eyes to meet Lesley's gaze. Lesley was smiling a crooked little smile. 'Money? Now you're talking. Money is the root of all evil, and so on. Are you sure?'

'No, I'm not sure,' said Ellie, getting cross. 'You said to enquire within and that bubbled up. I doubt very much that it's true, except' – she shifted uneasily – 'something isn't right. The way the men reacted is overkill. They got together and conspired to get rid of their wives. Maybe they thought they had cause, but honestly! It was just a joke that they took the wrong way. Except, of course, that Bunny died.

'What I mean is that a joke is a joke. Someone seized on the joke to . . . to do what? To get themselves a younger and prettier set of wives? That sounds all right if you look at their marital history, each of them having had at least one spouse before. Is that really what this is all about? I tell myself it must be, but they were awfully quick off the mark, weren't they? They wouldn't have been half as efficient if Evan's first wife hadn't been such a good organizer. I like Monique. I understand her. She was brought in to help Evan and that's exactly what she did. It's true she doesn't think much of Diana as a mother and wife, but—'

'Mm. Who does? Sorry. Rhetorical question.'

Ellie reddened. 'Diana has been a good mother to the little boy, she really has. She's devoted to him and he to her. She's looked after her husband to the best of her ability, has kept his estate agency going, and never looked at another man.'

Lesley raised her hands in submission. 'All right, Ellie. I'll go along with that. So why do you think it's to do with money?'

'Kat was Rupert's housekeeper. He's a miser, counting every penny. He married her to save himself the cost of her wages. It was he who took the emails to Evan in the first place. Why did he do that? Kat has been a good wife to him, so why would he throw her out? It doesn't make sense, unless he's hoping to gain more by losing her than he's getting now. I don't understand it.'

Lesley thought about that. She nodded. 'Right. You've

convinced me that something is very wrong there. Show me the emails and I'll see if there's something that I can latch on to. If so, I'll have a word with the wives while they're here.'

'Help yourself to a cuppa. I don't think there's any biscuits left, but you can look.'

Ellie collected the emails from her handbag in the hall. The house seemed unnaturally quiet. There was no sound from upstairs where Barbie and Russet were presumably settling in. She peeped into the sitting room and saw that Kat was tucking the throw around Trish, who was fast asleep.

Kat saw Ellie and came to join her in the hall. 'I help make up beds?'

'Thank you, yes. I'd appreciate that. I'll just take these papers through to the kitchen for a friend who's popped in for a cuppa, and we'll go upstairs to see what we can sort out.'

Ellie dropped the emails back into Lesley, who was indeed in the process of making herself a cuppa, collected Kat and led the way upstairs to the linen cupboard on the first floor.

'We'll deal with the big room at the end of the corridor first. A bottom sheet for the double bed, yes. I think the duvet and some pillows are still on the bed there. Here's a matching duvet cover and pillow cases. Can you take those along for me?'

Kat did so, while Ellie found linen for the single bed in what used to be her old housekeeper's room over the kitchen.

Kat returned, smiling. 'Russet and Barbie are settling themselves. Barbie will make up her own bed. She is good housewife.'

Ellie handed her another set of linen. 'We'll make up another bed for Trish in the room over the kitchen, and that just leaves you. This evening I will arrange that too. Hopefully. This way.'

Kat followed Ellie round the stairwell, saying, 'I can sleep on sofa downstairs, or anywhere.'

Ellie opened the door into what had once been the housekeeper's bedroom. 'I'll try to arrange something better. This one will do for Trish tonight.' Ellie slid up the sash window and looked around. 'It needs airing and redecorating but I don't suppose Trish will mind.'

They set to work together to make the bed up.

Ellie thought this was a good opportunity to get Kat talking. 'You are worried about Trish?'

Kat grimaced. 'That husband, that Terry! Not good, I think. He say, "You must lose weight. You must look more like Barbie and Russet". Trish, she is built different from them and she try, oh, how she try to please him. She eat nothing. She lose weight too quick, I think. Still he is not pleased. He say, "It is not enough". It is not possible to please that one, I think.'

Ellie was horrified. 'She's been on one of those crash diets? No wonder she's fit for nothing. Poor girl! I thought she was too thin for perfect health.'

Kat shrugged. 'The men want, what do you say . . .?'

'Stick insects?'

'What is that, please?'

'Too thin. You can see the bones.'

Kat nodded. 'As thin as a stick. I remember that.'

Ellie ran a finger across the chest of drawers. No dust. Good. Her cleaners were supposed to do every room once a month, but it was good to check.

Oh, horrors! Her cleaners were due tomorrow morning, Tuesday, to give the house its weekly seeing-to. But with all these people staying, the cleaners would be very much in the way. Ellie took her mobile phone out of her pocket. She would cancel their visit tomorrow. 'Kat, I have to make a phone call. Can you finish up for me?'

Ellie hurried out on to the landing. She'd got her cleaners to put their mobile phone numbers on her own phone. She'd never phoned them before. She hoped she'd remember how to do it . . . Ah, a voice on the other end.

Ellie quickly explained that she'd unexpectedly got a house full of people, so could she cancel tomorrow's session? She would, of course, still pay the agency fee.

'Good news for once,' said the voice. 'We've been run off our feet today. See you next week then.'

Ellie clicked off the phone, and then stared at it. Could it be that the cleaners she'd used for years had been the same people who had helped evict the wives that day? Ellie was angry with herself. She ought to have asked. But now Kat was hovering, asking a question, and Ellie must answer it.

'Oh, yes, there's a shower room and toilet next door. I'll get you some towels.' She delved into the linen cupboard again and handed Kat the appropriate items. Mission accomplished. Trish could be comfortable here tonight.

The curtains flapped in the breeze from the open window, and Ellie shut it to keep the warmth in. It looked like more rain to come.

Ellie said to Kat, 'I'm worn out, aren't you? Let's find somewhere to sit and have a quiet chat before anything else happens.'

Ellie led the way down the stairs. She tried to think where they could be alone, and turned into the dining room, which was only used once a week for the board meetings of her charitable trust. Pulling out a chair, she said, 'Now, Kat, could you bear to tell me exactly what your husband said to you this morning when he threw you out?'

Kat went a dull red. 'He say I am thief. He say I steal money from him.'

'I'm sure you didn't. Why would he say that?'

Kat looked away.

She's going to lie. Or perhaps, she's too embarrassed to say?

Kat gave a long, long sigh. 'He give me money for this and that. I write it down in a little book. In my country, on the farm, we wives are very careful. We bargain in the market. We get a little discount. That is our money to keep for ourselves. You understand?'

'Yes, I do. In the old days the farmers' wives in this country had the right to keep the money from any eggs or butter they sold.'

'So I do that. It is not much, you understand, but I have no money to buy anything with. He pays all the household bills himself. He is very clever. He gets cheap deals. He leave money for the gardener, and the window cleaner. For the food shopping I have a float. He checks the bill and takes the change. Sometimes I go to cheaper supermarket. It is much further to walk but I do it, and he is pleased to save a few pennies. I ask if I can keep that money that I saved him or the money for the bus, but he say it is what I should do as a good wife. One day he give me money for the window cleaner, but the man did not come that day because it rained. I put the money in my tin to pay him next time. My husband did not know the window cleaner did not come because he was at work and did not see. So next month he left me the same money again and I forgot to tell him I already had it, and he found the money and said I stole it. He said I should go back to my own country or he would tell the police on me.'

'That's ridiculous!'

'He say I should tell him the window cleaner did not come. He say I steal from him.' She began to rock. 'Is true. I thought to keep the money myself. So yes, I am a thief. All for a bar of . . .' She stopped abruptly.

'A bar of . . .?'

Kat reddened. 'Nothing. I am silly. I stuff my face with sugar, which is not good for me. He is right. I have no willpower.'

Ellie said, 'You mean, you wanted to buy some sweets for yourself?'

'Some chocolate. I love chocolate. In the beginning, I get some from the supermarket, but he saw it on the bill. He said to take it back, that he would not buy me things to ruin my teeth and have to go to dentist.' She began to rock again. 'Once I ate a big bar, all by myself, all in one afternoon.'

Ellie was puzzled. 'Back to this morning. Didn't he say anything about you wanting to kill him?'

'No.' She thought about it. Light dawned. 'Yes, he did. Right at the end. He say that I poison him and I say "Nonsense!" because I am good cook, and he laugh and say to forget it. Then he say again that I must go. So I did.'

Well, well. So Rupert, who had taken the emails to his friends, didn't really believe the suggestions were meant seriously, either. Rupert was only interested in saving himself money, which surely he would not do by getting rid of Kat. Poor Kat!

Ellie leaned forward and took Kat's hands in hers. 'You were in an intolerable position. It's slavery. You worked full-time and received no wages. That's against the law.'

'No, no!' Kat produced her sodden hankie and used it. 'He is my husband. He has the right to say what I do.'

Ellie thought about that. 'Kat, you know I said I had a friend who'd dropped in for a cup of tea. She happens to be in the police—'

Kat recoiled. 'She is come to arrest me?'

'No, no. Of course not. Please, don't be afraid. Nothing like that. She is a good person, Kat, and she understands the law better than I do. I think what your husband has done to you is against the law and he ought to be told. He had no right to treat you like that.'

'Yes, yes. He is my husband.'

'I don't know how it would be in your own country, but here we regard what he has done as wrong. It is unreasonable conduct and I think it would give you grounds for divorce.'

'No, no. I not divorce. You not understand. It is forbidden.'

'It is also forbidden to keep a slave without pay.'

Kat wrung her hands. 'Please, I am not slave. I am wife. I have papers to say I am married. Barbie and Russet tell me I must have proof of wedding. They show me how to have safety deposit box in bank for my passport and papers. I have the right to live in this country. I not have to go back home, no? There is no work. Will you help me get another job? I work hard, I not steal again. I swear it.'

Ellie sent a kind thought to Barbie and Russet, who did indeed seem to have looked after Kat well. 'Kat, I am pretty sure you have every right to stay here, and that you do not have to go back home. Of course you can get another job, but in the meantime I think it would be good for you to consult with my friend from the police so that your mind can be put at rest. She is definitely not here to arrest you.'

'Who is to trust? Is all so difficult!'

Ellie thought of how it would be if she had landed in a foreign country where she did not speak the language well and did not understand the laws of the land. To add to that, Kat had been brought up to believe marriage was for life and look where that had landed her!

'Trust me,' said Ellie. 'I guarantee that Lesley will not arrest you. She will be able to tell you what your position is with regards to getting some kind of payment from your husband. Do you understand?'

'You are sure?'

'Yes, I am sure. Come through to the kitchen and meet Lesley.'

Kat followed Ellie. Reluctantly. But she did.

Lesley looked up from studying the emails. Ellie introduced Kat and explained her position. Lesley was no fool. She did her best to put Kat at ease and managed to get the woman to sit down at the table, even though Kat gave the impression that she was longing to flee.

Ellie left them to it. She wanted to speak to Diana before she did anything else. Back in the hall, she tried ringing her daughter's number again, and again it went to voicemail. She tried her solicitor, Gunnar. That call went to voicemail, too. She tried his chambers. They were shut for the day.

She could have wept with frustration. The hall was full of other people's luggage. Thomas was . . . who knew where?

Her ginger tomcat, Midge, suddenly appeared from behind a pile of luggage and wound himself round her feet. Where had he been? He didn't like visitors much. Correction, he approved of certain people who would feed him titbits, but he avoided Diana and he was probably finding this influx of people and their belongings rather too much to cope with.

He purred, loudly. She told him he'd find Lesley in the kitchen, and that Lesley would probably feed him if he asked nicely. She pointed and shooed him in the right direction. He gave her an old-fashioned look but, seeing that she was not prepared to indulge him, he slunk off to see who else might pay him some attention.

Ellie went into the conservatory at the back of the house. If she could do nothing else, she could finish potting up the geraniums. Where had she left her gloves? Well, never mind them. Best get on with the job. She'd worry about everything else later. She set to work, her topmost mind concentrating on the plants, while the underpart of her mind worried away . . . Diana . . . her grandson . . . Thomas! All those women . . . poor Trish! Oh dear!

She looked at her watch. Susan, who the women had called her 'cook person' was not scheduled to cater for Ellie and Thomas tonight. In truth, it was not in the terms of her tenancy agreement that Susan should cook for them at all. The fact that she did so every now and then was a bonus and much appreciated. It could not be taken for granted. Susan would probably be out tonight with her fiancé, whom she was due to marry in a few months' time.

Thinking about young Rafael, Ellie wondered if he might help in finding some accommodation for these homeless women. He was an unusual young man who had ploughed an inheritance into buying a rundown block of flats, which he was doing-up himself. Perhaps he might like to accommodate one of these dispossessed women?

A stir in the doorway and there was Trish, blinking herself awake, trying to smile. The bruise on her jaw had turned almost black. 'Can I help?'

Ellie indicated a collapsible chair which had ended up in the conservatory instead of having been put away in the garden shed. 'Seat yourself. Relax. Talk to me.'

Trish had her mobile phone in her hand. Ellie wondered who she'd been talking to, or was planning to talk to.

'You've contacted your parents?'

'Tried to. They're out. I left a message saying I'd ring back later.' She fidgeted with her phone. 'Terry rang. Checking up on me. He seemed to think I wasn't going home to my parents' house but moving in with some man or other.' She reddened. 'I really don't know why he thinks that. He's terribly angry. I told him I was here with you tonight and was going back to my parents tomorrow.'

She gave a long, long sigh and sat down to watch Ellie. 'What are you doing? Are those geraniums? I don't know much about gardening. Terry said . . .' She looked down at her hands. 'I'm hopeless at it.'

'You just need to be shown, that's all,' said Ellie. 'Tell me, how come you women ended up as friends? You're all so different from one another.'

SIX

Trish said, 'How did we get to know one another? Yes, I suppose it does look odd. It was our husbands, really. The five of them are always together, thick as thieves. The golf club is their second home, and they like us to go with them but not to join in their conversation. To show us off, I suppose, while they talk business. Sometimes it's a bit tiresome, going out when I'd rather have a night in, watch telly, that sort of thing. Terry didn't want me to be left alone at home. He said he wouldn't know what I was up to. I thought it meant he wanted me with him at all times because he loved me, but now I see . . . perhaps . . . It's difficult.'

'He was jealous?' Ellie knew that people talk more easily if their hands are occupied at the same time. 'Trish, would you like to help me with these cuttings?'

'I don't know how.'

'These geraniums have got a bit leggy and the stems have gone brown, so I want to start new plants from them. Can you see that the growing points are still green? Take this double pink geranium. You cut off the green shoot at the end, maybe six inches or more, use these scissors, and take off the lower leaves. That's right. Now, you were saying . . .?'

Trish slowly and carefully selected a geranium shoot and cut it off. 'Terry seemed to think that I started flirting with someone else the moment his back was turned, so he was happy to take me to the club if I sat with the other wives. Barbie and Russet were already friends – they go to the gym together and the same beauty parlour. They were kind to me, included me in their group. They'd both known Terry's first wife, and they were worried that I might also end up in hospital. They were right, weren't they?'

Ellie demonstrated. 'Now you dunk the cut end of the green bit you've cut off in this powder, which helps it to root. Like this, see? Kat was also part of this group?'

Trish dunked as instructed, with the tip of her tongue poking out of her mouth in concentration. 'Am I doing this right? Well, Kat . . . Poor dear Kat. Rupert brought her along one evening and asked us to look after her. She looked so lost, so out of place. Barbie wasn't there that evening, I remember. Russet and I tried to make small talk with her and didn't get far. Then she told us that Rupert didn't want to leave her at home because she might be on the landline to her mother back home, who was poorly. Kat was so worried about her mother. She did have a mobile at one time but had run out of credit and he wouldn't give her any money for it. How could he!' She held the cutting up. 'Now what do I do with it?'

Ellie pushed some empty pots towards her. 'Fill one of these with compost from that bag over there and tap it to make the earth settle. Then you poke a pencil down into the middle to make a well for the cutting to drop into. That's right. Firm the compost down around it using . . . No, not your fingers. Use your thumbs. That way you don't damage the shoot. Splendid! You've got the idea. Do you want to try another one?'

Trish did. She selected another shoot and cut it off the plant. 'Ah, well, we all knew Rupert was a bit of a tightwad though the word is that he's stinking rich. He wouldn't let Kat run up a bill on his landline so of course we lent her our phones so that she could talk to her mum. Not for long. Kat was always careful about that. I suppose you could say we sort of adopted her, but it wasn't all one way. She's a brilliant seamstress. She alters our clothes for us, taking the skirts up, that sort of thing. We make sure to pay her well for what she does, in cash. She found an old sewing machine in the loft at Rupert's and I think that was the one thing she liked best about living in his house. She'll miss that. Perhaps I can find another for her somewhere.'

'You paid her so that she could buy chocolate?'

Trish laughed. 'She loves chocolate. Why not?' She filled another pot with compost, made a well and dropped in her cutting, firming the earth around it.

'How does my daughter Diana fit into this group?'

Trish looked hard at Ellie. 'She's not like you at all, is she? I mean, she's a real businesswoman. She didn't often join us, partly because of babysitting and partly because she runs the estate agency for her husband. I don't think he goes in more than once in a fortnight, if that. He's pretty well retired, isn't he? Yes, she did join us sometimes. Barbie and Russet have known her for ages. They told me Evan had been a bad picker in his second and third marriages, but that he seemed to have done better for himself this time.' She reddened. 'Sorry, I shouldn't have said that.'

Ellie passed her another geranium. A white one this time. 'They were right. Diana did look after Evan well. I think he's going to miss her. She was with you the night you all started talking about murder, wasn't she?'

Trish looked down at her hands, feeling awkward about

speaking about Diana behind her back. 'Yes, she was. Looking back, I wonder how we could all have been so silly. It just seemed a bit of a lark at the time. Do you think the men would have taken it so hard if we hadn't put our ideas on emails? But you never think something you put on email or on text will be made public, do you? We included Diana in the group because it seemed only polite since she'd been there that time.'

'You didn't text one another for that sort of thing?'

'Oh yes, of course we did. We texted for the usual, making arrangements for the times we met for lunch, or coffee, or checking if anyone else had an invitation to a party or . . . all sorts. We'd email one another if we found a cheese the others liked, or needed a carpet cleaner, that sort of thing. Household stuff. We used emails and not social media because we needed to include Kat. That is, until Barbie got her a smartphone and showed her how to use it. Diana didn't bother with chit chat on email or on her phone. She works hard, doesn't she?'

Ellie said, 'I suppose the right question should be, "What brought those five men together?"'

'Oh, that. They've all been members of the golf club for ever, and they've got some kind of business deal going on. Not for women's ears. "Women don't understand business".' She grinned, quoting the men rather than believing in what they said. She winced and rubbed her jaw. 'Ouch. I must not do that.'

'What sort of business?'

A shrug. 'Barbie asked once. Got her head bitten off. She's pretty bright is Barbie. Clued up financially, plays the markets but keeps it quiet. She said it was something big that the men had all put money into and which they said was going to make them a fortune. She tried to explain the stock market to me once, but I'm a real dum-dum about that sort of thing. Terry says I've no head for business and he's right. I don't think Diana was there when the subject came up.'

'Do you think Diana knew about this big scheme that was going to make the men so much money?'

A shrug. 'Might have.'

'Your friend Russet said something about her husband promising her a swimming pool next year. Is that right?'

A half laugh. 'Well, yes; she likes to go to the gym for a swim most days but there's been some changes there, a new owner or something, and it's not as good as it was. So yes, she's mad keen to have a swimming pool, and he did say she should have one some time.'

'What did you do before you married Terry?'

'I was a primary school teacher.' She smiled, remembering. She'd liked that job, hadn't she?

'How did you two meet?'

'Singing carols in the Avenue, just before Christmas some years ago. I found myself sharing a carol sheet with Terry. He's a right softie about carols, as I am. A nasty old man came to stand next to me. He was being a bit annoying, putting his hand on my bum, stuff like that. Terry got rid of him. Some of us went on to a Greek restaurant for supper. Terry sat next to me and it went on from there. It was a real whirlwind romance, like in books. I couldn't believe this wonderful man wanted me, silly old me. I mean, I'd been going out, sort of, with a teacher from school for months but he was so laid back about it that . . . Well, when I met Terry, that was it. We met and wed within eight weeks. He took me for the most wonderful honeymoon anyone could ever have, in the Bahamas, but he'd booked it in term-time so I had to give up my job. I did think I'd go back to it because I loved the kids, but he was earning so much that it made my salary look silly. Also, he wanted me there at home. I'd thought, I'd hoped, we might have a child someday, but . . .'

Suddenly she looked older. 'That's not going to happen, is it? Barbie said he wanted to be the child in the marriage, and maybe she's right. Barbie's clever about people, you know. Maybe I'll go back to teaching now. If they'll have me. I'll probably have to wait till next September to get a job, won't I?'

'Can't you do supply teaching at any time?'

'Mm. Yes. Of course. Why didn't I think of that?' She rubbed her forehead. 'Sorry, I'm not making much sense. It was a shock, you see. I'm sure Terry didn't mean it. He gets upset and acts without thinking. His father used to beat him regularly. I believe it can be handed down, this idea that it's perfectly all right to discipline someone by physical means.'

'Discipline is one thing. Laying your hands on someone in a temper is quite another.'

'Yes, but . . . I know you're right, but . . . Yes, I know you're right.' She shivered, torn between wanting to forgive a man she still loved and the fear that he'd beat her again if she returned to him. 'I know in my head you're right, but in my heart . . . I feel so torn . . . I never thought I would ever contemplate divorce but now . . . Yes, I see that unless he agrees to see a shrink . . . Do you think he will?'

'I don't know. I think it would be good for you to spend some time apart. Don't get pushed into making a hasty decision.'

'No, you're right. I know you're right. It's what the others have been saying, too. I'm not sure I have the strength to resist him, though. If he comes round—'

The front door crashed open.

Ellie heard it and shot out into the hall. A well-built man with a beard was propelled into the hall, followed by two people looking over their shoulders . . . And then – of course! – Diana in a fury, shouting, '*Will* you let me pass!'

Barbie and Russet appeared on the landing above while plump little Kat and policewoman Lesley bobbed up from the kitchen, and Trish came to the door of the conservatory.

'What!' The bearded man was, of course, Ellie's husband, Thomas, who'd used his key to let himself in, only to be pushed forward by the others. Thomas was brought up short by the piles of luggage. He said, 'Ellie, what . . .?'

Diana thrust past him. 'Oh, out of the way, do! Mother, I need you to—'

Barbie and Russet descended to the hall, both talking at once. 'Diana, this is all very well, but you do realize—!'

'Diana, did you manage to—?'

Ellie held up her hands, which she noticed were grimy from potting up the geranium cuttings. 'If you'll all be quiet for a minute, perhaps—'

Diana seized Ellie's arm. 'I said, I need you to—'

'*Quiet!*' Thomas had a good yell on him, when necessary.

And there was quiet.

Resentful glances were thrown at him. Mouths were opened to expostulate. 'But . . .'

'Quiet!' Thomas said, again. He let his eyes wander around the hall, finishing up on Ellie, who was wiping her hands on her skirt in an effort to get them clean. Thomas said, 'Ellie?'

Ellie tried to keep it simple. 'These ladies are all friends of Diana's. One of their husbands died. Diana may or may not have suggested the means by which he died—'

Diana opened her mouth to object, but Ellie carried on. 'The police may or may not become involved in that, which is why Lesley is here, to make enquiries. Meanwhile, all five of the wives have been thrown out by their husbands or their families, and Diana invited them here to consult. They have nowhere else to go and I have offered to find beds for them for one night only. Their belongings will have to stay here in the hall till tomorrow when they move on. Meanwhile, Diana has—'

'Diana,' said that lady, 'has been waiting, first at the bank to get her cards reinstated, and then for my mother's solicitor to condescend to give me five minutes of his time. I need to know what rights I have if it comes to a divorce, and I want my son. I need—'

Ellie broke across this. 'You need money to retain Gunnar, and you haven't got enough, so you want me to ring him and promise to pay his bill. Is that right?'

'Well, yes. I'm sure you'll want to. I suppose you think it's a bit much, having everyone descend on you, but what else was I to do? I don't have many friends, I'm always so busy, and this lot . . . Besides, having them here might make Evan think again about what he's done.'

'It's not Evan you have to persuade. It's Monique.'

Diana blinked. 'Ah, so that's it. Right, I'll phone her and let her know we're all here and what is she going to do about it? You'll phone Gunnar again, right? After all, it's your grandson who's at risk here, isn't it?'

Ellie could have said that she wanted to retain Gunnar herself so that she could have access to her grandson and that she didn't necessarily want to retain him on Diana's behalf – or not without thinking the matter through – but she decided this was not the moment to have that conversation.

Thomas opened his mouth to speak and closed it again. He shook his head, wordless.

Ellie remembered he'd shot out that morning to deal with some crisis affecting the magazine. Hadn't the printer threatened to go bust, or something? He must have had a difficult day. Now he'd come home to find himself in a sea of distraught women, his difficult stepdaughter requiring money and support, Lesley representing the police and luggage blocking the way through to his sanctum in the library.

Thomas, being a man who liked peace and quiet, might well have roared his disapproval and demanded that Ellie considered his problems first and foremost. He might have turned the discarded wives out.

Thomas, being a man of integrity, managed to put his own problems aside to help others. As Ellie hoped he would.

He said, 'A council of war. Good idea. Yes.'

The girl with the red-gold curly hair who had come in behind Thomas now stepped forward. 'Mrs Quicke, I know I said we were going out tonight, but that's not important. Can I help at all?' Susan, the 'cook person' who was Ellie's and Thomas's lodger, currently studying at university.

Thomas perked up. 'Yes, what about supper? Can we feed the five thousand?'

Diana said, 'Thomas, you really are something else. As usual, you've got things out of proportion. Food is not the most important question at the moment. Retaining Gunnar is.'

Ellie hated it when Diana got at Thomas, especially in front of other people. He had the patience of an ox, but when she was rude to him in front of other people it was enough to make Ellie's blood boil. 'Diana, manners, please. I will have to consult with Thomas before I make any arrangements to speak to Gunnar about anything.' And to Susan, she said, 'Are you sure? Haven't you got theatre tickets for something?'

Susan dimpled. 'No, we were going out on a pub crawl.'

Ellie grinned. Susan did not, repeat not, do pub crawls. Susan liked an evening out at a pub, chatting to friends, but she was a thrifty, sensible girl who was saving hard for her wedding in a few months' time. She was a thoroughly nice girl, and Ellie was very fond of her, especially when she exercised her skills in the production of food for Thomas and Ellie. She said, 'Well, if you really don't mind?'

'Of course we'll help.' That was Rafael, her half-Italian fiancé, who'd been keeping in the background. Rafael had a lively sense of humour and Ellie suspected that he was probably enjoying every minute of this unusual situation. 'May I help you ladies up to the bedrooms with your gear? You don't want to get it mixed up with anyone else's, do you?'

Barbie got in her bid a fraction before Russet. 'Oh, if you could. Those three suitcases and—'

Russet homed in on Thomas. 'If you could help me? I'd be so grateful. This tote bag and that. I can manage a couple of these bags if—'

'No, that one's mine!' Barbie straddled the disputed piece of luggage.

Thomas was not his usual ebullient self. He was having to make an enormous effort to smile and appear agreeable. Ellie wanted to ask him what was wrong but decided she must wait till they were on their own.

Rafael, who was a young man with an unusually keen understanding of people, managed to get himself between Barbie and Russet, who were going nose to nose over one of the bundles. 'Judgement of Solomon coming up. What's in this bag, ladies? Tell me, and I'll check.'

'Clothes. I think.'

'Paperwork. Photograph albums.'

Rafael looked. 'Clothes it is. Now, ladies, which room is occupied by who?' He started up the stairs in Barbie's footsteps, while Russet angrily delved into some of the other black plastic bags on the floor, opening them, inspecting the contents and flinging them down again. Thomas hovered, dividing his attention between her and Ellie.

Ellie thought Thomas was being unnaturally quiet. Alarming!

Diana clicked off her phone. 'Well, I've told Monique, and she'll tell the others, I'm sure.'

Ellie was watching Thomas, who was trying to pretend nothing mattered bar finding the right luggage for Russet. 'Very well, Diana. Your friends are welcome. I think you'd better speak to the police before you decide what to do next.'

Lesley, who'd been keeping mum, said, 'Yes, that would be a good idea.'

Diana wasn't playing. 'Police? What for? I can't be bothered with all that now.'

Ellie considered a scenario in which Lesley might arrest Diana for murder. No, of course she didn't mean that, exactly. But Ellie knew that when Diana wanted something she went at it with the persistence of an electric drill until she'd achieved her end, and at this particular moment Ellie would welcome a respite. She met Thomas's eyes across the hall. With the empathy born of a happy marriage, she became aware that he was desperately worried about something and that it was nothing to do with the marital discord that had turned their house into a hotel.

She remembered he'd left her a note about the printer of his magazine going bust. He'd gone out to see them and returned with no good news clearly written on his face. Ellie tried to remember exactly when the next issue was due to go to press. Soon, she thought. Which meant . . .? She couldn't work out what it meant for the moment.

Meanwhile, Lesley was at her elbow, in full police mode. 'Ellie, do I have your permission to use the dining room for some interviews? I'll speak to Diana first.'

'This is ridiculous!' Diana was outraged. 'What do you want me for?'

Lesley was placatory. 'Just a quick word, right?'

'Of course you can use the dining room,' said Ellie, trying to think if it had been dusted that week and deciding that it didn't matter. 'Go ahead.'

Susan appeared from the kitchen, slipping into an apron. 'How many for supper?'

Ellie said, 'Can't think. Four wives, one widow, Thomas and me, plus you two. Lesley, do you want to eat with us?'

A shake of the head from Lesley, who was wearing plain clothes but had the trick of authority. 'I hope to be out of your hair before long.' She waved Diana into the dining room. 'I promise this won't take long.'

In other words, Lesley didn't really think there was any call to yell for a formal police investigation but wanted to dot the i's and cross the t's. So Kat must have convinced Lesley that the whole joke thing had not been done with criminal intent. It was something of a relief to know that.

'I can spare ten minutes!' Diana stalked into the dining room, calling back to Ellie, 'Don't forget to ring Gunnar!'

Susan disappeared. In her place stood Kat, wringing her hands. 'How can I help?'

A shriek of rage from Russet. 'Look! My precious scent!' An exotic scent perfumed the hall. 'The bottle's been broken! How could they! I'll sue the lot of them!'

'Yes,' said Thomas, being patient. 'Perhaps we can rescue some of it, upstairs? Will you lead the way?'

Grumbling, Russet grabbed a tote bag and started up the stairs. Thomas, heavy-laden, followed behind her.

Ellie dithered. What to do first? Ring Gunnar? No. She must talk to Thomas first.

Kat swam into Ellie's field of vision again, pleading for something to do. 'Perhaps I can lay the table? That would be helpful, yes?'

Ellie shook her head. 'Lesley is talking to Diana in the dining room. I think we'd better eat in the kitchen but Susan is better left alone when she's cooking. Look, have you a mobile phone with a camera? I think someone should take a photo of Trish's jaw before the bruising fades.'

'I have smartphone, yes, but I do not know how to take pictures yet.'

'Get Trish to show you how to take the photo. Now that would be really helpful.'

Kat brightened up at the prospect of action. 'Where is Trish?'

Yes, where indeed? Last seen, she'd been in the door leading to the conservatory, but she hadn't come into the hall like the others. Ah, there she was, crouched in a chair in the sitting room, sobbing. One poor, overtired, overwrought girl who'd had a really bad day.

Ellie said, 'Kat, Trish is worn out. Can you look after her?'

'The poor, poor thing,' said Kat. 'She loves that frog of a husband.' Seeing Ellie's reaction, she asked, 'Is "frog" right? Is it tadpole?'

Ellie said, 'It's probably "toad", and I agree. You will take care of her, right? Take her up to her room, the one we've just got ready, and see her settled there.'

As Kat chugged off to look after Trish the men came back

down the stairs, with Russet chivvying Rafael along. 'That one over there, and the blue case . . .'

Ellie would have interfered, but Rafael still seemed amused rather than annoyed, so she kept her mouth shut. Barbie came out on to the landing above, calling out, 'Oh, Rafael, can you bring up the black carry-on case for me?'

Ellie left Rafael to decide which woman to obey and towed Thomas down the corridor to his study. She pushed him into his big chair. 'Tell!'

He washed his face with his hands, looking every day of sixty-plus. Usually he wore his years lightly, but not today. 'I feel such a fool.'

Ellie couldn't be doing with this. 'Skip that. What's happened?'

'The printers. We've used them for years. The old man retired, but the new manager seemed to know what he was doing. A few things hadn't been . . . Well, they were late a couple of times which was infuriating, but there was nothing to indicate . . . Then last month, you know we've always paid our bills on time, we've never . . . But this time he asked for payment in advance because they'd had a problem with the press. He was very apologetic but said they'd guarantee . . . Stupid! How could I have been so stupid?'

'You paid the bill early, and now he isn't going to produce the goods?'

Thomas nodded. 'It's the end for the magazine. Even if I could find another printer in time, we don't have enough working capital to pay for another printing.'

He knew that Ellie had considerable funds in her charitable trust, but he'd never asked her for money before, and she understood that he did not wish to do so now. Thomas had been squeamish about marrying a woman who'd inherited money. He'd been meticulous about paying his way in the household expenses.

Ought I to offer him a loan? No. He wouldn't accept it. Or would he?

He said, 'I got there to find the shutters down. No one there. Deserted. I tracked him down to his home. The old man, that is. Not the manager. The old man was distraught. He's retired, walking with a stick, got Parkinson's. He only learned what had happened this morning. Like me. His manager has cleaned out their accounts and taken off for pastures new. I was afraid he, the old man, would have a heart attack there and then.'

Ellie took his hands in hers and pressed them. 'What do you propose to do?'

'On the way back, I was thinking how to get the magazine out. The subscribers have all paid, I can raise the money at the bank, find a new printer. I'll probably have to pay in advance, but that's all right. I'll have to see about it tomorrow.' He returned the pressure on her hands. 'I'm not asking you for money, Ellie. You understand that? I'll be all right. Just for a while, I felt I'd been knocked senseless. It's my own fault that I've got into this mess. I ought never to have trusted the man. My mistake, and I'll get myself out of it. I won't take any remuneration from the magazine for a while, but if you can manage without my contribution to the household finances for a few months, I'll repay as soon as I get everything working again.'

Ellie understood that he really did want it that way. She loved him all the more for it while feeling irritated that his pride refused to let her help him out. Love and irritation, that's what life was about in a family, wasn't it?

He said, 'It's not as bad as it might be. I wasn't due to email the text of the next issue to him till later in the week so tomorrow I can find another printer. I'll have to ask around, see if I can get some recommendations.'

She nodded. He was picking himself up, dusting himself down and starting all over again.

He said, 'I'm sorry I . . . Just now. It all looked so black. I couldn't see my way.'

'You came back to find chaos and a wife who was so distracted by what was going on that she couldn't find time to look after you.'

He did his best to smile and it wasn't a bad effort. 'Yes. What a shambles! I'd forgotten to pray about it. Can you imagine? Completely, utterly forgot my biggest resource. I was so locked into self-pity . . . It was only when I carried those bags up for that woman . . . Who is she, by the way? No, don't bother to tell me now. On the stairs I realized what a fool I'd been. I only had time for an arrow prayer or two. I must spend some time in the Quiet Room this evening. That is, if you can spare me.'

'I think I'll join you. Thomas, I need your advice. Diana and her friends have all been thrown out by their husbands or families on the shaky pretext that they were plotting to murder them. They need a solicitor. Some of them have money. Some haven't. As you know, Diana wants me to pay Gunnar to help her. She thinks I can access the trust fund to help her but I can't do that. It's not my private purse. I cannot take money from it whenever I fancy. I pay so much from my pension towards the bills, and what with the rent Susan pays me, and what you put in the bank every month, it's enough to keep the house going and for us to be comfortable. I really don't think I can subsidize Diana.'

'Has she no means of paying Gunnar herself?'

'I don't think she has enough. She seems to be able to make money but not to keep it. I cannot let her draw on the trust. That money is not intended to finance my daughter's divorce or a custody case. I'm quite clear in my mind about that. I do have some money put away for a rainy day, and I'm asking you if you agree with me that this is it. I was going to suggest we have another holiday abroad this year, and update various things in the house but, if you agree, I will use that money to see what can be done in relation to—'

'The little boy. Of course. He must be so confused, so distressed. What a dreadful business.'

'What I think we might do is retain Gunnar to help us, you and me, to understand what rights we may have regarding access to our grandson. That shouldn't cost too much, should it? Diana will be furious, but if you back me up, I can cope with that. I cannot and will not draw on the trust funds for Diana. I will have to pay what I can afford out of my own money.'

'And here's me making matters worse for you. I can't believe how stupid I've been.'

She kissed his bearded cheek. 'Things happen. We'll survive. Let's go and see what's for supper.'

They didn't get any further than the door when there was a tearing scream from above.

There were still some heaps of luggage in the hall, although they had diminished in size and were more scattered around than they had been.

Susan's fiancé, Rafael, was halfway up the stairs, carrying some bags under his arms. He was looking up at the landing.

Russet stood there, swaying.

Phone in hand.

It was she who had screamed. Her mouth was open and working, her eyes rounded with horror.

Her eyes turned up in her head.

She was at the top of the stairs. She was going to fall!

SEVEN

Monday evening.

Rafael dropped whatever it was that he was carrying, sprinted up the stairs and caught Russet as she collapsed. He was stronger than he looked and managed to lift her away from the top of the stairs.

Barbie appeared from her bedroom along the corridor. 'What the . . .!'

Kat and young Trish appeared on the landing from the other side of the house. 'What's the matter?'

Ellie started up the stairs. 'Russet appears to have had some bad news. Rafael, can you carry her back into her room?'

Rafael half supported and half carried Russet along the corridor. Ellie followed. Russet had ended up in the small bedroom used for Ellie's grandson, and it was crowded with his and her belongings. Rafael negotiated his way through the luggage to lay his burden down on the bed against the wall.

Russet's mouth worked but no sound emerged. Her colour was patchy. Shock.

Barbie hovered in the doorway. 'What's happened?'

Russet's phone was still in her hand. It quacked. Someone said, 'Hello? Are you still there?'

Ellie reached for the phone, but Barbie was quicker. She picked it up and spoke to the caller. 'Who is this speaking?'

Russet began to shiver. Her jaw juddered.

Rafael, ever cool, took Russet's pulse. 'She's in shock. We should get her into bed?'

Ellie nodded. She pulled off the woman's shoes and skirt and, with Rafael's help, got her under the duvet.

Rafael said, 'Brandy?'

Ellie shook her head. 'Tea. Sugared.'

Rafael disappeared. Trish and Kat crowded in. 'What's wrong? Can we help?'

Barbie clicked off the phone. In a dead tone, she said, 'That was a neighbour of Russet's. I've met her. She's a horrible woman, an avid gossip. She'd watched Russet being thrown out of her house this morning. She doesn't like Russet, because Russet is beautiful and kind, and she's neither. She intended to ring Russet to "commiserate". As if you can believe that! She was glorying in what had happened! Fortunately or otherwise, she had an appointment at the hairdressers this morning so she put off ringing till she got back, which is when she saw an ambulance arrive at Russet's house and, after that, a police car. That did it. She couldn't bear not to know what was going on, so she went round to ask a policewoman who was standing by the front door what had happened. She was told there'd been an accident and to go away but she managed to look over the woman's shoulder and saw Walt lying on the floor in the hall with paramedics standing around, doing nothing. It was obvious he was dead. So naturally she had to ring Russet to see if she'd heard the bad news.'

Trish had her hands to her mouth. 'How awful! Was it a heart attack? I know he takes pills for high blood pressure.'

'I suppose so,' said Barbie, in that same detached voice.

There was a sudden chill in the room. Ellie glanced at the window, but it was shut. Barbie clicked the overhead light on. The 'click' sounded extra loud. Barbie drew the curtains across the window. Barbie's face was pale, but she was still functioning.

Trish turned away and leaned against the door. Tears came. 'Whatever next?'

Ellie looked around. Four discarded wives were there, but where was the fifth? Diana must still be in with Lesley. They'd missed all the fun, hadn't they?

Ellie looked at Kat and jerked her head towards Trish. Kat

understood. She put her arm around Trish. 'You come along with me, Trish. It is one horrible day, no? You have a nice lie down in your bedroom now.' She nodded to Ellie and Ellie nodded back. Kat would look after Trish.

Russet stopped shuddering. Her eyes were closed, but she gasped for breath. Hyperventilating? Ellie pulled her to a sitting position. 'Take a deep breath. And another. That's it. You'll soon feel better.'

Gradually Russet began to breathe more easily.

Rafael arrived with a mug of sweetened tea and a pack of aspirins.

Barbie said, 'Aspirin won't touch it. I've got some sleeping tablets somewhere. Shall I see if I can find them?'

Ellie stopped her. 'Not on an empty stomach. Has she eaten anything today apart from a couple of biscuits? Probably not. She ought to eat something first, don't you think?'

Barbie nodded. She sat on the bed and lifted the mug to Russet's mouth. 'Take a sip, now. That's it!'

Russet shot upright, pushing the mug of tea away. 'Walt . . .? It can't be true. That awful woman would say anything to . . . He can't be dead, surely! It's his heart! I've told him and told him he ought to lose weight. I should go to him. If they get him to hospital in time, they may be able to revive him.' She threw back the duvet and made as if to get up, but Ellie and Barbie coaxed her to lie down again.

Ellie said, 'I'll check for you, shall I?'

Russet wasn't listening. 'I was so angry with him this morning! I could willingly have throttled him! How could he! And now . . . Oh, surely it's not true! Tell me it's not true!'

Barbie soothed her. 'Mrs Quicke will find out.'

Russet's scarlet fingernails clutched the duvet in desperation. 'I ought to be there. With him. Which hospital do you think they'll have taken him to? I've just remembered, I'm short of cash. Can you lend me some, Barbie? I was going to draw some out, but . . . I can't think why I didn't. Oh, I know. I'd seen some of the claret that Walt likes best. It was on sale in the wine shop window. I thought I'd get a case for him as a surprise, and I forgot about drawing out some more cash. I was thinking about how pleased he was going to be when I turned into the drive and then everything went wrong. Oh, how could he!'

Barbie rocked Russet to and fro, saying, 'There, there.'

'I'm so angry with him! Tell me he's not dead!'

Barbie looked up at Ellie. 'She comforted me when Bunny died. I couldn't believe it at first, either. It takes time.'

Neither of these women had expected their husbands to die on them. They may not have loved them deeply but they were fond enough of them to carry on with their marriages, even though they had no illusions about their men.

Ellie said, 'I won't be a minute.' She hoped Lesley would still be in the dining room talking to Diana, and indeed she was, poring over some papers on the table before her. Or rather, Lesley was there, but Diana wasn't.

Ellie shut the door to the hall behind her. 'Lesley. A problem. One of the wives has just had a phone call from a neighbour, who claims that Russet's husband has been found lying in his hall this afternoon, and that he's dead. An ambulance was called, and then a police car. Can you check?'

'What?' Lesley looked from Ellie to the printout of the emails she was holding. 'You're having me on.'

'I wish I were. His name is Walt. Short for Walter. I'm not sure what his surname is but it may be somewhere on the emails.'

Lesley looked. 'Wade. The surname for Russet appears to be Wade. As in Wade's Pharmaceuticals, I suppose?'

'Russet is in shock. She's in denial, hoping he's not dead, that it's just a heart attack and he's been taken to hospital. She wants to go to him, but she's not fit. I'm wondering whether to call a doctor for her.'

'Doctors don't pay house calls any more, do they?' Lesley stabbed at one of the emails. 'Someone – not her – in the emails suggested Walt might take a dive down the stairs.'

Ellie winced. 'No, it wasn't her, and I don't know how he died. She's half out of her mind, not knowing what's happened.'

Lesley picked up her phone.

Ellie hovered. She didn't believe in this many coincidences. One coincidence – that of Bunny's getting his pills mixed up as foreshadowed in the emails – was suspicious but could just about be ruled acceptable. If Walt really had tumbled to his death down the stairs . . . No, that would be one coincidence too many. If true.

Let's hope it was a heart attack.

Lesley spoke into her phone, listened. And spoke again. She put the phone down. 'Police were called to an address in Uppercross Road this afternoon. A gardener had arrived by appointment to cut the hedges. He needed access to a power point so tried to rouse someone in the house. He knocked in vain, used his phone. Heard it ringing inside, looked through the glass in the front door and saw a man lying in the hall at the foot of the stairs. He called the ambulance and the police. So it's true.'

'It doesn't mean Walt fell down the stairs.'

'No, it doesn't. There will have to be an autopsy.' Lesley grimaced. 'If we go by these emails and they discover he was pushed . . . Could his wife have done it?'

'No. She returned home from the shops about eleven, not expecting trouble. Walt then told her to get out. She says there were contract cleaners in her house already, clearing out her things. They can bear witness to the fact that Walt was still alive when she left. The neighbour also saw her leaving. As she was on the point of departure, Diana phoned Russet and suggested they meet up here. She was the first of the wives to arrive. Thomas was here and let her in. We can ask him what time that was, but I think it gives her an alibi, because she's been here ever since. Walt did have high blood pressure. It could be that.'

Lesley was doubtful but trying to make sense of events. 'She could have arranged to be out of the way so that someone else could kill him for her?'

Ellie shook her head. 'No. She's in shock. She had no idea.'

Lesley drew the papers towards her and picked up her pen. 'Which cleaning firm was it, do you know? They could confirm if she left when she said. I must speak to Thomas to verify what time she arrived.' She dropped her pen. 'No, I can't, can I?'

'Why not? He's got his own troubles at the moment, but he's here. I'll call him for you, shall I?'

'No, I mean that I can't get involved.'

'Why not? You talked to Kat, and you talked to Diana. Where is she, by the way?'

Lesley shrugged. 'She said she had to make a phone call. Look, Ellie. I talked to Kat and to Diana informally, off the record. Bunny's death had been written off as misadventure, so I could chat to them about it without cautioning them.'

'So? Now you have read the emails?'

'They left me wondering about coincidences but not at all sure it changed anything with regard to Bunny's death. I was acting out of curiosity as a private person and a friend of yours when I talked to Kat and Diana, not as a police officer.'

'That's splitting hairs.'

Lesley thrust her fingers back through her hair. 'Yes, you're right. I've made a mistake. Two accidental deaths is one thing, but not when you add the emails to the mix. I have to take the emails back to the station and see what the super says. If he says it's all just a series of coincidences, then that's all right. If he decides they're evidence of motive for murder then I can't – as your friend and having some prior knowledge of Diana – compromise any investigation by speaking to anyone else. It's not my case and the odds are against it being given to me. Look, I'll get back to you as soon as I can. Until then, you'll keep the women here, won't you?' She gathered up her papers and left, banging the front door behind her.

Ellie told herself that she mustn't feel let down. Lesley was a good police officer. She could not jeopardize her career by ignoring the emails. It was not up to her to decide which cases needed investigation and which did not. This latest death might well be an accident. Well, it might.

Though Ellie did not believe that it was.

What a mess!

Ellie climbed the stairs again, only to meet Barbie coming out on to the landing, carefully shutting the door of the room in which Russet lay.

Ellie said, 'I'm afraid it's true. He is dead.'

Barbie nodded. In a low voice, she said, 'Yes, she remembered the gardener was due today. She had his number on her phone and I've just got through to him for her. He says he's on his way home now after having made a statement to the police. He says the police are still there, but Walt's body has been removed. He wants to know . . .' Barbie gulped but managed to control herself. 'He wants to know if Russet wants him to come back and do the hedge tomorrow.'

Barbie swayed. Ellie caught Barbie's hands and held her steady.

Barbie closed her eyes for a count of five. She took a deep breath and opened them again. Barbie was not going to let this get her down. She said, 'Do you think the police will want her to return home? She's still got her keys, and the car.'

'I don't know,' said Ellie. 'I'm in touch with the police. I'll ask them, if you like.'

'I'm not sure she's fit to deal with it yet.' Barbie removed her hands from Ellie and flicked back her hair. Barbie was not accustomed to asking for help from anyone else, was she?

Ellie said, 'No, I could see it was a shock.'

'I know I wasn't capable even of making a cup of tea when Bunny died. Poleaxed, I was. Sat in a chair and stared at the television set and it wasn't even on. Russet came round and got me to go for a walk with her, twice a day, and forced me to eat something. She helped me with the funeral arrangements and phoning around to everyone. She was great.'

Barbie looked back at the closed door. 'As we speak, she's ringing her brother. He lives in Ipswich. It will take him for ever to get over here tomorrow even if he can get away, and then I'm not sure what good he'll be. He's not exactly the world's most . . . She's his elder sister. She pretty well brought him up. He relies on her for everything. Now it's the other way around and I'm wondering whether he can cope. He's married with three young children, but his eldest daughter has more sense in her little finger than he has in his whole body. His wife's not much better. Feckless, both of them. Knowing that pair, I don't suppose they'll even offer to have her stay with them for a while.'

'It's good to have family around you in times of trouble. Just having him here will help her.'

That wasn't entirely true, but it was the thing one was expected to say.

Barbie tried to smile. 'Not my family, I can tell you. Not hers, either.' She took another deep breath. 'Mrs Quicke, you've been very kind. Beyond the call of duty. How dreadful of us to impose on you. If I'd had a chance to think . . . But being thrown out like that . . . I wasn't myself. I'll get out of your hair as soon as I can. I'm sure I can find somewhere to go tomorrow.'

Lesley wants the women to stay here. Do I tell Barbie that?

No, she doesn't need to know they're all under suspicion, especially if the police decide there's no cause for alarm.

Ellie said, 'You're very welcome.'

Barbie was thinking hard. 'Russet might not want to stop on in that big house by herself. If she wants me to, maybe I can call in some favours, find someone who'll lend or rent me a flat somewhere nearby so that I can stick around to help her through the next couple of weeks. Just till she can sort herself out.'

'It's early days.' *Do I mention that Rafael might be able to help? Not yet.*

'I'll find some work, somewhere. I still have contacts in the arts world. Only a few weeks ago someone asked if I'd help out, part-time, with an exhibition he's staging in Bond Street. I'm sure I can pick up something.'

Ellie admired Barbie's resilience. 'You're a survivor.'

'I hope so. I cling to that thought. Mrs Quicke, I hate to add to your problems, but I think Russet ought to stay in bed for a while. May I scrounge some food for her and me, and bring it back upstairs to eat with her? You're right. We haven't eaten today and could do with something, anything, to keep us going.'

'I'll see what I can do.'

I must find Diana and shake some sense into her!

Barbie turned away, and then turned back, frowning. 'Trish; I'm worried about her, too. She's not going back to that ghastly husband of hers, is she? We've been trying to talk some sense into her, but she's far too soft. Perfect victim material.'

'Kat is looking after her.'

Barbie nodded. 'That's a relief. Kat needs someone to look after, and she's got a lot of common sense. She won't let Trish sacrifice herself.' She went back into Russet's room. Ellie checked that the big guest room to which Diana had taken her things was empty – it was – and went downstairs to look for her daughter, trying not to worry. For one thing, she didn't know where she'd put Kat to sleep tonight.

Diana came out of the downstairs cloakroom and crossed into the sitting room. Ellie called out, but her daughter seemed deaf and blind. Ellie followed Diana into the sitting room to find her standing at the window, gazing out into the dusk. It was raining. Inside and out.

'Diana?'

No response. Diana had discarded her black jacket, and the collar of her white blouse was undone. Unusual, that. Diana was as pale as her shirt. Her face looked puffy. She was not her normal immaculate self.

Ellie remembered seeing Diana look like that before. She reached for the nearest chair and subsided into it. 'You're pregnant.'

Diana responded with the tiniest of nods.

'How many weeks?'

A shrug. 'Nine. My dear husband was very active just before his birthday.'

'You haven't said anything because . . .?'

'I had a miss at the end of last year, and another six months ago. I might have had another. I was going to wait for the three-month scan.'

Ellie didn't know whether to be pleased or sad. Diana hadn't been a good mother to her first child, who lived with her long-divorced first husband, but she'd been a devoted mother to the little boy who was the result of her union with Evan, the Great White Shark.

Ellie wanted to know, 'Was it a mistake?'

A shrug. 'Perhaps. Sometimes I thought one was enough because I wanted to get stuck in at work, but occasionally I thought it might be nice to have a little girl, though I suppose Evan would want another boy. I didn't really think much about it, since I've had at least two misses. I wasn't nauseous before, but this time . . . I thought I had plenty of time to decide whether I wanted an abortion or not. Today has decided me.'

Ellie's stomach plunged. 'You don't want the baby now?'

'Of course I do. Don't be ridiculous, Mother. Of course I want it. Her. I'm pretty sure it's a girl. You'll say I can't possibly tell yet, but I know, and Evan will have to lump it.'

'You have to tell him.'

'Do you really think it will make a difference? How little you know him. He's got another piece of arm candy in his sights. All of thirty-five, bleached blonde, a figure which has been expensively enhanced and pound signs in her baby-blue eyes.'

'If you knew about her . . .?'

'I knew and I didn't know, if you see what I mean. It's this new nanny he engaged when I was busy with the sale of the penthouse in the town centre. It did cross my mind once or twice that he fancied her, but she's got a boyfriend already and I thought he wouldn't dare divorce me because it would be too expensive. Only, he's found a way around that too, hasn't he, by accusing me of murder?' She did up her blouse. 'So. I've got to fight him for custody of my son. You've spoken to Gunnar about representing me, haven't you?'

'Not yet. I'm not sure I can afford him. There's a problem with finance. You know I can't access trust money for my own personal use.'

'So, mortgage this house, why don't you? It's absurd you living in such a big place, anyway. You must downsize. Move into a small flat somewhere.'

Ellie was shocked. 'Certainly not. Let me remind you that I couldn't put you and your friends up, even in makeshift fashion, if I didn't live in a big house.'

'Don't make difficulties, Mother. This is important.'

'Indeed it is. I shall do nothing without thinking things through. What about you? Have you enough money to retain a solicitor?'

'I put everything I've got into a big new scheme for the town centre. I mean, everything.'

'Was that a good idea?'

'Yes. I don't expect you to understand. It's the golden pot at the end of the rainbow.'

Oh dear. It's fairy gold time again. Diana has always cut corners and placed her faith in projects which fail to deliver.

Diana was restless. She stood at the window, tapping on the glass. An irritating habit. *Tap, tap, tap. Tap, tap, tap*. She said, 'I rang home just now. They refused to let me speak to my son. I could hear him crying in the background. They said – she, Monique, said – that he's got his nanny and doesn't need me any more.' She swung away from the window. 'I'll get him back. Of course I will. If necessary, I'll collect him from the nursery and bring him here.'

Ellie opened her mouth to say that Russet was occupying the room in which the boy usually slept but decided against doing so. She didn't think Diana would find it that easy to kidnap her son, and if she did, wouldn't the police become involved? Ellie shuddered at the thought of the boy in the centre of a tug-of-war. Diana might relish it, but the toddler wouldn't.

One thing: Evan didn't know that he was about to become a father all over again. Would that make a difference to his attitude? Surely it must do so. If Diana didn't tell him, then Ellie would. Evan had the right to know.

Ellie said, 'What I don't understand is why you invited your friends to meet you here? You don't seem to have much in common with them.'

A shrug. 'I thought that if we got together to form a united front, we could fight for a better deal from the men. A couple of the other women have money and we could put together a fund to secure a solicitor who could act for all of us. Then I realized you could do that for me, so I abandoned that idea. I can manage without their help, if you'll only get Gunnar on to the job.'

'Diana, that's a bit steep. You got them here, and now you turn around and say you're not interested in them? They're in shock. They need looking after.'

Diana was so focused on her own needs that she didn't seem to hear what her mother was saying. Instead, she went on, 'Until I can get a proper settlement from Evan, I'll make do with the top-floor flat here. It's not terribly convenient, but at least I can shut the door on the rest of the world and recreate some kind of home for my child. I've told your cook person that she'll have to move out straight away so that you can redecorate before I—'

'What!' said Ellie. 'You've done what?'

EIGHT

Monday supper.

'You can't turn Susan out,' said Ellie, trying to keep calm. 'This is my house, and you cannot go around telling my tenant what to do. Susan is part of the family and, what's more, she has a valid tenancy agreement. Surely you understand what that means? She has a legal right to be here.'

A shrug. 'Give her notice to quit. Tell her she has a week to find another place. That's fair enough, isn't it?' Diana looked around her. 'Anyway, it's about time you downsized and let me take this house over. Until then, I'll make do with the top flat.'

Ellie closed her eyes and took a deep breath to control her impulse to murder. She understood now what a blind rage meant. 'No! That. Will. Not. Do.' She opened her eyes again to see if Diana understood.

Diana was looking at her with an expression of faint surprise. 'Why ever not?'

'Because . . .' Ellie brought her voice down from the stratosphere. 'Because I say so. Because this is my house and I decide what goes on in it. Because you expect too much.'

'I can't believe what I'm hearing. You are my mother, and naturally you will support me in this terrible situation.'

'Support? Yes. Within reasonable limits. I have told you again and again that I cannot access trust money for private use. I have helped you out many times in the past from my own money; I gave you the house we used to live in. What you now want is a step too far. I need the income from the top flat to run this house. Thomas helps . . .'

Except that he can't help for the immediate future. Diana doesn't need to know that.

'Oh, Thomas!' A twist of the lips. 'I suppose it's him who's turned you against me.'

Ellie told herself to count to ten and made it to five. 'No, Thomas is all for family solidarity. He has not said a word about you coming to stay and has been sympathetic to your problems. Neither has he objected to your inviting your friends to come here without asking permission. Are you going to defray the cost of their stay here?'

'You cannot be serious! These are my friends, who are in great distress. No one but you would object to helping them—'

'I'm not objecting,' said Ellie, wearily aware that she was going to lose this argument, as she always lost arguments with Diana. Diana didn't play fair. She never had.

'It sounds like it to me,' said Diana. 'I suppose I ought not to be surprised at your mean-minded attitude. Your thought processes are stuck in the last century. I begin to wonder if you should be tested for Alzheimer's.'

Ellie couldn't find words to reply. Did her daughter really think that? And if so . . .

Diana nodded to herself. 'Yes, that's it. Obviously. It's time someone else took charge of your affairs. Have you signed a Lasting Power of Attorney yet, so that I can do the necessary for you? Well, have you? Because if not, we'd better see to it tomorrow.'

Ellie almost laughed. She shook her head. 'Diana, forget it. Thomas and I have both made proper provision for our eventual descent into old age. Also, I changed my will some time ago, remember? Thomas is looked after, and the trust gets the rest. You've had enough already. You get nothing more.'

Diana didn't even blink. 'Don't be so ridiculous. Of course you'll leave everything to me. Mother, it really is about time you faced up to it; you're fast losing the plot. This nonsense has got to stop! I'll take you to see a doctor tomorrow. Let me know when supper's ready.' So saying, she stalked out of the room.

Ellie felt like sinking into a chair and having hysterics. Or indulging in a major bout of tears. Or throwing something.

Instead, she found a hankie, blew her nose and marched out to the kitchen in fire-fighting mood.

Yes, Diana had definitely been here and wreaked her usual havoc. Susan, flushed of face with her red-gold hair in wild curls around her head, was kneading dough as if she'd like to strangle it.

Rafael, on the other hand, was calmly at work on his laptop. Rafael was a wealthy young businessman who had recently bought up a block of substandard flats, which he was turning into desirable properties. Half-Italian by birth, he was intelligent, six foot something, long and lean with a quirky sense of humour. And, Ellie noted, he was now wearing a pair of rimless glasses. That was new.

Midge the cat was perched on the table, superintending whatever Rafael was doing on his laptop. Midge liked Rafael, and vice versa.

Susan was so hot with rage that Ellie imagined she could see steam coming off her. She didn't look at Ellie, but said, 'All right, all right! I know! I'll be out tomorrow!'

Rafael was keeping his cool. 'Much as I'd like that, Susan; no, you won't.'

Susan swiped her forearm across her forehead. Still not looking at Ellie, she said, 'Diana explained everything. I quite understand the position you're in, Mrs Quicke. Rafael has a spare room in his flat that I can move into.'

Ellie said, 'No, you won't.'

Rafael said, 'It's the marshmallow test, isn't it?'

Susan glared at him. 'What?'

Rafael was unmoved. 'It's a test given to children to see if you can predict which will be successful when they grow up. You give each child a marshmallow and tell them that if they wish to do so they can eat it straight away, but if they are prepared to wait ten minutes, they will be given a second sweet. Some can't wait. Others can and, if they do, they get their reward. The ones who wait are the ones who have sufficient self-control to defer immediate gratification, and that earns them a bonus. If you moved into my flat, Susan, I'd not be able to control myself. You wanted to wait till we're married, and I agreed to your terms. So, we'll wait.'

'Grrr!' said Susan. 'I'm not listening!'

Rafael said to Ellie, 'Mrs Quicke, I've tried the magic word on her and she nearly swiped me into the middle of next week.' He looked at Susan over his glasses and shook his head. 'Temper!'

That was a bit provocative, wasn't it? But perhaps Rafael was right, and they all needed to let off steam somehow or other. But how? Ah, an idea . . .

Ellie marched over to a cupboard containing odd pieces of china which were rarely if ever used. She pulled out some thick old plates and slammed them down on to the table. 'There you are, Susan! Smash them for me.'

'What?'

'Throw them down on the floor! Stamp on them. Make a noise! Scream!'

'What?' Susan picked up a plate. 'Do you mean it? You want me to smash this plate?' She lifted it up high, and hesitated.

'Oh, dearie me,' said Rafael. 'Are we so conditioned not to make a fuss that we can't break a plate or two?'

Susan grimaced. She lowered the plate to waist level and dropped it on to the floor. It rolled under the table, unbroken.

Midge decided this was no place for a cat and disappeared.

Ellie said, 'That wasn't much of a smash. Try again!'

Susan tried again. This time the plate broke. Susan looked appalled at what she'd done, but Rafael clapped. Then he looked at Ellie out of the corner of his eyes. 'Go on,' he said. 'You know you want to.'

Ellie grabbed a plate, held it high over her head, yelled, 'Yaroo!' and threw it down on to the floor where it smashed into several pieces. It felt wonderful!

'Yaroo!' yelled Susan, getting into the swing of things. Her next plate crashed against the skirting board and broke.

'May I?' asked Rafael, taking off his glasses to join in the fun. His plate disintegrated in a most satisfactory fashion.

'One more,' said Ellie, handing one to Susan and having another go herself. 'Yarooo!'

'Yaroo!' echoed Susan. Smash, bang wallop! Crash!

A sharp voice broke in. 'What . . . is the meaning of this?' Diana, in full black and white fury. 'What childish—!'

'Oh, shut up, Diana!' Ellie was surprised to hear a note of authority in her voice. 'This is not your house, not your crockery and none of your business.'

'Well!' For once Diana couldn't produce the right words but turned on her heel and left.

Susan tried a laugh on for size. It was a reasonable effort. 'Sorry, everyone. I seem to have lost my sense of humour for a while. I'll clear the mess up.'

Rafael reached for the long-handled broom. 'That was most enjoyable. I've always wanted to know what it felt like to smash things. Susan, you get rid of that dough you've been pummelling to death and wash your hands. I'll clear the bits and pieces up.'

'And I,' said Ellie, 'will put your mind at rest. Susan, you have a tenancy agreement for the flat.'

Rafael said, 'That's what I told her. She wouldn't listen.'

Ellie went on, 'Forget what Diana said. I'm holding you to our agreement. I am not letting you get out of it. You have to stay here for another three months, until you leave this house to get married. Understood?'

Rafael tumbled pieces of china into the rubbish bin. He put his arms round Susan as she washed her hands at the tap, kissed her first on her neck, and then, turning her round, on her lips. 'Of course I want you to live with me now, but I know you have this dream of doing everything in the correct order. You want to take your time, deciding colour schemes, buying furniture for our new home, unpacking wedding gifts, having fittings for the wedding dress, making your own cake, planning the buffet, choosing the hymns for the church. Strangely enough, I want that dream, too. It appeals to my old-fashioned, orderly mind. And I do believe wholeheartedly that pleasure deferred is pleasure doubled. I know you want to come to the marriage bed in a long white dress with nothing on underneath . . . A fantasy which keeps me awake every night, I may say. But I can wait. No need to rush it.'

Susan dried her hands. Her colour had returned to normal, and she was her sensible self once more. 'If you two think it's all right, then that's it. Settled. Supper won't be long. Mrs Quicke, have you time to fill us in on what this is all about?'

Rafael resumed his seat. 'Exactly, Mrs Quicke. If we can help in some way, consider us at your service.'

Ellie ran her fingers back through her hair. 'As far as I can work out, five neglected wives joked among themselves about how to dispose of their husbands. Their discussions ended up on email and one of the men actually died in the way that Diana had suggested.'

'Really?' Rafael was amused. 'I'm having trouble getting my head around that. What did she suggest?'

'Mixing up the man's pills. The other women came up with a wide range of plans from shoving someone down the stairs, setting him on fire, poisoning or drowning.'

Rafael rubbed his chin, which sported a fashionable dark shadow. 'They dreamed up wholesale manslaughter?'

Ellie said, 'Of course not. It was all a joke till one of them died in the way described. The husbands then took fright. They plotted to protect themselves by throwing their wives out. None of them had children at home, except for Diana. Evan kept their child and has barred Diana from the estate agency. She dumped her stuff here and went off to check with the bank that her own private account was still in working order, and to consult my solicitor. On the way, she contacted the other wives, who were getting the same treatment as her. Diana suggested that they join her here with some idea of forming a group to fight their expulsion. I was out – I'd gone to try to make Evan see sense at the time – but Thomas let the first arrival in, and she admitted the others. Later on today, another husband died. Walt, husband to Russet. He was found at the bottom of his stairs. That may have been a natural death, or it may not. It will take an autopsy to decide.'

'Phew!' That was Rafael. 'That's two down. What's left? Poisoning, drowning and fire. Do you think—?'

Ellie was grim. 'I think they'll discover Walt died from a fall down the stairs. He did have high blood pressure, so that may have been a factor in his death.'

Susan was round-eyed. 'You think he was pushed?'

Rafael said, 'Once is coincidence. Two is what?'

Ellie said, 'I don't know. One thing is for certain: today's victim was not killed by his wife. All the women were here and alibi one another. My friend Lesley in the police force is looking into the matter, because if it's not a coincidence it could be something more serious. She's told me not to let the women leave here because the police may want to interview them. Anyway, I can't turn them out, for pity's sake. They're in shock. They really are. I'm trying to find beds for them all tonight. Tomorrow is another day. Hopefully, they'll move on then.'

She was not aware that she had crossed her fingers till she saw Rafael notice what she was doing.

Rafael said, 'Pardon my French, but isn't your daughter being rather high-handed?'

Ellie stiffened, then relaxed. He was being tactful, but he was quite right. Rafael was looking at her with a quizzical air, and Susan with compassion. They knew what Diana was like because they'd experienced her at first hand. They were not going to embarrass Ellie by voicing their low opinion of Diana, but they were not going to be fooled by flimflam. They were waiting for her reaction to Rafael's question. She could pretend she didn't know what they were talking about. On the other hand, Ellie had come to regard Rafael and Susan as friends whose judgement she respected. She thought she could trust them.

Some people might think it would be disloyal of Ellie to criticize her daughter to people who were not family, but Ellie had found Diana's recent behaviour disturbing. It was true that her daughter had been under great stress, but even so, she had made what amounted to threats to her mother.

Ellie tried to make her voice colourless as she decided to share some of her burden. 'Currently Diana expects me to fund a divorce for her. She believes I can access the trust fund to subsidize her. I've told her that I can't do that, but she doesn't listen. She sees me living in this big house and she wants me to move out and leave it to her. It might sound sensible if Thomas and I were ready to downsize, but we aren't. I do sympathize with Diana. She's in a difficult situation.' That sounded weak. She knew it, and so did they.

Rafael put his glasses back on, then took them off again. The businessman in him was back in control. 'You could, perhaps, think about giving Thomas a Power of Attorney? Just in case anything should happen?'

Delicately put, but the meaning was clear. What would Diana's position be if Ellie met with an accident and was incapacitated, or worse . . . if she were to die?

She said, 'Already done. With my solicitor. Diana won't get any change out of him.'

Rafael somehow refrained from saying, 'Good girl!' though Ellie thought he was going to do just that.

Susan was concerned. 'Rafael, if Mrs Quicke is short of money, do you think you might help her out?'

Before Ellie could speak, Rafael scotched the suggestion. 'Susan, Susan! Mrs Quicke is a woman of many parts. If she had wanted to borrow money from me, I would have been delighted to oblige, but my instinct tells me she has a substantial rainy-day account.'

Ellie grinned. 'I do, but that's a secret. This house eats money. I had planned to paint the outside next year, and the boiler is going to need replacing some time, so I do put money aside for maintenance every year. Thank you both for your concern but honestly, I'm all right.'

'Oh, good. Sorry I spoke.' Susan blushed, embarrassed at having spoken out. She busied herself opening the oven door, releasing a wonderful aroma of lamb and herbs into the kitchen. 'How many did you say there's going to be for supper?'

Ellie gulped. The aroma of freshly baked meat made her realize she hadn't eaten anything but a sandwich since breakfast. Oh, and a biscuit or two. Neither had her guests.

Ellie counted on her fingers. 'Diana for one. She's in the guest room next to ours. Then there's Barbie. She's in the room at the end of the corridor. Her husband, Bunny Brewster, was the first to die and he did so in the way suggested, in jest, by Diana. Bunny got his pills mixed up and died, verdict misadventure. Only, his first wife and son have thrown Barbie out of the house which she thought was going to be left to her and have denied her access to her valuables. She's probably the oldest of the women, but she's a survivor. Somehow, she'll cope. Also, she's had longer to come to terms with her husband's death and is beginning to look to the future.

'Then there's Russet, auburn-haired and a smoker. She's in the room my grandson uses when he sleeps over. Russet is not as old as Barbie but getting on. She is in shock. It was her husband who died this afternoon and I have no idea what the verdict on that death is going to be. Strangely enough, if he was pushed, then that was the death jokingly prescribed for him by Trish. She's the youngest of the evicted wives, and she's in the old housekeeper's bedroom upstairs. She seems to be a really nice girl married to a not very nice man called Terry. She was a primary school teacher and wanted children, but he didn't. He's been abusing her. Trish certainly didn't mean Walt any harm.'

'Barbie, Russet and Trish. That's three,' said Susan.

'Number four is Kat, short for Katarina. She came from somewhere in middle Europe to act as housekeeper for her husband, who is a right old skinflint called Rupert. Apparently he married her to save himself the price of her wages. I think Kat will probably have to doss down on the sofa tonight. She won't object. She's a capable woman, and a born carer.'

Rafael said, 'You say the five wives can all alibi one another for this afternoon's death?'

Ellie winced. 'Four of them were here. I joined them

mid-afternoon, made them tea, tried to calm them down and phoned Lesley to ask if there were any basis for suspecting foul play. If it weren't for the emails, I'm sure the verdict on Walt's death would be that it was an accident. But with the emails . . .' Ellie raised her hands in a helpless gesture. 'Lesley is looking into it.'

Rafael said, 'You've left one wife unaccounted for.'

Diana. He meant that Diana had not been with them this afternoon during the time when – or if – Walt had been pushed down the stairs. Did Rafael really think that Diana might have been responsible for Walt's death? No, surely not!

But she could read a flicker of doubt in his eyes.

Susan could do the maths, too. She wasn't going to say anything, though. Instead, she turned away to busy herself checking the contents of various pans on the stove.

Ellie said, 'Diana went to the bank and then to my solicitor's chambers. She waited around for him all afternoon, because he was in court.'

Noncommittal, Rafael nodded. Susan tasted the contents of one pan and added a half teaspoonful of salt.

Were they both mulling over the idea that Diana might have committed murder? Were they wondering if, when Diana had learned Gunnar was in court, rather than wait around for him, she had taken herself off somewhere for a couple of hours . . . and called on Walt . . . and did what?

'No,' said Ellie. 'I don't believe that Diana pushed Walt down the stairs, not for a minute. Why should she? What would she gain by doing that? Besides which, she was in great distress. She's been separated from her little boy, is homeless and without a job. It's nonsense to suspect her of, well, of anything.'

Rafael rubbed his chin. 'Do you think any one of the women would be prepared to kill for a friend?'

Ellie shook her head. 'No, I don't. I've talked to each one of them in turn and the idea is ridiculous.'

Susan said, 'Supper's ready. Will you call them down?'

The aroma of the meat cooking had already wafted through the house. Kat came in, shepherding a shaken Trish before her. Kat looked more settled now she had somebody to look after. Trish looked as if she'd disintegrate any minute.

Ellie ushered them to the table, introduced everybody and said she hoped nobody was a vegetarian. They shook their heads. Kat seated Trish next to her. 'It smells good, no? You will feel better when you have eaten.'

Thomas arrived, putting his own worries aside to play host. 'Ladies, you are all very welcome. Now, which is which?'

Ellie said, 'This is Kat, and next to her is Trish.'

Rafael had put his laptop away and now dealt out knives and forks. Susan dished up and passed hot plates around.

Barbie appeared in the doorway. 'I'm sorry to be difficult . . .'

Ellie introduced Thomas. 'Barbie, this is my husband Thomas. Thomas, this is Barbie.'

Barbie managed a social smile. 'It's very good of you to have us. Mrs Quicke, would it be possible for me to take some food up to Russet? She's still very weepy, wants to return home, wants to see her husband. She's not fit to go anywhere.'

Ellie hesitated. 'I think it would be best if Russet came down and joined us. No matter how little she eats, it's important for her to be with her friends at this time. Do you think she can make it?'

Barbie nodded. 'You're right. I'll get her into a dressing gown or something and bring her down.'

As Barbie left, Diana passed her in the doorway. She ignored Thomas, and everyone else at the table to say, 'I'd like mine brought upstairs, please. I have various phone calls to make which won't wait.' It was an order, not a request.

Before Ellie could object, Rafael got his word in. 'I'm not having Susan wear herself out carrying food up and down those stairs.'

Diana blinked.

Ellie wondered if Diana was thinking, *What! Are the peasants revolting?*

Ellie hastened to smooth things over. 'If you'd like to take a tray upstairs, Diana, then please do so, but bring it down again afterwards, right?'

'Really!' Diana paled with anger, and then flushed. 'Oh, very well. I'll hang around till you've all fed your faces and take what's left over, shall I?'

Susan handed Diana a plate. 'No need for that if you'd like to help yourself?'

For once, Diana had not got her own way. Ellie wondered whether this was a good time to knock Diana off balance even further. 'Diana, you didn't wait for Gunnar in his office all afternoon, did you?'

'No, of course I didn't. What a waste of time that would have been. I went to see the bank manager, and then I thought . . .' She paused to lick her lips. 'I went over to the nursery. I thought that when my son came out at the end of the day, I could whip him into a taxi and . . . But he wasn't there.'

'You waited outside the nursery? For how long?'

'I don't know. An hour, I suppose. What's with the questionnaire? I hope there's no onions in that dish. I can't abide them.'

Susan didn't even lift her head. 'No onions. Shallots. They're rather good at this time of year.'

Onions and shallots. Same difference. Fortunately Diana didn't seem to know that. So she'd had an opportunity to go round to Walt's house and push him down the stairs? No . . .

Ellie's landline rang, and she hurried into the hall to take the call. Barbie and Russet passed her on their way to the kitchen. Russet was in a velvety green housecoat. She looked like a feeble old woman, her hair lustreless, her gait unsteady. Barbie had her arm around her friend, saying, 'Just a few more steps.'

Ellie picked up the phone. As she'd hoped, it was Lesley on the other end. Ellie shut the door to the kitchen quarters. 'What's the verdict on Walt's death?'

'Awaiting the result of the autopsy. I didn't get back to the station in time to submit the emails, so there is as yet no cause for suspicion from the police point of view.'

'There is no doubt about the manner in which Walt died?'

'It's routine to have an autopsy when someone hasn't seen a doctor recently. I will suggest they look to see if there's some bruising on his back which might indicate he was pushed, but no one's ringing alarm bells yet. Are the women still with you?'

'Yes, all five of them. Russet is in shock. So is Trish. Barbie and Kat are looking after them.'

'Your opinion?'

Ellie crossed her fingers. 'They alibi one another and none of them benefited by their husbands' deaths.' Diana had no alibi, but Ellie wasn't going to mention that, was she?

Lesley said, 'I'll submit the emails to my boss tomorrow morning for consideration. Independent of the autopsy, I do believe we will want to take the case further. Whether or not I'll be on it is another matter. It complicates matters that I've spoken to two of the wives without cautioning them first.'

'If you're not put on the case, who will be in charge?'

'Um, your devoted admirer "Ears", I suppose.'

Ellie had feared it might be him. The man she'd nicknamed 'Ears' was Lesley's superior officer, who lacked imagination. And that was putting it kindly. His ears turned bright red when his blood pressure rose, and most unfortunately Ellie had, in a senior moment, referred to him by this idiosyncrasy. He had never forgiven her, as the nickname had run around the station in minutes. 'Ears' hated Ellie. He didn't like Lesley much, either, since she was considerably more intelligent than him.

At times this created a difficult situation for Lesley. Every now and then Ellie worried that she'd harmed Lesley's prospects in the police force. 'Ears' would certainly enjoy finding fault with Ellie for anything from putting the rubbish bins out before the correct time, to murder. Yes, he would love to get her for murder.

Or arrest Diana for it. Ellie winced at the thought.

'Lesley, isn't it common practice for the police to inform the victim's wife if he's found dead? No one official has been round to see Russet yet.'

'What? I agree. They should have been.' Lesley didn't actually grind her teeth, but Ellie got the impression that that was what was happening. 'Someone ought to have called. Perhaps they didn't know where to find her?'

'They could have reached her through her smartphone, or her neighbour. Russet learned of her husband's death when her nosy neighbour phoned her. And the gardener who found Walt's body, he's also got her number.'

Lesley sighed. 'Anything else you'd like to throw at me before I am thoroughly put off my supper?'

'The neighbour or the gardener might have seen a strange car or noticed a visitor?'

'Yes, we'll have to do house-to-house if we decide there is a case to answer.'

'Also, the woman who masterminded the expulsion of the five

wives is called Monique. She was Evan's first wife. She is intelligent and powerful. I suspect that she employed a cleaning agency to do the dirty work. If so, the cleaners might have noticed something which would help. I haven't checked yet, but it is possible Monique would have gone to the one I use, which is run by a friend of mine.'

'There are lots of cleaning agencies around.'

'Not many that are good. There is another reason why Monique might have used Maria's agency. Maria is happily married to Diana's first and long-divorced husband. Monique doesn't care for Diana, and it would be just like her to use Maria's agency to get rid of Diana's things. A subtle form of revenge, if you see what I mean.'

'You're guessing.'

'Yes. I'll check in the morning, shall I?'

Lesley said, 'The end of a perfect day. I'm going to go home to my husband and listen to him grumbling about the other teachers at school. Or maybe – let's look on the bright side – he'll be talking about cricket. Or maybe it'll be football, because that seems to be on all year round nowadays. We shall turn on the telly, pick a ready cooked meal from the freezer, have some ice cream for afters.'

'Sounds good. Speak tomorrow.'

Diana pushed open the door from the kitchen and came into the hall, carrying a tray heaped with food. 'Who's that on the phone? You've been speaking to Gunnar? When is he going to tell Evan he can't keep my little boy?'

NINE

Monday supper.

Ellie knew that she ought to allay Diana's fear, but she couldn't quite manage it. It had been a long and tiresome day and the immediate future looked grim. She realized she was being curt but couldn't help herself.

'Diana, that was the police on the phone. They have the emails and there's to be an autopsy on Walt. I know you've spoken to Lesley informally, but I think the police will want to see you again about your suggestion to kill a man by mixing up his pills. In the meantime, my supper awaits.'

Without waiting for a reply, Ellie swept down the corridor and into the kitchen. And relaxed.

Rain was beating at the windows, but Susan had switched on the lights and lowered the blinds with the result that all those sitting round the table seemed to be enclosed in a warm, golden glow. Tantalizing aromas rose from the dishes of food which Susan had placed on the table.

Rafael swept Ellie into a chair beside Thomas and Susan put a plate full of food in front of her. 'Enjoy!'

'Yes, enjoy!' said Thomas, pushing his own worries aside and including everyone at the table. 'It may be raining outside. You've had a bad time today and the future is uncertain, but you are all here, safe and sound. Take the time to rest and recover. Be thankful for the meal. Let tomorrow bring what it will. Tonight you are among friends.'

'You are very kind.' That was Trish, hollow-eyed and badly bruised.

The strained looks of the women began to fade as they took their first mouthfuls of food.

Kat patted Trish's arm. 'You can manage a bit more to eat, yes?'

Trish looked at her clean plate in surprise. Then smiled. 'Yes, please.'

The women had each taken only a small portion, perhaps fearing they would have no appetite, but as they cleared their plates, they began to realize that they might manage seconds.

Susan beamed. She liked her food to be appreciated. 'Seconds for you, Mrs . . . Bunny, is that right?'

Ellie thought Barbie might take offence, but she didn't. She even managed a low laugh. 'Mrs Bunny it is. I'm Barbie, short for Barbara. And you are Susan? Who is not a cook, I gather?'

Rafael spoke up. 'Susan is training to be a chef. As soon as she finishes, we're getting married. She's refused to wear my ring yet, but she has agreed that the Reverend Thomas will marry us.'

This struck the right note, as the women all switched from contemplating their own troubles to congratulate Susan on her cooking and on her engagement. Each and every one of them had a second helping. Ellie told herself not to eat too fast; Susan's cooking was, as ever, delicious.

It was Russet who picked up on Rafael's hint. 'The Reverend Thomas? You are a minister? You have a church? I haven't been to church for ages. Not since I was a child.'

'I'm retired from parish work,' said Thomas. 'I don't often wear a dog collar now. Anyway, the beard hides it when I do.'

Kat, who was probably a Catholic by upbringing, said, 'Rupert didn't like my going to church. I tell him that I pray wherever I am. It is good, but not essential, to go to church.'

Ellie thought, *Good for Kat*.

Everyone had cleaned their plates of the first course. Susan removed the few leftovers and placed a huge bowl of fruit puree, yoghurt and cream on the table, together with a plate of her homemade biscuits. There was a further slackening of tension. Clever Susan. Nothing in the meal was too heavy for these distraught women to eat. Nothing was indigestible. Individual glass dishes were provided, and the dessert went round the table for everyone to help themselves.

Thomas said, 'If you go past the dining room on the other side of the hall you will come to a quiet room. It's not a chapel. It's not consecrated. I go there for my thinking and prayer times. If any of you would find it helpful, you are welcome to spend time there.'

There was silence while the women absorbed this information.

Barbie said, 'Would you be there? If, for instance . . .' The words died away.

'Your choice,' said Thomas, in his usual comfortable fashion. 'If you want to sit and think, that's fine. If you want to talk to God, that's all right. If you would find it helpful to talk to me about anything, no problem.'

Rafael couldn't resist. 'May I come and talk about cabbages and kings? Or politics?'

All four of the wives cracked a smile. Rafael knew how to release tension, didn't he?

Thomas said, 'Your choice, ladies.' He looked around at their dishes. 'No coffee for me tonight, I think. I'll need my beauty sleep.'

Kat started.

Ellie realized that she hadn't yet arranged a bed for Kat. Must she really sleep on the sofa? Before Ellie could speak, Susan laid a hand on Kat's arm. 'I have a small flat on the top floor here. You are welcome to occupy my spare room. You don't mind climbing some stairs, do you? Show me which are your things in the hall, and we can take them up together.'

Kat hesitated. 'Trish, will you be all right?'

Trish said, 'I'm fine.' She didn't look it, but she was a brave lass. 'I'm going to ring my parents and then take myself off to bed.'

Kat had risen to go with Susan, but now she said, 'First I must help clear the table.'

'No, you don't,' said Susan. 'You have an early night. You'll feel better in the morning.'

Kat's eyes watered. 'You are all so kind. Blessings be on you.'

Russet also got to her feet, holding on to the table to stabilize herself. 'Kat has the right idea. Thomas, will you give us your blessing before we leave this room?'

Thomas looked round at each one of them. 'May God bless this house, and all in it. May He grant us a quiet night, and peace in our hearts. Amen.'

Russet brushed tears from her cheeks and followed Susan, Trish and Kat out of the room.

Ellie helped Rafael stack dirty plates in the dishwasher.

Barbie sat at the table, her eyes down.

Thomas said, 'I'm off for a few minutes in the Quiet Room. All right with you, Ellie?'

Ellie nodded, and he left.

After a moment, Barbie followed Thomas out of the door and down the corridor.

Now that was a surprise. Ellie hadn't expected it to be Barbie who would take up Thomas's offer.

And then there were two: Rafael and Ellie, working together to dispose of the supper things.

Susan came down to say she'd settled Kat in her spare room,

poor thing, and would have an early night herself. Ellie clattered saucepans into the sink while Susan had a murmured conversation and exchanged a few kisses with Rafael. Then Susan, too, left.

Midge the cat reappeared now the house was quiet, and Ellie fed him. She glanced at the clock and yawned.

Rafael said, 'Can you find me a duvet and a pillow, Mrs Quicke? I'll sleep on the settee in the sitting room, if you don't mind.'

Ellie's mind went to Full Alert. 'Surely there's no need for that.'

'Alibis, Mrs Q. Too many dodgy deaths. What's next? I ask myself. Poison, drowning or fire?'

Ellie felt rather faint. 'You really think there's going to be another death?'

'Don't you?'

'No, surely not.'

'Someone tried to frame these women for murder, right?'

'Someone took advantage of their silly game to get rid of them, that's all.'

'Where would the finger of blame be pointed if the police decided that one or more of the husbands had died in suspicious circumstances? At their wives.'

'Well, yes. Always supposing that the deaths are going to be regarded as suspicious, which is not yet the case. Fortunately they've all got alibis for this afternoon when Walt died.'

Rafael didn't point it out, but they both knew that Diana hadn't any such alibi. Instead, he said, 'Another thing: these women are vulnerable, homeless and without a man to stand up for them. They joked about killing their husbands, and the joke has turned sour. Once the men discovered the emails, they threw their wives out, which indicates to me that these particular husbands didn't have much of a sense of humour about their wives' "jokes". Instead of laughing, they reacted with anger. Even with violence in Trish's case. I'm wondering just how far their fear may drive them to go. I wouldn't want any of them trying to harass their wives further when the situation is so . . . Shall we say, fluid?'

Ellie translated this in her head, and gasped. 'You think one or more of the husbands might believe that Russet was responsible for Walt's death and take it out on her? No! Surely not. Anyway, would the men even have heard about it by now?'

Rafael was reason itself. 'The gardener saw the body and summoned an ambulance. The neighbour saw the body, the ambulance and the police. Don't tell me the neighbourhood isn't seething with speculation by now. Don't tell me someone hasn't phoned the remaining husbands. And what action are they going to take? Are they going to sit on their behinds and wait to be poisoned, drowned or set on fire? No, of course not. They will take action in some way.'

Ellie looked wildly around. Were all the ground-floor doors locked and the windows ditto? 'I suppose the men might get together and talk it over.'

'Take it from me, they'll be worrying which of them is going to die next.'

'You think Diana's husband, or Kat's husband – Rupert the skinflint – or the wife-beating Terry might come looking for Russet here? I think, I hope he doesn't . . .'

'I think, I hope, they don't. But, with everyone having mobile phones nowadays, always texting and keeping in touch, I wouldn't like to bet that they don't. For a start, when Russet's nosey neighbour and her gardener spoke to her on the phone, they would have asked where she was, and she would have told them. And why shouldn't she? If she told them, she might as well have told the whole world.'

Yes, the neighbour probably had told the whole world, and one of her gossips would think it only right to phone whichever of the other husbands they knew. Oh dear.

Ellie told herself not to panic. 'No, no. I'm sure you're exaggerating. It's far more likely that the men would take their suspicions to the police and we can assure the police that Russet never left this house.'

'I think we should make sure she doesn't go out tonight, too. Perhaps I'm being overcautious, Mrs Quicke, but I do think it would be a good idea for someone to sleep downstairs tonight, just in case one of our guests fancied a midnight walk outside, or a stranger came knocking on the door asking to speak to them. The women have alibis for this afternoon. Let's make sure they maintain them tonight. And, it had better be me who sleeps downstairs because Thomas looks tired.'

Ellie had noticed that Thomas was flagging, too. Rafael didn't miss much, did he?

'All right. You have a key to the front door, as has Susan. So have I, and so does Thomas. Diana has one, too, but no one else. We can double lock the front door, so that would make it difficult for anyone to get in or out easily. We can shoot the bolts home. They're a bit high up for me, so could you attend to that?'

Rafael didn't say it, but they both understood that if Diana wanted to leave the house, he'd be there to prevent her doing so, if he could.

Ellie found Rafael a duvet and a pillow and made up a bed for him on the big settee downstairs. Then she followed Midge the cat upstairs, leaving the lights on in the hall. Sleep didn't come quickly. She tossed and turned. It was ages before she heard Barbie come up and walk along the corridor to her room.

Finally Thomas came in. 'What's Rafael doing, sleeping in the sitting room?'

'Acting as our guardian angel.'

Thomas was amused by that. He shucked off his clothes, threw them roughly in the direction of a chair, padded into the bathroom for a lick and a promise and returned, smelling of good soap. He removed Midge the cat from his side of the bed to a chair and slid in beside Ellie.

Ellie found it irritating that Thomas could never tell her what had transpired in his private conversations with people like Barbie who went to him for help. After all, as his wife she told him everything – or almost everything – that happened to her. She did understand, though, that he couldn't betray a confidence, and one thing she could do was to check that he was at peace afterwards.

'Good?' she said.

'Good,' he replied, as they made themselves comfortable. She spared a thought for the discarded wives who tonight would sleep alone. How very fortunate she was to have Thomas! He switched off the bedside light as the chiming clock in the hall told the household that it was now midnight.

Minus five minutes. It's running slow. I hope Rafael can sleep through it, or not sleep, if . . . Dear Lord, look after us all this night. This house feels like sanctuary, so many distressed souls under this roof, with two strong angels to watch over us. At least, they're not really angels. They're make-believe angels. No, that's wrong. There's nothing make-believe about either Rafael or Thomas. Well, you know what I mean, Lord . . .

Tuesday, breakfast time.

A misty morning promising another warm day, possibly without rain for once.

Ellie lay in bed, watching the second hand of the clock edge its way towards the moment when the alarm would go off. Midge and Thomas had disappeared some time ago. Thomas would be in his Quiet Room saying his office, and the cat would be out, making sure his territory was secure against invaders.

It seemed to Ellie that the house was quiet with the expectant silence you can sense before a storm. In a moment of fancy, she imagined her home holding everyone in its walls safe and sound, while waiting for the enemy troops to come storming along the road.

What nonsense! She slapped the alarm off and forced herself to get out of bed. On the top floor, a toilet flushed and a shower began. Susan, getting ready for the day. In these old houses, the plumbing grumbled and sometimes clanged as different parts of the system came into use, which reminded Ellie that the shower in the end bathroom on this floor could be slow and needed to be checked. She hoped Barbie and Russet managed to use it without any trouble. Oh, and was there enough cereal to feed everyone for breakfast?

She ought to spend some time on her knees asking God to look after them all that day, but . . . No, she mustn't panic. Doors were opening along the corridor. She must get downstairs as fast as she could to look after her guests. She dragged a brush through her silvery hair, knocked over her lipstick and let it lie. Slipped into some shoes.

Dear Lord, you know I must be busy this day. If I forget you, please don't forget me. The old warrior who wrote those words knew a thing or two about prayer when he'd got a busy day ahead of him. Of course, he was going into a real battle. Was it the battle of Worcester? She couldn't remember. Anyway, the present situation felt like war, too.

Someone rang the doorbell. Who could it be, so early in the morning? A car horn tooted. What was that? Dogs barking? Ellie hurried out of the bedroom and made it down the stairs a step or two ahead of Susan to find Thomas unbolting the door while Rafael, fully dressed, cradled an alarmed cat in his arms. Yes, it really was dogs barking.

Dogs barking? Whose dogs? Surely not Trish and Terry's dogs?

Thomas tried to pull back the catch on the door to open it. Ellie cried out, 'Stop, Thomas! I'm not sure it's a good idea to open it till we find out who's there. The door's double-locked, anyway. Let me find my key.'

Before she could search for her handbag, Thomas produced his own key and set it in the lock but didn't turn it. 'You think you know who's there?'

Trish appeared on the landing above, dressed in a T-shirt and jeans. Her jaw was green and black, and she was visibly trembling. 'That's Terry's dogs. I'd know their bark anywhere. What does he want? He shouldn't have come here. I'd better go out to him, hadn't I?'

The doorbell rang again. Strongly, indicating impatience.

'No!' Barbie came to Trish's side, shrugging herself into a housecoat. She wasn't wearing much underneath. Barbie had a lithe, well-cared-for, sleek body. She'd brushed her hair out but had not yet made up her face. No eyebrows, but good bone structure. Even without make-up she was a handsome woman.

Barbie said, 'Remember what we agreed, Trish. He's got to learn to respect you.'

Trish was conflicted. 'If he's really sorry . . .'

Barbie put her arm around Trish. 'He won't respect you if you go back to him too quickly. Agree to see him in a few days' time.'

Ellie said to Thomas and Rafael, 'If it is Terry, how did he know where Trish was to be found?'

Thomas stroked his beard. 'I'll go out and talk to him, shall I?'

Russet appeared, a towel around freshly washed hair. 'What's happened? Is it Terry's prize pooches out there making a racket?'

Someone pounded on the door. Thomas looked at Ellie. 'Do I let him in?'

Rafael said, 'There's two of us to one of him,' and put the cat down. Midge streaked for the kitchen quarters. He didn't intend to hang around if dogs were going to be let into the hall.

Ellie nodded to Thomas. 'Let him into the hall but only so far. Trish, you stay up there with Barbie.'

Thomas slowly and carefully opened the front door a foot or so and stood in the doorway. Thomas was very solid. He didn't shift more than an inch as a man drove into him and rebounded.

'How dare you! You! Lout! Stand aside. Out of my way!' Two dogs raised their voices in concert.

Through the half-open door, Ellie could see a well-built man in his forties, with thinning, wiry dark hair and a high colour. He was dressed in good casual wear, with two dogs' leads around his wrist. The dogs were beauties, silver-grey in colour. They were big dogs, satin-skinned and intelligent. Weimaraners? They snuffled and yapped around Terry's feet.

Thomas folded his arms. 'This is my house. Who are you, and what do you think you're doing here?'

Rafael stepped up to Thomas's shoulder, taking out his mobile phone. 'Shall I ring the police?'

The intruder said, 'Where is she? You have no right to obstruct me in searching for my wife. Produce her now! Or else!'

'Or else . . . what?' said Thomas.

Rafael said, 'I have the police number on speed dial.'

'What do you want the police for?' The voice climbed down an octave. 'There's no need for police. I just want to see my wife, to make sure she's all right. She got some bee in her bonnet, quite ridiculous, and took herself off in a huff. Now she's had a chance to calm down, I've come to take her home.'

'What makes you think she's here?'

'I rang her parents and they told me she was staying here overnight.' Yes, he was calming down now. 'Would you kindly tell her I'm here?'

Yes, of course, Trish had rung her parents and told them where she was. Why wouldn't she? Did that mean the other men knew where their wives had gone as well? Well, was there any harm in that?

Thomas was calmness itself. 'What do you want to see her for?'

'So she is here! I couldn't think why . . .' He turned away and there was the sound of a slap. 'Shut up! Shut up!' A dog whined. Another yelped.

He'd hit them? How could he!

Terry returned to the charge. 'Is she here? I have a right to know.' Then, in a softer tone, 'We had words yesterday. I may have said things . . . She took them the wrong way. You understand that I need to see her, to make sure she's all right.'

'Oh!' Trish tried to move towards the stairs, but Barbie held her back.

Terry had heard that. 'She is here, then? You're holding her against her will?'

'Certainly not,' said Thomas. 'She took refuge here after you threw her out—'

'That was a mistake. I was told . . . You've no idea of the stress I've been under, and then she attacked me! You didn't know that, did you? She's no shrinking violet.'

'That's enough,' said Thomas. 'Yes, your wife is here. She is safe and being well looked after. Now I must ask you to leave.'

Instead, Terry raised his voice. 'Trish! Trish love! Let me see you for a minute! I promise not to touch you! I'm so sorry. I was out of my mind. I didn't know what I was doing. Trish, I'm going mad!'

Trish broke free of Barbie and would have run down the stairs if Barbie had not caught her back. Barbie said, 'No!'

Thomas looked up the stairs and that was his mistake, for Terry thrust him aside and got himself and the dogs into the hall. He looked about him, the dogs plunging and jumping around him.

Ellie stepped in front of him. 'Thus far, and no further. Trish stays upstairs. You can talk to her from where you stand. If you try to go any further, we'll ring the police. Understood?'

'Of course, of course. Down, dogs!' He looked for Trish and found her on the landing, Barbie's arm around her. 'There you are! Your parents told me some stupid story about your being hurt. It was you who attacked me. Perhaps you didn't tell these people that, or they wouldn't have been so keen to take you in, would they? I could have you charged with assault, but I won't, because I know you're sorry you did it. You overreacted. That's right, isn't it?'

Trish had both hands over her mouth. Tears in her eyes. She trembled from head to foot but did not speak.

Terry said, 'Well, well. That's all water under the bridge. I can see you're sorry for what you did, and I'm prepared to overlook it, just this once. After all, who knows what goes on behind closed doors between a man and his wife, eh? I bet you didn't tell these people what you've been up to, have you?'

Trish shook her head but still did not speak.

Terry spread his hands, speaking to Thomas and Rafael, ignoring the women. 'She's a little free with her favours, you know? But she's young and I'm prepared to forgive her, in spite of everything.'

He was persuasive. Ellie could see how he could charm most people into believing what he said was true. He hadn't fooled Thomas, whose wide experience had taught him to look below the surface, nor Rafael, who had unusual insight into people's motives. Nor had he fooled Ellie, as the hairs on the back of her neck had risen on Terry's first attempt to brush Thomas out of the way.

A movement above. Ellie looked up to see Susan and Kat had joined the other women on the landing.

'Enough!' said Terry, holding out his hand in a commanding gesture. 'Trish, let's go somewhere that we can talk in private. If you've got a problem, if you've misunderstood anything I've said, then we can deal with it.'

Trish said nothing. Her eyes were huge. She shook her head.

'Come on! We can't hang around all day. I have to get to work and . . .' His voice rose, and the dogs yapped. He scowled at the dogs. 'And you have to walk the dogs. You can't leave them locked up in the house all morning.'

Trish whimpered, but didn't move.

Barbie said, 'They're your dogs, Terry. You're always telling us how clever you are to have picked out such well-trained animals. You walk them for a change.'

His face altered from bonhomie to rage. 'Bitch! I might have known you'd try to put your oar in. Well, we all know your nose is out of joint now. Evan told me you've been turned out without a penny. I shall enjoy seeing you down the Job Centre, begging for a job to clean houses, or stack shelves in a supermarket. Come, Trish. We're wasting time, and time's money.'

Once more, Trish shook her head.

His colour rose. 'If you don't come now and take the dogs for their walk, you'll force me to do something desperate! Understand? And it will be all your fault!'

Barbie kept her cool. 'And what will you do, Terry? Employ a dog-walker?'

'If she can't look after them when she knows perfectly well that I'm far too busy to do so, then . . . then I'll have to have them put down!'

TEN

Tuesday morning.

Everyone froze. Did Terry really want to try to have those beautiful dogs put down? Surely not.

Trish crumpled to the floor, whimpering.

The dogs, puzzled and unhappy, whined and yelped at Terry's feet.

Russet swept down the stairs like an avenging angel. 'How dare you, you piece of dog shit! Walt never wanted to bring you to the house and now I understand why! I also understand exactly why your poor first wife landed in hospital not once, but three times!'

The dogs began to bark as she raised her voice.

Terry laughed. 'Get away with you, you tired old hag! I told Walt, it's more than time he got rid of you and picked something juicier. I'm happy to see he's done just that!'

Russet shrieked, 'Walt was worth a dozen of you, you nasty little boil, spitting out poison every time you open your . . .' She stopped and reached for the newel post at the bottom of the stairs to steady herself. She dropped her voice to a whisper. 'You don't know, do you?'

'What? Quiet, dogs!' They whined, cringing away from him. Were they expecting another slap?

'You really don't know?' Russet broke into a painful laugh. Then stopped herself, fighting for self-control. She leaned against the banister for support.

Ellie stirred herself. 'This has gone on long enough.' She checked that Barbie was looking after Trish, and that Susan and Kat were too far away to help Russet. Ellie helped Russet to sit on the bottom stair. Then she faced Terry. 'Your friend Walt died yesterday afternoon by falling down the stairs.'

He blustered, 'What absolute nonsense! That's ridiculous! I don't know who you are, but what you don't seem to know is that my good friend Walt had a very good reason to throw Russet out yesterday morning. And as for you . . .'

Thomas moved closer to Ellie on one side, and Rafael stepped up on the other.

Ellie said, 'My name is Mrs Quicke. This is my husband, Thomas, and this is Rafael, a good friend of ours. Together we have been looking after your wife and her friends. I understand that you didn't know Walt had died when you came here, but that's no excuse for your bad behaviour. I suggest that you check with the police at the earliest opportunity to find out what's been happening. They will no doubt want to ask you various questions. Now I must ask you to leave. Your wife's injury has been photographed and can be used in evidence against you if you try to contact her again without her permission. She needs a period of recuperation among friends before she decides what to do in the future, so—'

Terry sneered. 'Walt's dead? I don't believe it. I'd have heard if that had happened. Trish has fooled you with some wild tale or other. She's not quite the thing, you know. She sleeps around. She needs to be with someone who knows how to make her behave herself. So, get out of my way, old woman.'

Old woman! Ellie winced. Thomas drew in his breath sharply. Ellie felt rather than saw that Rafael was smiling. Not nicely.

Terry called up the stairs. 'Come along, Trish. Playtime's over. You've wallowed in your fantasy long enough, with your "so-called" friends egging you on, no doubt. When you're ready to admit your mistakes, I'll forgive you. Right. So, it's time to get back to real life. You can leave your car here while you take the dogs for a walk. I've a meeting in fifteen minutes, but I'll be back for lunch and I expect you to be home with food ready for me by then, right?' He grinned, revealing prominent eye teeth.

Everyone looked up. Trish was holding on to Barbie . . . or Barbie was holding on to Trish. Someone whimpered. Maybe it was the dogs, who were also looking up at Trish. They'd recognized her, hadn't they? One of them tried to get to the stairs, trying to reach Trish. The other, kept on a shorter chain, tried to follow but was held back with a curse from Terry.

He said, 'Come on, girl! I haven't all day.'

Trish managed to get to her feet. She pushed Barbie away and made it to the head of the stairs. She took two trembling steps down and stopped. 'Let the dogs come to me.'

Terry released them, and they shot up the stairs to press themselves against Trish. She cradled their heads and hugged them. She wept. Perhaps the dogs did, too. It was clear they loved her, and that she loved them.

Trish wanted children. Terry didn't give them to her. She'd made the dogs a substitute for children. She won't be able to let them go.

Trish stood up, her hands on the heads of the dogs. 'Terry, I swear I've always been faithful to you. I need some space to think about what's been happening in our marriage, so I'm going to stay with my parents for a bit.'

His mouth turned ugly. 'So you'd walk out on me, would you? And the dogs? I was serious, you know. If you refuse to look after them, you leave me no option but to have them put down.'

A sharp intake of breath from Russet, and a 'No!' from Barbie.

Ellie tried to think. Surely vets refuse to put down healthy dogs, although they would offer to rehome them. Did Trish know that? Apparently not. Would she give in? Probably.

Rafael said, 'That's blackmail!'

Trish swiped tears from her cheeks. 'Terry, this is not like you. I know you love the dogs, too. But I can't . . . I won't . . .!' She bent to kiss the dogs again, and then gave them a little push. 'I love you. Go back to your master. Off you go.'

Obedient as ever, they descended the stairs but kept turning their heads back to check that she really intended to dismiss them.

Terry's colour rose. 'I mean it, Trish. You will be responsible for their deaths, not I.'

Rafael stepped forward. He picked up the trailing dog leads and gestured the dogs to his side. Rafael was the sort of person whom people obeyed, and the dogs knew it. They pricked up their ears and eyed him with the whites of their eyes showing but made no resistance when he twitched on their leads to get them standing at his side.

Rafael said, 'You have handed the dogs over to Trish to care for, so care for them she shall. Trish, I know you have nowhere to take them for the moment, so may I suggest that until you can make proper arrangements for them, I put them into kennels for you?'

'What!' Terry couldn't get his head round this. 'You can't do that!'

'Yes, I can,' said Rafael. 'We've all just heard you hand them over to her.'

Not exactly, no. Terry didn't say that, and he didn't mean that. But if Rafael's words made Terry rethink . . .?

Russet gave a hard little laugh. 'That's right. You did. I heard you. Terry, you said you couldn't keep the dogs and you said you were giving them to Trish to look after.'

Barbie hung over the banisters. 'I heard him, too.'

Susan shouted down from above, 'Rafael, I love you!'

'Ditto, ditto,' said Rafael, teeth gleaming as he looked up at her.

'What . . .!' Terry gibbered. Then swung round on Thomas. 'What lie is this? I didn't mean I was giving them to her, and you know it. He's twisting my words. What he's proposing is theft!'

Ellie saw Thomas struggle with his conscience. He knew Terry hadn't meant to give the dogs to Trish. He also knew that what Terry had been doing amounted to blackmail.

Ellie spoke up. 'Terry, you did say you wanted Trish to look after the dogs. You said that if she didn't take them, you were going to have them put down. In effect, you condemned them to death. As you have said they should die, then they are as good as dead. What Rafael is going to do with two dogs he's rescued from death is his own business.'

Terry gaped. 'That's not what I meant at all! These are two very valuable, pedigree dogs. I paid a pretty penny for them on the understanding that she would look after them and, well, I don't slobber over them as she does, but . . . Well, they're mine. They're part of the household.'

Rafael said, 'Shall I buy them off you?'

'No, I . . .' He looked wildly around. 'Trish, I didn't mean . . . This is not how this is supposed to work.' He turned on Rafael. 'As for you, you keep out of this, Mister whatever your name is!'

'My card,' said Rafael, producing one from his back pocket. 'As you have condemned the dogs to death, you won't have the cost of feeding them in future. On the other hand, if you want to return them to life at some point, then I'll let you have the bill from the kennels for their keep. Understood?'

Russet applauded. Barbie laughed, and joined in. As did Susan and Kat.

Finally, Thomas shrugged. And smiled.

Ellie pulled the front door open and gestured for Terry to leave.

Terry hesitated. Would he leave without the dogs? How much did he really care for them?

He said, 'No, I can't . . .' He grabbed the dogs' leads from Rafael, and said, 'Heel, boys!'

The dogs obeyed him, and Terry whisked them out of the house.

Ellie watched Terry put the dogs in the back of his car and get into the driver's seat. Spurting gravel, he drove away, narrowly missing the gatepost as he did so.

She closed the door on the outside world and turned to find Trish had come down the stairs and was hanging on Rafael's neck. 'Thank you. You were brilliant! He didn't really mean it about putting them down. He does love them, you know. The first thing he does when he gets home at night is to take them out to the common and throw a ball for them to catch.'

Barbie said, 'It was all a bluff, Trish. Someone primed him to lean on your love for the dogs so that you'd return to him.'

Ellie said, 'You think someone has been putting ideas into Terry's head?'

Barbie said, 'On the button. It's that slimy toad, Rupert. Always going on about men being the master of the house and women needing to be shown their place in the world. Rafael, I'd like to shake your hand. Shaking hands may be old fashioned, but some sort of gesture seems to be called for.'

'Oh, no!' said Kat, welling up with tears. 'It's not Rupert. I'm sure not.'

Of course it is!

Trish hung on Rafael's arm. 'I did wonder if he'd let me take the dogs, but when I spoke to my parents and my sister last night I realized it wasn't possible. My parents have just downsized to a second-floor flat, and my sister's a worse case because she lives miles away and works from nine to five. I'd never in a million years have thought that Terry would want to kill them. I'm sure he never thought that up himself.'

Barbie nodded. She rolled her eyes at Russet, who nodded in agreement. They were both of the opinion that Rupert had been getting at Terry.

Trish went on, 'I do see that I have to let things calm down. When I've spent a few days with my parents, maybe I can come back here and get a job so that I can take the dogs out now and then. I'm sure I can get some work as a supply teacher. If I can't, then I'll go in as a teaching assistant somewhere.'

'Atta girl!' said Russet. 'Congratulations on standing up to Terry for once.'

Ellie thought, but did not say, that neither a supply teaching job, nor that of a teaching assistant would give Trish enough money to live on in their expensive neighbourhood. But if she divorced Terry, he would be forced to make her some sort of allowance so maybe her scheme would work.

Susan and Kat came downstairs to join them. Susan looked at her watch. 'I'm sorry to hurry everyone, but I've got half an hour before I have to be in college. I could do coffee or tea and toast for you all if you'd like?'

There was a general move towards the kitchen.

They all heard a key turn in the lock on the front door and turned to see who it was. Diana. She was dressed for the office in her usual black and white, but there were dark shadows under her eyes.

'What?' said Ellie. 'You've been out already? Diana, don't you realize that—'

'I wanted to see my son before he went off to nursery, but they wouldn't let me into the house and he didn't come out. I think they've moved him somewhere.'

Ellie said, 'But, how did you get out of this house?'

'I came down early. That long streak that's engaged to your cook person was on guard. He doesn't like me for some reason and I didn't want to have to explain where I was going to him – or anyone else for that matter. So I went round the landing and down the back stairs into the kitchen and got out that way. I thought it was going to be a nice day but it looks like rain again. I did go on to the nursery just in case he might have gone there early. I waited till they were all in, and I checked with the organizers, who were very rude, I must say. I mean, who's been paying the bills, eh? Apparently my son is not going there any longer. So I dropped into the doctor's to make an appointment for you to see him with me this afternoon at three sharp, and came home. So, is breakfast ready?'

Without waiting for a reply, Diana marched off to the kitchen.

Ellie tried to grapple with this and failed. A doctor's appointment? Diana had been out and about, without reflecting that this might deprive her of an alibi? Ah, but she didn't know there was any need for her to have an alibi, was there?

Rafael had been having a quiet word with Susan, but now broke off to speak to Ellie. 'I haven't much on today. I've got an errand to run, but I'll drop back later, right?'

Thomas was also looking at his watch. 'Can you manage, Ellie? I'll be off, too, if you don't mind. I've had a cup of coffee already and I've set up an appointment with a different printer for half nine. Ring me if there's a problem.'

Exit the two men.

Russet fingered her phone. 'Barbie, what do you think? I've got to get back home. I need to see Walt. Where do you think they'll have taken the body? And the house. Did the ambulance men have to break in to attend to him? I ought to be there. Heavens! I've got to start ringing round, making arrangements for the funeral. I suppose I have to see his solicitor, too. Walt made a will in my favour when we got married so that's all right, but there's so much to be done. The bank, his credit cards and driving licence. I know you've just been through all this. It's all rather daunting, isn't it?'

Barbie said, 'You're right, there. I'm thinking I shouldn't have let them walk all over me yesterday. I'm sure I can rustle up enough paperwork to prove that the miniatures are mine, but it will take time to organize. Would you like me to come with you, see you through the worst of it? I could book into a hotel, stay somewhere local for a couple of days if it helps.'

'Would you? Stay with me, of course. I didn't like to ask, but that would be . . .' Her eyes starred with tears.

'Come on.' Barbie shepherded Russet up the stairs. 'Let's get dressed and put our war paint on.'

As they went their way, Ellie heard Russet say, 'I know Walt was a right old whatsit, but I'm going to miss him, I really am. I was just thinking – there's his case of wine that I bought for him, and I must collect his dry cleaning, too, though what I'm going to do with it I don't know. My brother's going to try to come over later today – you've met him, haven't you? He says he can't stay long and he's not that good in an emergency, but . . . Then I ought to ring the people we were supposed to be dining with last night.'

Ellie told herself that she had to take control of the situation, which was getting out of hand. Nobody should be making plans till they knew if the police were going to act or not.

First things first. Breakfast.

In the kitchen, Ellie found a red-faced Susan emptying the dishwasher and spinning plates and mugs on to the table while a kettle screamed and Diana lectured her about the correct way to lay a table.

Ellie said, 'Leave it, Diana. Thank you, Susan. You've done more than enough. Off you go or you'll be late. We'll manage. I'll make some tea and a cafetière of coffee, too.'

Diana flounced into a chair, saying, 'There's a right and wrong way to do things, and there's such a thing as letting things get too slack. Susan takes advantage of your good nature, Mother. Now I'm here, things are going to have to change. I'll have a boiled egg and some dry toast, tea without milk, nothing else.'

Susan ignored Diana to say, low-voiced, 'Mrs Quicke, it's that time of the month for Kat. She needs tampons and her husband didn't think to pack her toiletries. I've fixed her up for now, but she needs to shop for her own.'

'Thank you, Susan. I'll deal with it.'

Susan seized her jacket and a tote bag and made her way out . . . which is when Midge appeared for his breakfast. At least Ellie knew what the cat would eat. What would the others want?

Barbie came in, looking immaculate. How on earth did she do it in the time? She was followed by a wan-looking Russet. Behind them came a pale-faced Trish, shepherded by Kat. They were all trying to smile, after a fashion.

Kat said, 'I can help, no?'

Trish tried to pretend everything was normal. 'We'll all help. Tell me what to do, Mrs Quicke. Do you have any cereal? Shall I boil some eggs or fry some bacon? Where is the toaster?'

'Cereal on the dresser, milk and fruit juice in the fridge. Saucepan for eggs under that counter, eggs are on the shelf above. Will everyone have cereal and eggs? And perhaps something from the fruit bowl as well?'

Somehow everyone got fed. Diana was good enough not to criticize her mother for serving tea and coffee in mugs and not in the best china. Ellie did make one mistake. She put the cafetière down on the table near Diana, who turned pale and moved it away from her. Ah, pregnant women often can't stand the scent of good coffee, can they?

There wasn't much conversation. They all had too much to think about.

Ellie made a note to do another shop as they were running out of staples. But how many should she cater for? Lesley wanted them all to stay but it might not be possible to arrange that? Ellie made another pot of tea and some more coffee before gesturing for silence.

'Now, ladies, a word. Some of you met my friend Lesley here yesterday afternoon. Apart from being a friend, she is also a police officer. She has taken copies of the emails you sent around to one another as a joke and will be presenting them to her superior officer this morning, to see if they consider the situation warrants investigation.'

Frowns all round. They were bemused, not frightened.

Barbie said, 'Bunny got his pills mixed up. I told the policewoman who came round. He was a bit of an idiot about his pills, I know, but—'

Ellie tried not to ratchet up the tension. 'I know. You explained. It was all perfectly understandable until it was revealed that one of your friends had suggested killing someone off in that way.'

More furrowing of brows. A couple of reluctant nods. Diana shrugged, trying to pretend that this was nothing to do with her.

Russet said, 'Yes, we see that it looks odd. But Diana wouldn't bother to kill Bunny. I mean, why would you, Diana?'

Diana shook her head. She wouldn't.

Ellie nodded. 'Agreed. It could be just a coincidence. But two deaths . . .'

Russet scraped back her chair. 'You mean they might query Walt's death? It was his heart, surely!' Her colour faded.

Barbie pressed Russet's head down to her knees. 'You are not going to faint. Understand?'

Russet took a couple of deep breaths and sat back in her chair again. 'I'm all right.'

Barbie released her. 'Mrs Quicke, you really think the police are going to investigate Walt's death?'

Ellie said, 'I don't know. There will have to be an autopsy. If he died of a heart attack, then probably not. But if there are bruises on his back, if they think it possible that he was pushed down the stairs, then . . . wouldn't you?'

An indrawn breath from someone. Trish?

Trish's voice rose. 'It was I who suggested we might push someone down the stairs, but I didn't mean it!'

'And you didn't do it, Trish.' That was Barbie. 'Keep your hair on. You can prove you didn't.'

'No, of course I didn't!' Trish said. 'I wouldn't. Oh, this is all so ridiculous! I could do someone an injury, I really could.'

Everyone managed a smile at that.

'Trish, you are expressing the frustration we all feel,' said

Barbie, 'but be careful not to make a threat like that before the police.'

Trish understood. 'My stupid tongue!'

Ellie was concerned about Russet. 'My dear, would you like some water?'

Russet took some more deep breaths to calm herself, and managed, 'I'm all right, really. It was just . . . I've just realized that we did foretell those two deaths in our emails. Not that we meant it. I still can't believe it. I'm trying to, but I can't.'

Barbie's eyes switched to and fro. Yes, she was going to take control of the group, wasn't she? 'Well, we know that neither Russet, Kat nor Trish could have killed him.'

Ellie agreed. 'True. None of you were there. You alibi one another.'

'Yes, that's right; we do,' said Barbie. A sudden thought. 'Except for Diana.'

No one looked at Diana directly.

Ellie stole a glance at Diana to see her biting her lip, colour flaring in her cheeks.

In an indistinct voice, Diana said, 'I didn't think I needed an alibi. Yesterday afternoon I went to different places, talked to this and that persons – I expect the police can find some people who saw me. I certainly didn't kill Bunny. Or Walt, either.'

'No, of course not.' Ellie let her declaration of faith in her daughter hang in the air. 'Another cup of coffee or tea for anyone?' Only Russet accepted.

Ellie said, 'The police may decide there is no case to answer, that these two deaths are unrelated and that the email suggestions were coincidences. May I ask whether you yourselves would agree with that decision?'

Uneasy looks were exchanged around the table.

'Reluctantly, no,' said Russet. 'Oh, this is a nightmare!'

Barbie shook her head. 'I'd like to believe it. I really would. It's a horrifying thought that someone might actually have arranged for poor Bunny to die . . .' She closed her eyes for a moment, frowning and then ironing out the frown. Frowning marred her good looks and at her age, it was important to avoid that.

Kat spoke up for the first time. 'Me, I do not believe it. It is, what you say, flying in the face of something big. One death, yes. Two deaths, nonsense!'

Trish mouthed some words to herself, shaking her head. 'I don't want to believe it. It can't be true!'

Ellie said, 'You do understand that the police may now wish to interview you all.'

Russet said, 'Thank God we can all alibi one another.'

Ellie agreed. 'Yes, you can. Except for Diana, but I'm sure people can be found who saw her at the relevant times. As of this moment, you are all protected from suspicion by having been with your friends. What I am going to suggest is that you don't now fly off to the four corners of the earth but stay here for one more day, continuing to give onc another protection. I want you to think twice before you leave this house, and if you do have to go out, you do so in pairs.'

An indrawn breath from Barbie. 'You think there's going to be a third death?'

Kat squeaked, and put both hands to her mouth. 'You think Rupert . . . or Diana's husband, Evan . . .?'

'Terry!' Trish looked wildly around. 'Someone's going to kill Terry?'

'I'm not suggesting anyone in particular,' said Ellie, 'but I do think it would be wise to take precautions. Kat, I know you need to buy one or two things and I daresay the others have found that because they left home in a hurry, they haven't got everything they need. I'm going to have to order in more food, so you might like to add on to my order with a local supermarket and have the stuff delivered. But, if you must go shopping yourselves, I really do suggest you go in pairs.'

Trish said, 'I could go shopping with Kat, if you like. She looked after me yesterday. I owe her one.'

Barbie as usual, was ahead of the others. She tapped on the table. 'Let's think sensibly. It would be best to order everything we need online. Even if two of us went to the shops together, suppose one got separated from the other, our alibis would be shot. Give me your list, Mrs Quicke, and I'll do it for you on the Internet. That is, if I may borrow a computer? Mine is still at home in the study, and I suppose that harridan will give it to that no-good son of hers. Unless you prefer someone else to do that?'

Here she gave a quick glance at Diana, clearly thinking that she would offer to help her mother out on this one, but Diana's gaze was fixed on the horizon and she didn't react at all.

Ellie was aware of the subtext but chose to ignore it. 'Thank you, Barbie. I'll show you where my computer is and give you the password.'

Barbie said, 'That's that, then. Now, Mrs Quicke, you've obviously given this matter some thought. If these two deaths are judged to be suspicious and we didn't kill them, then who did?'

'Indeed, that is the question the police will be asking. Before she left last night, Lesley suggested that none of you leave this house for the time being. I realize that's an imposition and possibly impractical. It's not just that Lesley wants to keep you here, but that she wants to keep you safe.'

Trish was round-eyed. 'You think *we* are in danger? Who would want to kill us?'

Barbie thrust back her chair. 'It's not us who are in danger. It's the men. We're not being killed off one by one. They are.'

'Murder? Really?' gasped Russet. 'But who? And why? For God's sake, why would anyone want to kill Walt, or poor Bunny, or any of us?'

'And,' Ellie drove the point home, 'who wants to put the blame on you? Because that's what it amounts to, isn't it? Without those emails, no one would think of connecting any of you with these deaths.'

Diana returned from wherever she'd been in her thoughts and slapped the table. 'That's right. Someone's trying to make out we killed the men!'

Kat said, 'It was Rupert who took the emails to Evan. You think Rupert has fantasy of a pretty young wife, like Trish? It may be so, but he is not a killer. No, that I do not believe.'

Trish reddened. 'No, really. Me and Rupert? Phew! Honestly!'

'In my book, Rupert's not clever enough,' said Russet. 'This is too subtle for him. Just look at how someone primed Terry to work on Trish by threatening to kill the dogs. Is Rupert bright enough to have thought that up? I doubt it. Kat, I agree with you that Rupert wouldn't go so far as to kill anyone. Besides, if he really did want a younger wife then he'd be wanting to get rid of you, not Bunny or Walt.'

Russet said, 'I've seen Walt looking at Trish, too. Looking is one thing. I don't think he ever got as far as touching, did he?'

Trish was scarlet with embarrassment. 'Of course not. I know Terry said I flirted with Walt, but I didn't, honest! And he didn't either, not really.'

Kat spoke up. 'Walt pinched my bottom once. He thought he was big shot. Men like to pinch bottoms. In my country, is a sign they like you but not enough to marry you.'

Barbie dismissed this. 'Juvenilia. Hormones. Nothing to worry about. What worries me is this: do the men realize the seriousness of their position? After all, Terry didn't seem to know about Walt's death. Do they realize that they are in real danger themselves? I don't think it's crossed their minds.'

Russet said, 'Surely Terry will tell the others.'

'Agreed, but will they understand that they're the ones in danger now that we've all left? If they were stupid enough to think we might have killed Bunny, they'll believe the moon is made of green cheese.'

Barbie focused on Ellie. 'They'd believe it if the police told them. How long do you think it's going to be before we're asked to make a statement about our movements?'

Ellie said, 'I suspect they'll wait on the result of the autopsy for Walt before making any final decision but, whether they decide to take the matter seriously or not, I expect my friend Lesley to let me know what's happening. At least, I hope so.'

Barbie was not convinced. 'We can't wait for the police to make up their minds. I think we should tell the men what we believe straight away.'

Trish said, 'Terry was horrid to me this morning, but I know he didn't really mean it. I don't want him to die. Shall I ring him?'

Barbie said, 'Would he listen? I doubt it.'

Ellie agreed. 'Well now; Terry might not listen to Trish, but I know someone who might be able to talk sense into the men.'

ELEVEN

Tuesday morning.

Trish pushed her chair back. 'I can't sit still and do nothing. I'm going to ring Terry. If he doesn't listen, well, at least I'll have tried!'

Barbie said, 'No, Trish. You'd only be setting yourself up for an argument. I don't honestly think we can ring Evan, or Terry, or Rupert, and tell them their life's in danger without proof. We can't just say, "We think this", and "We think that". They'd laugh themselves silly.'

Ellie agreed. 'Yes, they probably would. I'm going to tell Monique, Evan's first wife, what we know or suspect. Remember that it was she who masterminded your expulsion in the first place. She has never liked Diana,' and here there was a quick exchange of glances among the wives, which Ellie saw and pretended she hadn't. Diana put her chin up and pretended she didn't care.

Ellie continued, 'No doubt it gave Monique some satisfaction to organize Diana's removal from Evan's life, and she has gone along with his refusal to let Diana have access to their son. Monique had the evidence of the emails in front of her. The men wanted out of their marriages, and she was only too happy to help.'

'You know that for a fact?' asked Russet.

'She admitted as much to me. Monique has a good business head on her and is nobody's fool. I believe she organized the cleaning teams to pack up your belongings, but she is intelligent and fair-minded. If she is presented with the alibis which you all have for Walt's death, then I think she might admit to a modicum of doubt about who was responsible for what. She might not be convinced that Bunny's death was engineered' – again a frisson of doubt ran through the room, and again, Ellie ignored it – 'but she will be bright enough to accept that we are making a valid point in trying to get the men to be on their guard and yes, they will listen to her.'

Barbie wasn't sure. 'She will listen to you?'

'Yes.'

Barbie made up her mind. 'Very well. We would be grateful if you would do that, Mrs Quicke and, while we're on the subject,' she collected the eyes of the other women, 'I would like to apologize if we have been less than polite to you. We were under the impression that . . . Well, I don't think we behaved as well as we might have done when we arrived. In short, we are all profoundly grateful to you for taking us in and looking after us so well.'

Which, being translated, meant that Diana had told her friends that Ellie was a poor, weak creature, due to move into an old people's home? And that they now know better.

Diana's chin rose even further in the air. She got to her feet, looking at no one. 'My mother has always had my best interests at heart. I am glad you have all been able to take refuge here. I'm sure the men will see sense soon. Now, if you will excuse me, I have some phone calls to make.' She stalked out.

Ellie wondered if it would make a difference to the group if they knew that Diana was pregnant. Barbie and the others would make allowances for Diana's behaviour, wouldn't they? It was painful for Ellie to realize that her daughter was unable to make friends. It seemed unlikely that Diana understood what friendship meant. The other women knew and drew on one another's strengths. Diana's coldness and, yes, her self-centredness excluded her from such warm relationships. It was a minor miracle that she'd felt concerned enough for the others to offer them refuge at her mother's house. That was probably as far as she would ever go.

Barbie understood that, and so did Russet.

Ellie said, 'Thank you. You are all very welcome.' And meant it.

Trish, unfortunately, hadn't the same insight as Barbie and Russet. She had to take Barbie's group apology to Ellie further. 'You see, Diana told us this house was family property and she would be taking it over soon—'

Barbie cut her short. 'Yes, well. Diana doesn't always get it right. She told me that her stepfather Thomas was a . . .' She coughed and thought the better of what she had been about to say. She added, 'I think he's quite something, and definitely no pushover.'

Ellie said, 'You need say no more. I did inherit this house from a relative and when that happened, I gave my own house to Diana to live in instead. I did inherit a lot of money, but it's all gone into a charitable trust fund. I'm glad you like Thomas. He's my best friend as well as my dear husband. Diana finds it difficult to understand that she will not inherit this house nor any of my money, but she is my daughter and I love her and our grandson, and I will do what I can to help her, and you, through this.'

In other words: apology accepted.

'Good,' said Barbie, bracing herself for what was to come. 'Now, Mrs Quicke, in what way can we help you? For a start, do you want me to place an order for food and other things online?'

Kat spoke up. 'I can do that. You showed me how, and I can do it. Perhaps with a bit of help?'

Trish said, 'I'll help. I've got my laptop upstairs and we can use that.'

Russet tapped an unlit cigarette up and down, up and down. For two pins, she'd burst into tears again. 'This is all wrong. I need to know what's happened to Walt. I need to go back home. Ought I to ring the police and tell them where I am?'

Ellie said, 'I'll ring the police for you, and try to find out what's happening. Remember, if you do go back home, you ought to have someone with you.'

If I don't think of something for them to do, they'll all fly away to family and friends and it will be difficult for anyone to question them again. What can I suggest?

Ellie made up her mind. 'I'll get to work on phone calls straight away. Hopefully today will bring some good news and you can all begin to make plans for the future. In the meantime, you are welcome to stay on here, although I realize your quarters are not what you've been used to. While I'm doing the phone calls, I'm going to suggest that before you leave this room you work out what personal things you might need to get from the shops today and give Kat or Trish a list. I'll have a quick look in the freezer in a moment and work out what food we need. I know we're going to need milk, eggs, bread and cereal for a start.'

Trish woke from a brown study, possibly thinking about the

dogs? 'I promised to ring my dad again this morning, and my sister, to tell them when I'm arriving, but I can see it would be better to stay on here for another day. That is, if you don't mind, Mrs Quicke?'

Ellie said, 'Of course, Trish. Tell them you'll ring them again tomorrow when things are a bit clearer.'

Kat pushed up her sleeves and reached for an apron. 'First, we clean away the breakfast things, right? Then, Trish, if you will help me make a list of what we need to order? I can do it, but I need you to check that I have not made silly mistakes, right? I will cook quiches for lunch and a hotpot of chicken for tonight.' Kat was happy to be able to use her skills.

'Excellent,' said Ellie. 'There's a pad and some pens on top of the fridge that you can use to make your lists. Remember, whatever you do, do it in pairs. Now, Barbie and Russet, once you've told Kat what you need, I've got a job for each of you to do.

'Russet, we need to get the names and contact details of all the cleaners whom the men used to clear your belongings out of your homes. I have a feeling that Monique will have used my friend Maria's cleaning agency in the first place, but I doubt if Maria would have had enough people available at short notice to tackle five houses from her own workforce, because they will have been busy on their usual jobs. I will speak to Maria myself in a minute and find out what other agencies she might have recommended, and let you know. Would you then contact the agencies one by one and find out if they were employed on the job? Most importantly, we need to know what time the cleaners saw you leave, and when they left themselves. They will have submitted time sheets showing what hours they worked, and with any luck can confirm that the men – or, in Barbie's case, her husband's first wife and son – were alive when they left.'

'Got it,' said Russet.

Ellie said, 'You can use Thomas's study, which is at the far end of the corridor. He's going to be out this morning, so you can use one of the desks and his separate landline.'

Ellie made a mental note: Thomas had a part-time assistant and she herself had someone who came in to help her with the work of the trust. She would have to ring and tell them not to come in for a couple of days.

'Understood.' Russet put her cigarette away. 'I'll give you this morning, but if we don't get the all-clear by lunchtime, I'm off.'

Yes, and why shouldn't she? I have every sympathy for her wish to return home. If Lesley doesn't come up with the goods soon, then I'll cheer Russet on her way.

Ellie tackled Barbie next. 'Now, Barbie, if the police investigate Walt's death, I think they'll also want to take another look at Bunny's. It would be helpful if you could cast your mind back to the days before your husband died. Can you make a list of who might have had access to Bunny's pills then?'

Barbie blinked. 'You're assuming someone came to the house and deliberately mixed up his pills?' She swallowed. 'It's terrible to think that that might have happened. I can hardly get my head round it.'

'I understand, but logically it's what must have happened.'

Would Barbie faint? No, she was not the fainting sort. She took a couple of deep breaths. Then said, 'Right, what happened that week, it all seems so long ago, before . . . before everything went wrong. I can't even remember what I did that week. But I understand what you're on about. I've got my diary on my smartphone, and I'll see what I can come up with.'

Ellie said, 'My study is halfway down the corridor on the left. I'll be there for a while, making phone calls. If you need me, you know where to find me.'

The women brightened up at the thought of action. Ellie took a quick dive into the freezer to see what they might be able to use for their next meal, threw one or two suggestions in Kat's direction and left the women making lists of what they needed to order from the shops.

Down the corridor she went, thinking that the first thing she must do was to prevent her secretary and Thomas's assistant from leaving their homes. Explanations would take time, so she must think what to say.

But here came Diana, leaving Ellie's study. 'Mother, what's your password? I need to use the Internet. And why haven't you phoned Gunnar yet? His office says you haven't been in touch today. You really are losing the plot!'

Ellie told herself to keep calm. Count to five, at least. She made it to three and said, 'Diana, I don't think you realize the seriousness of the situation.'

'Of course I do! I need to have a list of all the nurseries in the area. I intend to visit each one till I find my little boy and then—'

'Listen to me for once! Or, if you won't listen to me, listen to your friends. They are all in the kitchen, making plans, working out how to deal with this emergency. Walt's death has put—'

'So what! You've lost your sense of perspective. You're completely off your rocker. The sooner I get you to the doctor's the better. Three o'clock sharp this afternoon, remember. If you see that feeble husband of yours you'd better tell him to find another cushy berth. I'm not having him cluttering up the place when I take over.'

Ellie thought kindly of murder. It would solve the immediate problem so quickly. The only snag was that she didn't think she could physically strangle Diana, who was taller and probably a lot stronger than she was. Moreover, if Ellie hit Diana, Diana might well hit back.

Restraining herself, Ellie said, 'I need to know something. The five men formed a group which met for social reasons, but also for business. Do you happen to know what that business was?'

'Oh, that! They thought I didn't know, but of course I found out. Evan thinks I can't access his laptop. Fool! He writes the password down on the back of the calendar in the sitting room every time he changes it. The men formed a company to buy a rundown shopping street near the town hall.'

'That's scheduled for rebuilding, isn't it? There was something in the local papers about it only last week. The development company had put in plans to build five tower blocks with shops beneath, and the council turned the plans down.'

'Of course. It wasn't a serious plan. The men knew it wouldn't be passed.'

'Then what are they on about? They're not developers, are they?'

'No, of course they're not.' Diana sighed. 'I wouldn't have expected you to understand, Mother. It's business and you've never been any good at figures, have you? In words of one syllable, they're holding on to the site until the price rises, when they'll sell out and make a nice profit. Get it?'

Ellie thought of saying that it was immoral but didn't. Diana wouldn't agree. Instead Ellie said, 'You've invested in it?'

'Naturally. At first, I couldn't think how, and then I thought that Rupert, the skinflint, might be wanting to hedge his bets so I asked my stockbroker to see if he'd sell some of his shares to an anonymous buyer and he was only too anxious to do so. He thinks of himself as a clever businessman, outwitting all comers, but in reality he lacks the nerve to play with the big boys.'

'Do the other men know that Rupert has been selling off some of his shares?'

A shrug. 'I have no idea. That's their business.'

'Diana, why did you invite your friends to come here? You must have had a reason. Is it something to do with their husbands' secretive financial dealings? In your rage at being thrown out, did you plan to get back at Evan by warning the others that in a divorce they should look out for hidden assets?'

Diana opened her mouth and closed it again. 'I don't know what you're talking about.'

'Yes, you do. That's exactly what you thought at first, but now you've changed your mind. You've hardly spoken to them since they arrived. Do you think you'll get better terms from Evan in a divorce if you promise not to reveal what you know to the other wives?'

'What an imagination you have.' Diana smiled to herself, which meant that that was precisely what she was planning to do. 'Now, if you don't mind, I need to get on your computer and find out what other nurseries they may have put my son into.'

'Where's your laptop?'

'Unfortunately, I left it at work.'

'And your phone? Haven't you one of those all singing, all dancing affairs?'

'Yes, but it's easier to use a computer.'

'Tough,' said Ellie. 'I need my computer myself this morning.' She brushed past her daughter into the study, closed the door and put a chair under the door handle to deter intruders.

Now, the phone. First, her secretary, then Thomas's assistant.

She told both there'd been a domestic problem which would have to be sorted out before normal business was resumed. She said she'd ring them later that day or early tomorrow to see when they should come in again. She spared a thought for Thomas, trying to find another printer for the magazine. Oh dear, oh dear. But he could manage it, if anyone could.

Finally, she got down to her own list.

Her call to Lesley on her mobile went to voicemail. Ellie left a message. She looked at her watch. Russet intended to leave at lunchtime. How long could Ellie keep her here?

Monique answered the phone at Evan's house. Ellie listened for a child's voice in the background but didn't hear it. 'Monique, it's Ellie Quicke here.'

Monique was amused. 'I understand you've taken in the refugees.'

'Ah. You've been talking to Terry? Yes, I have them here. There have been some interesting developments and I think we should talk. Shall I come over to you, or will you come to me?'

'I see no necessity for us to meet. Nothing has changed since yesterday.'

'Walt died.'

'So I hear. A heart attack. Distressing. I never knew him. So what?'

'It might not have been a heart attack. There's to be an autopsy. The police have the emails and are considering whether to take action or not.'

'Don't tell me you've involved the police!' A note of alarm for the first time.

'Looking back, don't you think you ought to have done so if you had suspected foul play after Bunny died? You didn't, which means you don't really think there was anything sinister about Bunny's death. Instead you used the emails as blackmail to get rid of wives who were surplus to requirements. *You* may have sat on whatever doubts you had about Bunny's death, but I am not prepared to do so. I repeat, this matter is now in the hands of the police.'

'I certainly didn't think it was serious enough to warrant . . . Oh, this is ridiculous! I'm sure the police will dismiss your suspicions out of hand.'

'You admit you didn't take the emails seriously, but that you used them to get Diana out of Evan's life. And, incidentally, to end the marriages of their friends? You didn't care who you hurt, did you?'

A long silence. Finally, 'I suppose you could look at it that way. It is true I was thinking mostly of Diana but as soon as the other men realized Evan was going to get rid of her, they all jumped in and said they wanted their wives out, too.'

Did the husbands have an ulterior motive? If they could divorce their wives before the truth came out about the secret development deal, they'd be quids in.

Ellie tried another tack. 'Diana's worried that Evan will forget his dentist's appointment, and can you remind him that he needs to have his warfarin levels checked?'

'You're mistaken if you think I'm going to nursemaid him.'

'He needs someone to look after him.'

A pause. 'It's true that I hadn't thought of moving in for more than a few hours. It's true that he does seem to expect . . . But that's nonsense, of course. I have my own life to lead.'

'Of course you do.'

'I must admit I hadn't taken the little boy's attachment to his mother into consideration.'

Ellie told herself not to panic. 'He's not ill, is he? Diana's been searching for him all over the place.'

'He's all right, but he is missing her. Well, he's been playing up a bit. He's rejected his favourite toy because his new nanny put it into the washing machine. Apparently it doesn't smell right now. They go a lot by smell at that age, don't they? None of us got much sleep last night – he was grizzling and his nanny had to walk him up and down in his buggy for hours. He's fast asleep now and she's fit for nothing this morning. Evan says he'll soon settle down.'

'Could you bring the boy over here? We usually have him a couple of times a week. You could let him stay with Diana for a few hours.'

'No. She'd kidnap him, take him off to the Outer Hebrides.'

Ellie had to admit Monique had a point there. 'Well, I'd like you to come over and talk to the women. We've discovered that they all have alibis for Walt's death.'

'You think that changes things? No, no. Walt's death was due to a heart attack.'

'Maybe it was. Maybe it wasn't. Don't you think the timing is significant? Two of the group have died within a fortnight in the ways suggested by the emails. Doesn't that make you wonder who's next? You said Evan wasn't well. What are the odds on his meeting with an accident of some kind in the next week or so?'

'That's absurd. Are you really suggesting that—?'

'Walt's death is also suspicious? Yes, I am. Will it be Terry next, or Rupert? I'll expect you in about an hour, shall I?' Ellie rang off.

Next she phoned the office of the cleaning agency which she used, only to learn that her friend Maria was not working that day. However, Maria's second-in-command was happy to confirm that yes, they had been approached to do some removal of personal effects for a couple of clients and had managed to find enough cleaners who had been free that morning to cover two of the requests. And yes, they'd recommended a couple of other agencies who might have been able to help the client out at short notice.

Armed with her lists of agencies, Ellie went to the library where Barbie and Russet were settling down to work. Ellie briefed Russet on what she had learned so far. Barbie was muttering to herself. 'She came early that day, didn't she? Must check. I'd better ring her . . .'

Ellie returned to the phone in her own office. She braced herself. She had to ring Gunnar on behalf of Diana. Oh dear, Gunnar wouldn't work for nothing, and Ellie could see that funding Diana's divorce might well be a costly affair, especially if Evan were going to try to hide his assets. Then there was the complication of Diana being pregnant again.

Gunnar was in court again that day, and uncontactable. Ellie didn't know whether to be glad or sorry about that. It was a relief to be able to defer that particular problem, anyway.

She decided she'd better see how Trish and Kat were getting on in the kitchen. On the way there, she came across Diana pacing up and down the hall, phone to her ear. When she saw her mother coming, Diana turned away and disappeared into the sitting room, shutting the door firmly behind her.

So who was Diana phoning that she didn't want Ellie to know about?

Ellie shrugged. She had enough to concern her without that.

In the kitchen, Trish and Kat had their heads together over their lists.

Trish said, 'Mrs Quicke, we've made a list of things we need ourselves, mainly toiletries, and we've made a start on a list of foodstuffs we think you need. Would you like to cast your eye over what we've done and see if there's anything we've forgotten, or that you've already got? I'll use my credit card to pay for it, of course. Which supermarket do you favour?'

Ellie cast an eye and nodded. 'Susan usually orders for me from Waitrose. Get their earliest delivery slot.'

Kat was polishing glasses. 'I tell Trish that we will survive. She is not sure about that, but then her father rings and says to come over tomorrow and bring me, too. He is a good man, no?'

'He is,' said Trish, managing to smile.

Kat put her head on one side. 'Is that someone ringing a bell?'

Ellie hastened back to the hall, only to be beaten by Diana on her way to the door, saying, 'That's my car in the drive!'

It was indeed Diana's car. Monique got out of the driving seat stiffly, rescued her cane and plodded towards the house. Diana wrenched the back door of the car open to extract her little boy, who had been strapped into a child seat.

'Mummy!' cried the toddler, holding out his arms to Diana.

'My little precious!' Diana held him close. And then, 'Pooh, you smell! And you haven't washed today, have you? Give Mama a big kiss!'

'I did it,' little Evan said, with satisfaction. 'All over. Pooh and wee. Lots.'

Monique sidled her way up the step and into the hall. 'He refused to use his potty, he gave his nanny a bloody nose, and sicked his breakfast up. He's probably dehydrated and got a nappy rash. He takes after his father, doesn't he?'

Diana gave her son some smacking kisses. 'You're Mummy's little darling, aren't you, my pet? Let's take you upstairs and get you changed and clean, and then we'll have a nice boiled egg and soldiers and some milk.'

'Not egg. Biccy.'

Ellie knew who was going to win that tussle and it wasn't going to be Diana.

Diana carried the lad indoors and up the stairs. Russet and her belongings now occupied the room in which the little boy occasionally slept over, but Ellie also kept a change of clothing there for him. Diana would probably complain about Russet's things being there, but tough! She'd have to cope.

Monique plodded her way into the sitting room and seated herself, looking around to see what was what. 'Big house. A bit lonely for you on your own?'

'I've remarried. Thomas is out today. Also, I have a lodger. Thank you for bringing the boy over.'

'I'm not up to looking after toddlers at my age. His nanny's in bed with a migraine and his father needs looking after, rather than being able to look after someone else.'

'There's room for negotiation about Diana returning?'

'I didn't say that. Why did you summon me?'

'I'm concerned about what happens next. You haven't left your ex-husband alone, have you?'

Monique shook her head. 'His friend Terry is there. They're drowning their sorrows in drink while swapping stories about how glad they are to be rid of their wives.'

'And Rupert, the skinflint?'

'I understand he's courting a widow with a substantial fortune.' An acid tone of voice.

Ellie had to laugh. 'Oh, poor Kat. I hope the new woman in his life can cook, or he'll be comparing her to Kat all the time. You do understand why the men should not be left alone?'

'You think another husband is going to die soon? By rat poison, or drowning? Or from being overactive in bed? I can tell you, Evan's hardly up for that at the moment.'

'Talking of which,' said Ellie in her creamiest tone, 'I understand he was feeling particularly well eight or nine weeks ago.'

'What!' Monique caught on quickly. 'You mean . . .? Oh, my . . .!' An indrawn breath. 'That'll put the cat among the pigeons. Are you sure?'

'Diana is. Evan doesn't know. Would you like to tell him?

And at the same time remind him about his dentist appointment and to get his warfarin levels checked?'

Monique said, 'Grrr . . .!' but got out her phone.

Ellie said, 'I'll make us some coffee.' She fled, but didn't get as far as the kitchen, for in the corridor she came face-to-face with Russet.

'Mrs Quicke, I can't rest until I find out what's happening to—'

'Have you discovered which cleaners did which house?'

'Oh, yes. At least, I got the names of the agency who did my place and Diana's. I haven't got through to the others yet because . . . I'm sorry, Mrs Quicke, but I really can't concentrate properly on anything till—'

'Understood. Come into my study and we'll try Lesley at the police station again.'

Ellie's study was small, but Russet managed to pace up and down while Ellie tried to contact her friend, who was in a meeting and couldn't be interrupted. Ellie insisted her call was urgent and was told that a message to call Ellie would be taken into the room and given to Lesley.

Ellie put her phone down and said, 'Russet, I'm so sorry. There's not much more I can do. All I can say is that if you feel you have to go home – and I do understand that – then it really would be a good idea to take Barbie with you, and to keep her as long as you can.'

Russet said, 'Well, she's nowhere else to go and I must admit, I'll be glad of her company. I'll tell her, and we can start getting some of our things down and into the car. We may have to leave some stuff here till tomorrow, if you can bear it?'

'You're very welcome. I expect you'll be glad to get out of here and able to smoke again.' At which Russet managed a weak smile.

Ellie continued down the corridor and this time made it to the kitchen, where Kat and Trish were concentrating on the latter's laptop. The kitchen was as bright as a new pin.

Thank you, Kat.

'Coffee anyone?' Ellie put the kettle on. 'By the way, Barbie and Russet are leaving this morning. Russet is anxious to get back home.'

Trish looked bothered at this rearrangement of their plans, but Kat said, 'All the better. I am not able to make quiches without cheese, which we do not have. I will make up several big dishes when the supermarket delivers and what we do not eat will go in to freezer.'

'Excellent,' said Ellie, her attention drawn to her landline ringing in the hall. She sped back to get there as the caller was about to be transferred to voicemail. 'Yes? Lesley?'

'It is. I got your message. As you know, there's to be an autopsy on Walt, but no investigation until the results are in. What do you think about that?'

TWELVE

Tuesday late a.m.

Ellie let herself down on to the hall chair. There were angry voices from the landing above, where Diana was arguing with Russet. That was foreseeable, wasn't it? Russet's belongings were in little Evan's room, and they were getting in one another's way.

Barbie raised her voice, too. She was trying to get past them both to bring some of her stuff downstairs. There were still piles of luggage lying higgledy-piggledy all over the hall. Ellie wished she could close her eyes and wake up tomorrow and find the house her own again.

On the phone, Lesley sounded alarmed. 'Are you there, Ellie? Can you keep the women with you?'

'No. Russet is preparing to go back home now, and Barbie is going with her.'

'Um, yes. Russet. Well, I tried to find out why she hadn't been contacted about her husband's death and was told by a neighbour that Russet had walked out on her husband but had probably gone to stay with her brother, who lives out of town somewhere. The police traced him, but he said he didn't know where she could be found.'

'She's been in touch with her brother, but I suppose that must have been after the police phoned him. Why didn't he give the police my address?'

'I don't know. Perhaps he thought he was protecting her. Listen, Ellie. I've been told not to poke my nose in where it's not wanted. I can't take any official action. I can't talk to the women. And yet—'

'You think, as I do, that Walt's death is just too neat and that the matter does need investigating. Does it help that the women all have alibis for Walt's death?' Ellie crossed her fingers when she said this, because Diana didn't, did she?

Lesley sounded frustrated. 'If one or more of them didn't kill him, who did?'

'We-ell, I've discovered that the men formed a company to redevelop part of the town centre. They don't actually want to do the job themselves, so they lob in outline plans for developments which they are sure will be rejected and watch the value of the site rise with every month that passes. They think they're going to become multimillionaires when they sell. I'm wondering if, when they set up their company, they included a clause that if one partner dies, the others inherit his shares.'

Lesley drew in her breath. 'Two down and three to go. You think one of the men is killing the others off, inspired by the emails? If so, the killer must be annoyed with you for proving none of the wives could have done it.'

'True. Any other bright ideas?'

'Warn the men?'

'Yes, I'm trying to do that. Must go.'

Little Evan came stumping down the stairs, one step at a time, towing his mother along behind him by clutching at her skirt. He'd been washed and was clad in a clean T-shirt and dungarees.

Diana was smiling and frowning, both at once. 'Mother, the sooner Russet leaves, the better. It's impossible to see to little Evan while all her belongings are in his room.'

'Biccy!' said little Evan, single-minded as usual. He towed his mother across the hall and down the corridor to the kitchen.

Ellie followed him to make a cafetière of coffee and put cups, saucers, milk and some biscuits on a tray. Little Evan ignored everyone else to make for the biscuit tin, and when he found it empty, took a deep breath to yell his displeasure. Ellie handed him a biscuit from the tray and carried the coffee things to the sitting room.

Monique was still there, talking into her phone.

Little Evan followed, towing his mother along. He ignored Monique to make for the box of toys which Ellie kept under the table for him to play with. Now he had a problem. He needed a free hand to play with the Lego, but he wasn't letting go of his mother, not for an instant. He solved that problem by cramming the biscuit into his mouth, showering crumbs around, to free himself for the next task. Diana wiped around his mouth with a tissue, but dutifully sat down on the floor beside him while he emptied the contents of the play box on to the carpet. Monique and Diana politely ignored one another.

Ellie settled herself down and poured coffee out for the three of them. From the hall drifted the sounds of luggage being bumped and hauled down the stairs and taken outside.

Little Evan tossed his Lego here and there, as if he were splashing water around in the bath. He laid himself across his mother's lap and fell asleep. Deeply asleep. Well, he'd been up all night, hadn't he? And ensured that the rest of his household hadn't had any sleep, either?

Diana stroked his hair off his forehead. 'Poor little mite.'

Ellie decided to throw a spanner into the works. 'Monique, have you invested in Evan's development company?'

Monique shifted in her seat and looked alert. 'What company?' She hadn't known about it.

Ellie said, 'Diana, perhaps you'd like to explain it to Monique?'

Diana frowned, but did as she was told. 'The men have gone into partnership to develop a parcel of land behind the cinema in the town centre.'

Monique blinked. 'A limited company?'

'Yes. A hundred shares each.'

'But the amount of capital they'd need for that sort of project . . .!'

'They mortgaged their houses and they borrowed.'

'How do you know this?'

'Evan used to keep on top of business affairs, but he hardly ever goes into the agency nowadays. He left it to me to run, saying he was ready to retire, but I knew he was up to something because the men kept getting into corners and sniggering, saying things like, "The little women don't need to know anything". So I did a little digging here and there, looked at his emails, and so on. It's a huge project.'

Monique breathed out slowly. 'Their combined ages are—'

'Quite. They're past it but still fancy they know how to make money in a big way. I wanted in. I thought Rupert would be the weakest link as he's always so worried about cash flow, and I was right. He'd been discreetly trying to dispose of some of his shares, so I bought them.'

'The idiots!' said Monique. 'They could lose everything!'

'Every now and then their tame architect produces a set of plans which fits the bill more or less, but which are so extravagant that they are bound to fail. With every month that passes the value of the land rises. I'm counting on the sale making me a tidy profit when it eventually goes through.'

Monique was adding it up. 'You think they've signed papers leaving their shares to one another in the event of a death? You think one of them is killing the others off, in order to get control of the whole company? First Bunny—'

'His death might or might not be murder. He could well have mixed his pills up.'

'And Walt.'

Ellie said, 'There's to be an autopsy. If he died of a heart attack, then nothing more will happen. If he was pushed, then the police will rethink.'

Monique sipped coffee. Her hand trembled. 'Mrs Quicke, was that why you wanted Evan to have company today? You think he's next for a trip to the crematorium?'

Ellie said, 'He's the partner in the poorest health.'

Monique rattled her cup into its saucer. 'Evan and I have known one another all our adult lives. I'm fond of him in a way, even if he is something left over from the last century.'

Diana said, 'Did he make his dentist appointment? He's been grumbling about a loose filling for ages but getting him there is always a struggle.'

'I am not his keeper,' said Monique.

Diana sighed. 'I don't suppose the office managed to clinch that sale I was working on. I've spent so much time on it, but . . .' She shrugged.

Is Diana trying to make Monique see that she was a good wife to Evan? And that her son loves her dearly? Is she plotting to get Evan to take her back? Wonders will never cease. But it would be a good solution to her part in this mess.

Monique seemed to have reached the same conclusion. 'Diana, your mother tells me you are expecting again. Is the child Evan's?'

'I've never looked at another man since I met him.'

Monique wanted to be sure. 'How far along are you?'

'Nine weeks. He was feeling raunchy on the night before his birthday. He wasn't capable of anything on the actual day, mind you. I remember he returned from the golf club with Bunny in the early hours. Both of them pie-eyed.'

Monique probed further. 'You've not told him about the baby?'

'No, because I've had a couple of misses this last year. I wasn't sure I could carry another baby to term and I wanted to be well on the way before I said anything. I was going to wait till I had the three-month scan to be sure, but Mother forced my hand.'

Monique digested this. 'So, do you want a divorce?'

'Not particularly. We rubbed along well enough and once I've taken on a job, I like to see it through.'

Monique manoeuvred herself upright. 'I came in your car because mine doesn't have a child seat in it. A mistake, because the controls are all wrong for me and it's put my back out again. I'll leave your car and the boy here for the time being and take a cab back. Thank you for the coffee, Mrs Quicke. Will you call a cab for me? I'll wait for it in the hall.'

Monique wanted a word in private?

The piles of luggage in the hall had changed yet again. Some piles had diminished, others had reshaped themselves. The front door was open and letting in cold air, but someone had propped it ajar so that they could ferry luggage out to Russet's car.

Monique turfed a tote bag off the hall chair and seated herself on it with the air of one prepared to chat.

Ellie closed the door to the sitting room and used the landline in the hall to call a cab. Barbie bustled down the stairs, bumping a suitcase on wheels behind her. She glanced at Monique, didn't recognize her and said to Ellie, 'We're nearly there. You'll be glad to see the back of us.'

'Not at all,' said Ellie, lying through her teeth. 'By the way, how did you get on with the list of visitors to your house in the week before Bunny died?'

'I made a start. It would be easier if I had Bunny's diary. I don't honestly think there's anything in your idea that someone from outside tampered with his pills. Why should they? Anyway, I can't think about that now. I've packed my stuff up again, but everything's in such a muddle that I may have to leave some things here till tomorrow, if you don't mind.' She took her suitcase outside.

Monique said, 'The men used me to get rid of their wives for them.'

'They used the emails as an excuse. They liked the thought of getting rid of wives who were past their sell-by date but wouldn't have done anything about it if you hadn't taken a hand in the game.'

'Except for Terry,' said Monique. 'From listening to him ranting away to Evan, I think he had a different motive. He thought Trish was playing away—'

'Ridiculous. She's a nice girl and faithful. He's the jealous type and his jealousy has made him abusive. He made a mistake yesterday when he hit her a little harder than usual because for once she hit him back. Now he doesn't know whether he's coming or going.'

Russet re-entered the hall, looking flustered. She glanced at Monique, and then turned to Ellie. 'Mrs Quicke; there you are. We're about ready to go but we can't get both Barbie's and my stuff in my car and I'm afraid we've had to leave some of our things in your hall. My brother should be arriving sometime this afternoon. Perhaps he could come round and collect the rest of my stuff then? And what's left of Barbie's, too?'

Monique said, 'Mrs Quicke has ordered a taxi for me. Take that as well. I'll pay. I owe you one. Mrs Quicke can order me another.'

Russet looked even more flustered. 'I'm afraid I . . .?'

Ellie introduced them. 'Russet, I don't think you've met

Monique. She's Evan first wife, long divorced. Evan used her administrative abilities to organize your expulsion and that of your friends. The men used her and she wishes to make amends. You can pack the taxi with the rest of your luggage and it can follow you home.'

Barbie had come in behind Russet and heard that. Barbie had excellent manners. 'You are Monique? I don't think we've ever met, but Evan has mentioned you now and then. He thinks a lot of you, doesn't he? A taxi has just arrived outside. If we can use that, too . . .? Well, thank you.'

'Don't thank me,' said Monique. 'Thank Mrs Quicke for making me see what a fool I've been. I'm sorry I've caused you so much trouble.'

'Strangely enough,' said Barbie, 'you did us a favour. If you hadn't arranged for us to leave, we'd all have been sitting at home on our own when Walt died. Since we were thrown out we were all together when it happened and that gives us an alibi for his death.'

'We really do appreciate everything Mrs Quicke has done for us,' said Russet.

Barbie added, 'True. I don't know what we'd have done without her.'

Trish and Kat came into the hall, both eager to help, both wanting to kiss and hug their friends and promise to keep in touch, as tomorrow they'd be scattered all over the place. There was considerable confusion about which piece of luggage belonged to which woman, but finally Barbie and Russet thought they had everything of theirs. Ellie assured them that if anything had been left behind, she would see that it was kept for them. Finally, Russet drove off in her own car, with Barbie following behind in the taxi.

Quiet descended. The hall was still strewn with packages, but the piles were less high than before. Kat started up the stairs, saying she'd strip the beds in the rooms Barbie and Russet had used and clean them. Trish retreated to the kitchen, saying she must phone her parents.

Ellie and Monique exchanged looks of relief, and Ellie ordered another taxi.

While they waited for it, Monique said, 'These women are

not fools. They're bound to start wondering who knocked Walt and Bunny off soon. I don't think it's Evan.'

'No. He's too . . . too . . .'

Monique snorted. 'Ineffective? Past it? Drink-sodden?'

'It's not Terry. I've observed him acting out. He's all bluster and no bottom. I can imagine him taking a swipe at someone in a temper, but Bunny's death required forward planning. It was premeditated. Not sure about Walt's. That might have been impulse.'

'You think it's Kat's husband, Rupert, who's doing it, then? Have you met the man?'

Ellie shook her head.

Monique said, 'A small-minded man of limited abilities. He inherited a great deal of money without any idea of how to deal with it, while being parsimonious in his private life. He has a pointed nose and several chins. His eyes are set too close together. I used to laugh when people said that close-set eyes were a sign of untrustworthiness, but he's got them all right. On the other hand, I've been wrong about everything once, and I could be wrong about him, too.'

'There's no alternative, is there? It must be Rupert. Perhaps only one of the deaths was an accident and the other was murder. Can you warn Evan and Terry, try to get them to take precautions? I can't do any more. We have to wait on the autopsy and see what the police want to do next.'

A taxi drew up outside and tooted. Monique plodded out, leaning on her stick. 'I'll be glad to sleep in my own bed tonight.'

Ellie accompanied her outside. 'You're leaving Evan on his own?'

'I'm not acting as his nurse. If I've read her aright, that new nanny of his doesn't want to sleep in an old man's bed. Let Evan get Diana back for that. She's up to his weight and, as you've kindly arranged for me to observe, she's a good mother to the little boy. I'm going home. Every bone in my body is complaining and I'm out of patience with the lot of them.'

Ellie helped Monique into the taxi. 'What will I do if Evan comes round wanting his son back?'

Monique settled herself. 'He's had one night of broken sleep. He's not going to endanger another by demanding his son back, is he? Driver . . .!' And she gave him the address.

As the taxi bore her away, a motorcyclist roared into the drive and its driver, clad in black leather, cut the engine. Susan's fiancé, Rafael, took off his helmet and shook back his hair. 'What's up?'

'I'm delighted to see you,' said Ellie. 'Russet has gone back home. Barbie has gone with her. Trish is talking to her parents about going to them tomorrow and taking Kat with her. Kat is stripping bedrooms upstairs. The cab you saw leaving took Monique, that's Evan's first wife, away. She's brought his and Diana's little son who has been creating havoc at home and is now asleep on his mother's lap in the sitting room. Oh yes, and the police won't do anything until after the autopsy on Walt, and possibly not even then.'

'I've been thinking. If the women were all together when Walt died and his death was murder, then whodunit?'

'Monique thinks it must be Kat's skinflint husband, Rupert, because his eyes are set too close together. No, I'm joking. She thinks that it's Rupert because Evan's too old and Terry too volatile.'

Rafael took a couple of packages out of the box on the back of his motorcycle. 'I noticed you have a fire alarm but the batteries seemed to be getting towards the end of their lives. I hope you don't mind, but I took the liberty of buying some more for you. As insurance, you might say.'

She gave him an old-fashioned look. 'Don't flannel me, young man. Why have you decided to do that today of all days?'

'This is a big house, and Susan is on the top floor with no fire escape. I'll replace the batteries now, if you agree. And see if anything else occurs to me. Poison isn't likely since you get your food from the supermarket. Drowning is out because you haven't a pond or a swimming pool. So fire is a possibility.'

Ellie took a deep breath. 'You think that whoever killed those two men will turn his attention to me because I took the women in?'

'It's a thought.'

'Two of the women have gone already.'

'Does the murderer know that?'

'I could get Kat to tell him.'

'You think it's Rupert, then? Have you met him? No?' He rubbed his chin, which sported the usual designer stubble. 'Suppose it's not him?'

Did Rafael think it was Evan or Terry? Ellie thought about that. 'You think it's Terry, because he threatened to kill his dogs?'

'I think he can't control his temper. If you agree, I propose to go round the house now checking that all the windows and doors lock as they should. All precautions should be taken, right? I wouldn't mind a sandwich for lunch, if you think you can manage it. Oh, and if you can't pay the bills for the little extras that I've bought, I'll be only too happy to lend you some money.'

That was provocative, wasn't it? He knew very well that Ellie had a comfortable rainy-day reserve, but he had made her laugh, which surely had been his intention. 'Thank you, Rafael. Have you any other crumbs of comfort to offer?'

He ushered her inside and shut the front door behind them. Eyeing the odd piles of luggage which still littered the hall, he said, 'Have you checked who's still got keys to this house?'

'Diana took my spare keys. The others didn't have any.'

'Are you sure about that?'

Now, there's a nasty thought!

THIRTEEN

Tuesday noon.

Ellie tried to think. 'Thomas has a key, Diana took my spare and I have a key in my handbag.'

'Mrs Quicke, where did you leave your handbag? Would you like to make sure you still have your key?'

'You mean, someone might have lifted it?' She cast a distracted look around. 'I left my bag here in the hall, didn't I? Or perhaps . . . You're right, I might have left it anywhere.' She tapped on the door to the sitting room before entering. Little Evan might still be asleep on Diana's lap. But no, he was awake, sort of. Diana was holding him upright, but he was rubbing his eyes and going limp. He wanted to go back to sleep, didn't he?

Diana said, 'I can't let him sleep any longer, or he won't last the night through tonight. I'd better take him for a walk.'

Ellie looked around for her bag, which was nowhere to be seen. 'Monique left you your car, so you could take him to the park for a while. Russet has gone back home, and Kat is cleaning the room she used, so you might be able to put little Evan down to sleep in his own bed in a while. Have you seen my handbag?'

Diana got to her feet with an effort. Little Evan was grizzling. Last night's lack of sleep was definitely catching up with him. 'I haven't seen it. Can your Susan person find Evan something to eat?'

Ellie set her teeth. Diana knew very well that Susan had gone off to uni. She started to say, 'No, and . . .' But Diana was already on her way out to the kitchen with her son and wasn't listening. Ah, her handbag! Ellie pounced. It had ended up under the high-backed chair in which she usually sat. The bag was open. Her keys? Yes, they were there. Thank goodness for that.

She found Rafael in the hall on a stepladder, replacing the battery in her smoke alarm.

She said, 'My keys are still here, but I've just remembered I'm out of cash.'

'Not to worry. How much do you want? Fifty? A hundred? I'll ask Susan to bring some in for you and you can repay her tomorrow. I'm planning to stop over again tonight and bolt the door for you when everyone's going to bed. All right?'

'You're quite mad. I'm sure it's not necessary. But, I love you, Rafael.'

'So you should, Mrs Quicke. I am a very lovable person, as Susan constantly assures me. Now, is there going to be a sandwich for me at any time? I'm famished.'

Lunch was a subdued affair.

Kat managed to produce a cottage pie by taking some frozen mince from the freezer, cooking it with onions and herbs and topping it off with the last of the potatoes. There was ice cream for afters. Little Evan grizzled but managed to eat his portion without spreading too much of it around and on himself. Trish was on the phone most of the time, first arranging her return to her parents' home on the morrow, and then updating her sister on what was happening.

Rafael bolted down a large portion and disappeared on his motorbike, saying he'd be back in a jiffy.

Kat was puffy-eyed but said she was fine. She'd turned out the room Russet had slept in so that Diana could have it for her little boy that night. Kat said she'd tackle the end room – Barbie's – that afternoon.

Diana devoted herself to little Evan, taking little part in the arrangements which Trish and Kat were making. After lunch, Diana took her son off to the park. The house seemed blessedly quiet in his absence, although there were still a lot of adults around.

Released from hostess duties, Ellie went upstairs and let herself sink down on to her bed. She would allow herself half an hour's relaxation and try to ignore the problems that kept edging into her mind. Diana and Evan. Trish and Kat. The husbands throwing their wives out and now, perhaps, regretting it. In spite of all her anxieties, she fell asleep.

She woke with a start when someone rang the front doorbell. Surely someone else would answer it? But no one did. It rang again. And again.

Feeling grumpy and bleary-eyed, she stumbled down the stairs and opened the front door to find a complete stranger standing in the porch.

Pointed nose, double chin and eyes set too close together. This must be Rupert, the skinflint who had married Kat to save himself her wages. He was wearing expensive casual clothes, so he didn't stint when it came to buying things for himself, did he?

'I suppose you're Mrs Quicke.' He pushed her back into the hall and stepped in himself. 'Where are you hiding her?'

'Your wife?'

'That thief. She's gone off with my grandfather's gold watch. I suppose she thought she'd pawn it and that I wouldn't miss it for some time. Well, she's wrong about that. It was the first thing I thought of this morning. I've let her live a life of luxury, far beyond anything she could ever have hoped for, and look what's happened! I'm having the law on her!'

Ellie tried to shake herself awake. 'What on earth are you talking about?'

'You're harbouring a thief, that's what! It's no good pretending innocence. It doesn't wash with me!'

'You're missing some item of value and you think Kat might have it with her? I'll ask her, shall I?'

'Not so fast! I don't want you warning her that I'm here, giving her time to hide it someplace. I need to search her luggage, and I need you as a witness so that when we find it, she won't be able to deny she had it. Where is she?'

He started towards the stairs. Ellie caught him back. 'What are you doing? You can't barge into someone else's house and demand to search it unless you are a police officer and have a warrant. You don't, do you?'

'I can get one if I need to.' He was huffing and puffing. A classic case of high blood pressure. 'Stand aside, woman, and let me search for my property!'

There was a disturbance on the landing. Trish and Kat came from down the corridor to the bedrooms, carrying the bed linen Barbie had slept in and a box of cleaning materials.

'What's up?' said Trish. 'Oh, it's Rupert. Have you come to see Kat?'

Kat stripped off her rubber gloves. 'I am here, Rupert.'

Rupert pushed past Ellie to climb the stairs, holding on to the banister. 'You crazy cow! I might have known you'd repay my kindness by stealing from me. Where are your cases, eh?'

'Upstairs, on the top floor,' said Kat, bewildered but not afraid. 'You think I have taken something from your house? I tell you, no. I would not. If something is missing then it is not with me. Why you not look to the cleaners you paid yesterday, the ones who packed up my things?'

He took no notice of that, but said, 'Bluster all you like. When I've found what you have taken, I am informing the police. They will arrest you and send you to prison. And, when you have served your sentence, they will deport you back to the farm.'

Trish said, 'Kat wouldn't steal, Rupert. You must be mistaken.'

'Which room are you in? Where have you hidden your cases?'

Kat put her cleaning things down. 'I have taken nothing. I have hidden nothing.' She looked worried. She twisted her hands one within another. 'I tell the truth.'

'Ha!' said Rupert. 'Show me!'

Ellie thought she could see where this was going, and she didn't like it one bit. The man was very sure of himself, which meant that he really thought Kat had something of his, while on the other hand, Ellie was equally sure that Kat wouldn't have stolen anything.

Rupert pulled open the master bedroom door. 'In here?'

'No, no.' Kat was also thinking ahead and not liking her thoughts. 'I am upstairs again. This way.'

'Don't show him!' said Trish.

Too late. Kat threw open the door to the small staircase which went to the top floor and led the way up. The others followed her. Ellie wondered where she'd left her mobile phone. Thomas would have known how to deal with this, but she didn't.

'This is the room,' said Kat, opening the door to Susan's spare room.

'At last!' Rupert pushed past her. It was not a large room but they all managed to pile in.

Kat had arrived with two suitcases, neither of them new. The black one she had placed on a chair by the bed, and the blue one was on the floor. The black one was open, revealing a small pile of underwear and ditto of cheap dresses. Rupert ignored the black one to heave the blue case on to the neatly made bed and throw it open, revealing a couple of winter jackets and some warm tops.

Rupert upended the contents of the blue suitcase on to the bed and felt around the suitcase lining till he found a hidden pocket at one side. 'There it is!' He held up an antique gold case watch for them all to see. 'I told you so!'

Kat gasped. 'I never see that before! That is not my case. That is your case that you lend me to take away my things. I not know there is hiding place there.'

'Of course you did!' said Rupert, grinning. 'Your friends are witnesses that I found my missing watch in your suitcase.'

Trish said, 'Hang about. That's not—'

Ellie intervened. 'Rupert, we are witnesses to the fact that you knew exactly where your property was to be found, that you knew in which of two suitcases it had been hidden, and that you went straight to it. If you try to make out that Kat stole your watch then you must be prepared for us to say that, on the contrary, it looked as if you planted the watch there yourself.'

His voice squeaked, 'Ridiculous!' He dabbed at perspiration with his handkerchief.

Kat had sunk on to a chair. She began to rock. 'I would not . . . Not ever . . . No, no!'

Trish put her arm around Kat. 'Of course you didn't. You didn't pack for yourself, did you? No, he got someone else to do that for you. He put that watch in there himself.'

'Why would I do that?' He dabbed at his forehead again.

Ellie said, 'It's all about money, isn't it, Rupert? You've kept it a secret that you and your friends formed a company to develop part of the town centre, and now that scheme is coming to fruition you are getting rid of your wives so that you don't have to share any of the profits with them.'

Rupert gasped, 'You know nothing about it!' His chest swelled and he had gone red in the face. A bantam pretending to be a cockerel. 'You know nothing! None of you know anything. Women cannot be expected to understand high finance. All women do is look out for a man to keep them. They say they want to care for a man but what they mean is that they want him to smother them with furs and jewellery and expensive cars and holidays abroad. A man has to be aware that women are only out for what they can get and act accordingly.'

Kat wrung her hands. 'But Rupert, I have never asked for such things.'

'I know your sort. You were biding your time, trying to fool me into thinking you had my best interests at heart while you were cooking the books and stealing money from the housekeeping. You thought I would overlook your thefts but that's where you are wrong. I have consulted the police . . .'

Poor Kat looked as if she were going to faint.

'And they told me it would not be easy to prosecute for a few pounds, but now I have proof that you stole my grandfather's watch they will take action, just you wait and see!'

Kat began to sob. 'Oh, oh! I am going to prison!'

Trish said, 'Nonsense, Kat. Rupert, what a nasty little man you are. You make use of Kat to bring down your household bills and throw her out when you think you can make a better match financially. You were worried that she might demand alimony, so you rigged this stunt to ensure she wouldn't ask for what is hers by right. You make me sick!'

'Is she right, Rupert?' Kat could hardly believe it. 'You would do that to me?'

Rupert made a gobbling sound, his eyes bulging.

Kat took a deep breath. Her bosom swelled. From being a poor downtrodden slave, she turned into a war-like Valkyrie. She began to make a low, moaning noise, which grew and climbed the scale to end in a shriek.

Ellie put her hands over her ears.

Kat grasped Rupert by his upper arms and shook him. 'You . . . rat's bottom! You . . .' Here she slipped into her native language.

Ellie did not know the words, but she knew very well what they meant.

Kat let go of Rupert all of a sudden. He stumbled and fell awkwardly, knocking the bedside lamp over.

'Ha!' Kat brushed her hands one against the other. She spoke some more words in her own language, ending up with, 'You watch! I take you to the cleaners!'

'By dose!' Rupert struggled to his feet, trying to get away from Kat, holding on to his face. Blood spurted through his fingers.

Kat said, 'Hah!' again. 'He has nosebleed? Always he has the nosebleed. But now I do not wash and clean his clothes for him. He must do it himself! So!'

Rupert deflated.

Kat waved her arm. 'Take him away! I do not wish him in my room.'

Trish giggled, hanging on to the end of the bed.

Ellie was torn between wanting to kick Rupert down the stairs – that is, if she could have managed it in her tight skirt – and thinking it was more than time this disgraceful scene was brought to a satisfactory conclusion. She helped Rupert out of the room by the simple process of hauling on his jacket. 'Come on downstairs and let me wash your face.'

'She hit be!'

'No, she didn't. Don't you try that on with me. We all saw you fall. Come on, another set of stairs. Try not to bleed all over the place. That's it, now. Across the hall and into the kitchen and sit down. Now, tip your head back.'

She ran a clean tea towel under the tap, wrung it out and handed it to Rupert to put over his nose. She tore off some kitchen towel and cleaned up his hands and face. There was nothing she could do about the blood on his shirt. He'd dripped all the way down his jacket. Oh, well. He'd have to take it to the dry-cleaners himself. Kat wasn't going to do it for him.

Ellie put the kettle on and made herself a cup of tea while Rupert snuffled away, keening to himself. She looked at the clock. It was getting on for teatime. Well, she wasn't going to feed or water Rupert. She drank her tea, watching him as he cautiously removed the towel from his face and checked that the bleeding had stopped. He was reviving, slowly. Watching her, wondering how he could take advantage of her having been kind to him.

Not a nice man. But was he a murderer? He didn't look like one, but what does a murderer look like?

Kat stormed into the room, the top buttons of her blouse undone and her shoulder-length hair, freed from its band, streaming behind her. She dumped a folded pair of socks on Rupert's lap. 'I go through my luggage and I find these, which are yours! I want nothing of yours! I spit on you!' She reared her head back to do so.

Ellie intervened. 'No, Kat. Don't give him the chance to say you attacked him.'

'He do worse to me!'

Ellie edged Kat towards the door. 'Yes, but that's not the way to get back at him. Leave it to me, will you?'

Kat hesitated, looking over Ellie's shoulder at Rupert. He cringed in his chair. Kat tossed her head and marched out.

Rupert gasped, 'I could do with a drink.'

'Tea, coffee or water?'

'Haven't you a decent whisky?'

'No.' She made him a cup of tea and placed it on the table before him.

His eyes went to and fro. 'You are a witness that she threatened me. She and that silly cow, Trish. Where are the other two hags, eh? I heard you had taken in the lot. Much good that may do you.'

'Russet has gone back home, and Barbie is staying with her for a while.'

'That is indecent! Russet rejoicing so soon after Walt's death? They have no idea of how to behave. As for Kat . . .!'

Ellie said, 'Russet is not rejoicing. She is distressed about Walt's death, and Barbie is helping her keep sane at this difficult time. As for Kat, I like and respect her. She is an excellent cook and a thrifty housekeeper. She has looked after you well. You will miss her.'

'Harrumph!' His colour was rapidly getting back to its normal pasty hue. He wasn't much of a one for exercise, was he?

'You were lucky to find her, though it wasn't so lucky for her. Now, let us look on the bright side – I am sure she will find a position where she will be appreciated and paid a good wage. There will be alimony when you divorce, of course.'

He bleated, 'She stole from me.'

'Nonsense. You planted that watch in her luggage. I wonder how much maintenance she can ask for when she divorces you? Half your worldly goods? That's the usual, isn't it?'

'No, no!'

'I understand you have another marital prospect in sight – someone with money of her own. Will she be as good a cook and housekeeper as Kat? Will she look after you as Kat has done?'

He tried to dab his lips with his hankie, but it was sodden with blood.

Ellie took the hankie off him, rinsed the blood off under the tap and handed him the roll of paper towel instead. Crossing her fingers, she said, 'I don't think you are a bad man or unkind. This has all got out of hand, hasn't it? I do understand that Bunny's death was upsetting, but you are probably regretting the day you took the emails to Evan and blew the whole thing up out of proportion. It wasn't you who suggested that you use the emails to get rid of your wives, was it?'

The rabbit ran for cover. 'No, no. Far from it. I was quite taken aback. But when the others . . . You must admit that it was enough to frighten anyone.'

'You didn't kill Bunny, did you?'

'Of course not!'

Ellie believed him. 'You didn't kill Walt, either, did you?'

'Walt?' He stared at her, aghast.

'You do know that Walt died yesterday afternoon?'

'Why, yes. But he wasn't *killed*, was he? I mean, he had a heart attack, didn't he?'

'Who told you that?'

'Evan, of course. Or was it Terry? They rang me. I was in a meeting. I have finger in many pies, and I attend board meetings of various businesses on a regular basis.' This reminder of his importance served to stiffen his back, and with returning confidence he began to preen. 'I am something of an entrepreneur, you know. I sniff out business opportunities and invest where appropriate. It is a skill I inherited from my father and from his father before him. You can ask anyone. They will tell you that Rupert has the Midas touch in business matters.'

'So you were in a meeting when Evan rang you with the news about Walt?'

'Yes, indeed. In the City. I didn't take the call until the meeting was over. I am strict about that. Mobile phones must all be switched off for the duration of the meeting. Nothing should be allowed to interrupt our proceedings. I am noted for this.'

'I'm sure you are. So it was Evan who rang you? Or Terry?'

'Both. They left messages, which I took on my way home in the car. I use a chauffeur-driven car when I attend meetings. It is false economy to travel by public transport.'

Ellie thought of Kat walking to a distant supermarket to save the bus fare, and she hardened her heart against this monstrous little man.

He twisted round in his chair. 'Is there a mirror? What do I look like? Have you cleaned off all the blood?'

To be truthful, he looked a mess. She said, 'I'll show you to the downstairs toilet in a minute.' While she had him at her disposal, so to speak, she might as well tie up a loose end or two. 'As a matter of interest, when did you discover the emails on your laptop? I suppose it was some time after Bunny's death?'

He stood up, fussing with his collar. 'No, no. Long before that. We had a good laugh when I first discovered them. Fenella said, just joking of course, that—'

'Who?'

'A friend of mine. We're both on the board of a company in which I have an interest. She said we should take precautions or we'd all be murdered in our beds. Then Bunny died, and it was no longer a laughing matter. I remembered it was Diana who had suggested that method of disposing of her husband, and that's when I showed them to Evan. Which way to the toilet?'

She showed him where it was and then cleared the table of the tea things.

If they'd known about the emails some time before Bunny's death, then . . . No, wait a minute, Rupert hadn't shown the emails to his friends until after Bunny had been found dead.

Was that right?

She looked at the clock. She must think about getting something ready for supper. She was a little surprised that Kat hadn't appeared to help. But then, Kat wouldn't want to go anywhere near her husband, would she? Kat would wait till he'd gone. And the sooner the better.

Ellie explored fridge and freezer which looked sad, almost empty. She found a couple of pizzas waiting to be topped up with cheese and tomatoes, but there were only two which wouldn't feed all of them, and there weren't enough chicken joints to go round. Susan often spent an evening trying out different recipes which Ellie and Thomas would taste, putting the leftovers into the freezer, but there were only small portions of such things left. There might be something under a stack of frozen vegetables in the corner but . . . She gave up.

When would Susan be back? Ellie checked her watch, which was running slow. Or had it actually stopped? She wouldn't be surprised if it had. So many things had gone wrong that day. In the back of her mind she was thinking over what she'd learned. She'd assumed that the emails had only come to light after Bunny's death, but Rupert said he'd found them earlier and hadn't taken them to his friends until after that tragic event. Which meant . . .

She couldn't work out what it meant.

Except that only the women and Rupert had been aware of the suggestions for killing off their spouses until after Bunny died.

Plus a woman called Fenella. But she had nothing to do with this business, did she?

Rupert came fussing out of the toilet, carrying his soiled jacket, and with a damp patch down the front of his shirt. He was stowing away his mobile phone. Had he been on the phone to someone while he'd been in the toilet?

He said, 'Tell that bitch to get down here, pronto. I'm taking her to the police station, now, this minute, and charging her with theft.'

Ellie stared at him. Was he mad?

'Get a move on!'

Ellie ignored him, so he went to the bottom of the stairs and yelled for Kat.

Ellie gasped, 'You can't do that! I won't let you!' A thought occurred to her. That phone call he'd just made. Was it to this Fenella person, whoever she might be? She said, 'Is Fenella the wealthy widow you're hoping to marry next?'

He gave her a narrow, suspicious look. 'She's an old friend. That's all.'

'I'm sure Kat's solicitor will be happy to hear about Fenella. Does she know you intend to make her act as cook and maid of all work as well as wife? Does she know you expect her to walk to the supermarket to save the delivery charge? Not many women would put up with that.'

He gave her a cold look. 'What would you know about it? Mind your own business. And, if you won't get Kat down here, I'll have to go up and fetch her.'

The thought of puny little Rupert dragging Kat's substantial figure down the stairs made Ellie want to laugh. But she didn't. The situation was rapidly getting out of control and she didn't know how to deal with it.

Normality returned when the doorbell rang. Ellie opened it to find the delivery had arrived from the supermarket. Ellie dithered. The food must all be put away in the fridge or freezer at once and Rupert was very much in the way. She said, 'Rupert, please go!'

Rupert gobbled, 'What, what?' He refused to move.

Ellie said, 'Go away, you nasty little man, or I'll . . . I don't know what I'll do, but I'll do something!'

The delivery man helped her out. 'Want him removed, missus?'

'Definitely,' said Ellie, and was amused to see that the delivery man did no more than gesture at Rupert to be on his way, and Rupert left.

Kat and Trish appeared in the hall. Ellie considered telling Kat what Rupert was threatening to do next but decided to wait. It was more important to get the food stowed away, and anyway, she didn't think anyone would take Rupert's babblings seriously. If they did, Trish and Ellie could bear witness that Rupert was making up his claim that Kat had stolen from him. So Ellie, Kat and Trish unpacked everything and put it away.

Finally, Ellie looked around the ground floor. Little Evan's toys littered the sitting-room floor. She picked up those she could see and dropped them back into their box. That made the room look better.

The hall was still encumbered with luggage, but the piles had been reduced in size though they did seem to have spread out more. An attempt had been made to make passageways through to the stairs and down the corridor to the Quiet Room and the library.

Ellie's anxiety levels remained high. Where was Thomas? And Diana? Had she returned little Evan to his father, or what? Ellie wondered if her home would ever be free of guests again.

Trish said, 'You've been so good to us, Mrs Quicke. I can't tell you how grateful I am. We've tried to clear up a bit and tomorrow we'll be out of your hair.'

Kat said, 'Can we help with supper?'

'Thanks, that would be good,' said Ellie. 'By the way, do either of you know a woman called Fenella?'

FOURTEEN

Tuesday late afternoon.

Trish and Kat looked at one another with raised eyebrows.

Trish shook her head.

Ellie said, 'Rupert says she's an old friend of his.'

Kat shook her head, too. 'Is possible. He does not entertain at home. Too expensive. He is always busy, busy, but he tells me it is no business of mine what he does, and I do not know about his friends except at the golf club.'

Ellie said, 'Rupert says Fenella is on the board of a firm with him. Is he on the board of many firms?'

Kat shrugged. 'He tells me that, yes. He is important man. Many firms ask for his advice.'

Then everything happened at once. The phone rang, and someone scratched at the door trying to use a key to get in.

'Mother, can you help!' It was a demand, not a plea. Ellie hastened to help her daughter open the door, to find Diana trying to fit her key into the door while holding a sleeping toddler in her arms.

The phone continued to ring. Trish said, 'Shall I answer it?' And, seeing that Ellie was fully occupied in taking little Evan into her own arms, did so. 'Mrs Quicke's house.'

'I took him to the park, trying to keep him awake,' said Diana, 'but he's so tired, poor little mite. I'm afraid he won't sleep tonight but I don't know what else I can do to keep him awake till bedtime.'

'Yes?' said Trish, on the phone.

Before Ellie could shut the front door, Thomas drew up in his car and parked. He trudged to the front door, eyes down. Exhausted. His day hadn't gone well?

Ellie found the toddler too heavy to hold for long. 'Diana, what do you want done with little Evan?'

'Give him to me,' said Kat. 'Poor little boy. He needs a nice hot bath and some food. Does he have a bottle of milk now and then? We will give him a little nap and then wake him up for playtime soon.' Little Evan half woke to find himself surrendered into a stranger's arms, but he didn't object. Ellie had the fancy that Kat probably smelled of comfort and had the sort of bosom which woke distant memories of breastfeeding in a small boy. Maybe Kat should have been a children's nanny instead of a housekeeper?

'Yes?' said Trish, with her finger stuck in one ear so that she could hear who was on the other end of the phone. 'Oh, yes, I think so. I'm sure that would be all right.'

A motorbike turned into the drive and coughed into silence. Rafael and Susan divested themselves of their helmets and came in to join the party. Rafael was burdened with several large bundles.

Thomas kissed Ellie. 'Are you all right?'

Ellie responded. 'I am. How are you?'

A quick smile from Thomas, and an even quicker hug. 'All right.'

Diana tugged at Ellie's arm. 'Mother! Pay attention. Have you rung Gunnar?'

Kat swayed, cuddling little Evan in her arms. 'Poor little boy. There, there,' she crooned to him.

Ellie didn't know who to attend to first. She said, 'Diana, you look exhausted. Why don't you let Kat deal with little Evan while you go and have a nice lie down?' Avoiding the subject of ringing Gunnar.

Ellie felt Thomas's arm around her and allowed herself to rest against him for a blissful second or two. Thomas surveyed the chaos in the hall and looked amused. 'Home, sweet home with you, Ellie, in charge as usual. I love it. You don't mind if I fire off a few emails before supper, do you? I have to send the stuff to the new printer tonight.'

Trish put the phone down. 'That was Barbie. Russet's brother has arrived and is taking them out for a meal. Barbie says can she come by and pick up her black tote bag which she must have left here by mistake.'

Rafael got himself and Susan into the hall and shut the front door behind him. 'I brought my sleeping bag, Mrs Quicke.' And pillows, as well?

Diana wrenched at Ellie's arm. 'Mother, I can't possibly relax until I know what Gunnar's prepared to do for me!'

Ellie thought that Thomas might think she was in control, but it didn't feel like it. She considered having a tantrum. She thought what a pleasure it would be to lie down on the floor and scream and wave her arms and legs about. She could imagine their horrified faces if she did. But of course she didn't.

She said, 'Diana, I haven't been able to speak to Gunnar yet but I'll keep trying. Go on – take a nap while Kat looks after little Evan. She knows what she's doing with children.' For a wonder, Diana obeyed her. She must indeed be exhausted.

Ellie turned to Trish. 'I ought to get supper started. Chicken casserole was suggested, wasn't it?'

'For how many?' That was Susan. 'Come along, Trish. I'll help. We'll all feel better when we've eaten.'

Ellie now had time to turn to Thomas. 'I'm so glad you've got it fixed, Thomas, even if it does mean you working late. Supper in an hour, right?'

He kissed her and departed to the library.

That left Rafael and Ellie. She said, 'I'm very grateful for your help, Rafael, but surely you don't need to stay tonight as well?'

'Have you discovered who's knocking off the husbands?'

She shook her head. 'I don't think any of them are doing it.' She considered what she'd said and shrugged. 'It doesn't make sense.'

'Then I stay.'

Ellie tried to think. 'Two of the wives left today. Little Evan will have his own room back, but the bedroom at the end of the corridor should be free now that Barbie's gone. Maybe Kat can move into that, or perhaps you'd like to use it?'

'I'll have a look.' He disappeared upstairs. The doorbell rang again.

This time it was Barbie at the door. A family-style Toyota was in the drive, with a youngish man in the driving seat and Russet sitting beside him.

'Sorry to be such a nuisance,' said Barbie. 'I did ring and Trish said it was all right if I came by for my black tote bag. Russet's brother is taking us out but I think I left my tote . . . oh!'

It wasn't where she'd left it. It wasn't surprising that it wasn't there, considering how much had been going on, but neither Barbie nor Ellie were in good shape to tackle yet another problem.

Ellie tried one or two piles and couldn't see a black tote bag. 'I'm afraid things have got moved around a bit. We tried to clear up but . . . And then there was a visitor.'

'Yes, of course. It's been a terrible time. Russet is coping quite well, but I'm not sure her brother is going to be much help. He has his own problems, just when we could do with . . .' Barbie was hanging on to her composure by her fingernails. 'I wouldn't worry about the tote, only it has some paperwork in it that I need.'

'Of course. Is it in this pile at the back of the stairs?'

'That's Trish's stuff, isn't it? I'm so sorry. I'm forgetting my manners. Is she all right?'

'Doing well. Is this it?' Ellie unearthed a red and black striped tote bag.

Barbie grabbed it. 'Yes. Thank you. I'm so sorry, I don't know why I said it was just black. I mean, I know it's red and black, but somehow—'

'You're still in shock. Think nothing of it. You'll feel better after something to eat. Keep in touch, won't you?'

Barbie produced a hankie, blew her nose and wiped her eyes. 'So stupid of me. So much to take in. You know?'

'Yes, yes. And now you have to support Russet as well. You're strong. You'll cope.'

'I don't feel strong, but you're right. I have to keep going.'

Ellie wasn't sure how it happened, but somehow she found herself embracing Barbie, who hugged her back. They disengaged to smile briefly at one another, recognizing a kindred spirit under stress.

Ellie accompanied Barbie to the front door. 'By the way, Rupert came round today. Mentioned someone called Fenella. Is she the woman he's proposing to marry next?'

'I wouldn't think so. She's Bunny's first wife. Dreadful woman.'

Barbie left, leaving Ellie staring into space.

Fenella, who was friendly with Rupert, was *Bunny's first wife*? Could that be true?

No, surely not. There must be more than one person called Fenella around. Except that it was an unusual name.

Ellie shook her head. Pull yourself together, girl! What did it matter if Bunny's ex-wife still met socially with the husband of one of Bunny's friends? Why shouldn't they? Rupert said they both sat on the boards of some company or other. They had interests in common. From passing the time of day they might suggest having a friendly drink together or going out for a meal. Fenella might ask Rupert for news of her ex-husband, and in turn he might ask her how she was fixed, financially. As she was on the board of at least one company, it followed that she had shares in that firm. Perhaps she had done well out of her divorce?

It sounded as if she were a strong, independent woman with a comfortable lifestyle.

It didn't follow that Rupert had designs on Fenella, even if she were a wealthy woman in her own right.

Of course, Fenella was going to come out of this business with Bunny's house and whatever other property he might have left, which made her a good prospect for Rupert to consider if he were to take a third dip into the marriage market. Poor Barbie had been left with nothing except the clothes she had been allowed to take away with her.

Fenella had been the winner in that game of ex-wives, hadn't she?

Presumably Rupert intended to come out of this affair smelling of roses, too. He'd got shot of penniless Kat and if, as gossip indicated, he succeeded in marrying Fenella, he would get Bunny's property, too.

According to Rupert, he was the only one of that group who knew about the emails before Bunny died.

Which meant . . .?

Could Rupert have engineered Bunny's death in order to achieve another wealthy marriage and acquire his dead friend's estate?

It sounded very possible.

Who would ever suspect another member of the group of devising the deaths of Bunny and Walt . . . unless they'd arranged for the surviving members of the group to inherit the dead man's shares? That really was a possibility.

Wait a minute. Didn't Rupert have an alibi for Walt's death? He'd been in a board meeting at the time, hadn't he?

Well, he might have been responsible for Bunny's death, if not for Walt's. Walt might have fallen down the stairs, exactly as they said.

If it hadn't been for the emails, no one would have thought to query either death. And the police were not really going to do anything about either death, were they? Or were they?

Ellie decided to ring Lesley one more time to see if there were any news.

But what was that?

A child's cry. Here came Kat carrying a clean and rosy-cheeked toddler down the stairs. She was singing something – a folk song? – to him and he was joining in now and then, off-key but to their mutual satisfaction. He was also clutching Eeyore the donkey, which was one of the soft toys Ellie kept for him to play with when he stayed overnight. What happened to the toy which had once been his favourite? The pink hippo? Was that the one which had been put into the washing machine by the new nanny and thereby lost its distinctive scent?

Diana appeared in the doorway to the sitting room. There were dark circles under her eyes and she looked far from her usual pristine self.

Little Evan held out his arms to her, and Kat skilfully transferred the boy into his mother's arms. 'There, now,' said Kat. 'I don't know who is more tired – Mummy or baby boy. Come along, Mummy; let's see what we can find to eat in the kitchen, and then you can put your little boy to beddy-byes. I don't think you'll be long out of bed, either.'

Diana recognized, as did Ellie and Evan, that Kat had taken them both under her wing and, for a wonder, Diana actually accepted the offer of help. Even more miraculous, she actually thanked Kat. 'You're very good with him. Yes, I must admit I am rather tired.'

Kat said, 'You should take it easy, no? You are being sick much?'

'A little.' With Kat carrying little Evan, Diana allowed herself to be shepherded down the corridor to the kitchen.

So Kat has worked out that Diana was pregnant again? Good for Kat.

Ellie made for the phone. It was getting late. Lesley would have left the police station for the night, but Ellie had her mobile number and tried that.

Lesley answered the phone. 'Yes, Ellie? What is it?'

'You sound worn out.'

'I am. I've been looking through hours of video trying to trace a suspect in an acid attack.'

'Nothing to do with Bunny and Walt, then?'

'Oh, that?' A long pause. 'No, nothing to do with that. We should get the results on Walt's death tomorrow afternoon. Actually, Ellie, I don't want to worry you, but if they find bruising on his back, I think they'll want to interview Diana under caution.'

Ellie caught her breath. 'You mean, they really think she could have a case to answer?'

'You must know that He Who Must Be Obeyed is enchanted with the idea that he can have your daughter up on a murder charge. If the autopsy proves that Walt was pushed, then you can expect him round tomorrow. He'll want to interview all the wives, I suppose, but he'll concentrate on Diana.'

'Two of the wives have left already. Russet has taken Barbie back home with her. No one seems to have objected. The other two are off tomorrow, to stay with Trish's parents up north somewhere.'

'That's awkward. Couldn't you have kept them?'

'No. How could I? And why should I?'

'You're right, of course, but I'm afraid my boss won't see it that way. He'll want to know why you allowed suspected criminals to escape.'

Ellie said, 'Tchah!'

Lesley managed a laugh. 'Yes, I know. Nobody's actually under suspicion till we get the results of the autopsy, and maybe not then . . . Which won't stop him trying to put you in the wrong.'

'You're off the case?'

'Yes. I'm so sorry, Ellie. I can't help.' Lesley sounded defeated, which was not like her.

Ellie said, 'Don't worry. I'll think of something,' and clicked off as Trish appeared from the kitchen, phone glued to her ear, looking as if she were on the verge of tears. On seeing Ellie, she said to the phone, 'I'll get back to you,' and shut it off.

Ellie decided she was too tired to ask what was wrong, but Trish had elected her as her best friend, and Trish needed to unburden herself.

'Oh, Mrs Quicke. It's my sister,' said Trish, holding back her tears. 'She's the eldest and so bossy, you wouldn't believe. She says I can't possibly be so selfish as to land back on Mum and Dad when they're having health problems and have just moved into a retirement flat. Of course she's right, but they do have a guest room and they did offer. They said they would expect me tomorrow and they said Kat could come, too, but my sister is right, and it would be all wrong of me to add to their troubles now.'

Ellie stiffened her back. 'Parents worry about their children. They worry even more if they can't do anything to help.'

'Do you think so? I was the youngest by so many years, and I forget . . . Because they are in their seventies now, and it's true, Mum has arthritis and Dad is waiting for a hip replacement. I do tend to spread myself around a bit, and Mum likes everything just so, which means she'll get in a state if I move back in, and I can see that it's all wrong for me to impose on them but . . . What am I going to do?'

'Grow up!' said Ellie, and then was appalled at herself.

Trish recoiled as if she'd been struck.

Ellie castigated herself. How could she have been so cruel! She said, 'I'm sorry, Trish. I didn't mean . . .' But of course she had meant it, and Trish knew it.

A tide of red swept up from Trish's throat and up to her hairline. She was silent. Quivering. Biting her lip.

Ellie winced. How could she have said that?

Trish took in a deep breath and let it out again. 'No, it's I who should be apologizing to you, Mrs Quicke. It's true. I've been behaving like a child.'

Ellie shot into speech. 'Your husband liked you to—'

'Yes, he did.' She was as pale now as she had been red before. 'But I ought not to have let him keep me a child. I see that now. Yes, it is about time that I grew up and took control of my life.'

'Don't jump into making a decision you might regret later.'

'I feel as if I'm swimming in a strange sea with no land in sight. There's nowhere to put my feet down. Nothing settled.' An attempt at a smile. 'I'm a Cancer, you see. I like my shell. I don't like change.'

Ellie was never quite sure whether she believed in such things as star signs, although she supposed some people she knew did face both ways, and others were clearly bull-at-a-gate. She didn't even know what sign she herself was supposed to be.

What she did know was that she was a woman whose lines had fallen in pleasant places. She was happily married to a wonderful man, had good friends, enough money to live on comfortably and plenty of charity work to keep her occupied. She didn't deserve such good fortune but there it was, and she was grateful for it. The least she could do was to try to help others when they were in trouble.

'I suppose,' she said, 'you could tell your parents that you appreciate their concern but would like to stand on your own two feet now. Ask their advice about what you should do? Perhaps you could check into a hotel or a B and B nearby. You could pay for Kat, couldn't you?'

'Yes. That's a good idea. I'll do that.' She accessed her phone, making her way up the stairs but stopped halfway up. 'Oh, Susan said to tell you that supper's nearly ready.' Trish continued on her way up to her own room.

Ellie thought of calling the girl back to say that if supper were ready, it was going to cause extra trouble all round if Trish went off by herself just as the food was being dished up. Instead, she shrugged and went along the corridor to call Thomas to the table.

Evening into night.

It had been a tiring day, emotionally and in every other way. So supper was raggedly served and quickly disposed of, almost completely in silence.

Diana had been withdrawn throughout, watching her son's every move, eating very little herself but accepting Kat's help. Ellie couldn't remember when her self-sufficient daughter had last been so quiet. Little Evan, on the other hand, was noisy, happily banging away with a spoon on his tray while Kat spooned food into his mouth. Kat was a natural with children but was wise enough not to exclude Diana from looking after her little boy. In fact, Kat fussed around Diana almost as much as she did around little Evan. She even asked Diana if she would like a massage to ease her tired body and a tisane to settle her stomach. Amazingly, Diana actually agreed to both! Kat took mother and child off to settle them down, and for a wonder little Evan didn't even grizzle when she carried him upstairs.

Kat decided to sleep in the room Barbie had been occupying. This meant that she could deal with little Evan if he woke in the night, allowing Diana to have a good rest. This left Susan's guest room empty. Everyone avoided looking at Rafael when he said he'd make his own arrangements for the night. Everyone but Ellie probably thought that he'd end up in bed with Susan, but that was their affair, wasn't it?

Thomas looked weary, too. He was preoccupied with his own thoughts and hardly spoke. When Ellie enquired, he said he'd done a good day's work and the magazine would go out on schedule with the new printer, but he didn't ask what had gone on in his absence and she didn't volunteer any information.

Trish wandered back into the kitchen and ate the plateful which Susan warmed up for her. Trish was distrait, and probably had no idea of what she'd eaten. She still had her phone glued to her ear, talking to her parents and then to her sister.

Once the table had been cleared and the dishwasher set going, Susan and Rafael went up to her flat and the house began to quieten down. Ellie felt restless and would have liked a few minutes in the Quiet Room, but Thomas felt better after he'd eaten and wanted to talk through the problems he'd met with that day. He did ask her how long she thought they'd be having guests, and he did make an attempt to listen when she told him what had been happening, but she could see it was an effort for him to concentrate on her affairs, so she kept it short.

He yawned mightily. 'As usual, you seem to have everything under control. Let's have an early night, shall we?'

Together they fed Midge his last meal of the day, turned off the lights and made sure that all windows and doors were shut and locked.

As they went upstairs – perhaps more slowly than usual – Thomas said, 'Bless this house and all who sleep in her.'

Ellie glanced at the door leading to the flat upstairs. Susan and Rafael would probably still be up.

Ellie decided to leave the landing light on, so their guests would be able to see where they were going if they had to get up in the night, which she sincerely hoped no one would have to do. Nevertheless, she left their bedroom door ajar so that she might hear if someone moved across the landing.

Thomas was fast asleep by the time Ellie got into bed beside him. She tried to pray a little, but she really was too tired to think clearly. She thought, *Bless this house and all who sleep in her . . . bless this house . . .*

And was woken by a bell screaming in her ear!

An alarm?

She sniffed. Was something burning?

A strange light flickered beyond the open bedroom door.

Thomas slept on. She shot out of bed and on to the landing.

A sheet of flame flickered across the floor of the hall!

The house was on fire!

FIFTEEN

Wednesday, very early morning.

Ellie screamed.

The siren yammered through her head, hurting her teeth. The house was full of people! Thomas! Little Evan! Susan, on the top floor, with no fire exit! Diana, Kat and Trish!

Ellie shook Thomas's shoulder. 'Fire! Wake up!' How could he sleep through that racket?

The cat was asleep on a chair by their bed. Ellie picked him up, thinking that she could at least rescue him – and then placed him on the floor. People were more important than pets.

She plunged back to the landing.

There was no fire exit anywhere, except by the main staircase, which was being fast approached by the flames.

Someone turned the lights on downstairs in the hall. Midge the cat shot around the landing and disappeared in the direction of the back stairs.

The siren was doing her head in. Was it Thomas who was shouting at her? She couldn't hear herself think!

Ellie screamed again. 'Susan!' She ran round the landing and pulled open the door to the top floor. 'Susan! Fire!'

The hall floor was normally kept clear, but the piles of luggage now strewn around could easily catch fire. All that those poor women had left in the world.

If the flames take the grandfather clock, I will be seriously annoyed! As if that mattered, when . . .

Thomas appeared in the doorway to their bedroom. He shouted over the siren. 'What . . .?'

Ellie yelled at him. 'Fire! Get Diana and little Evan out!'

Clutching the handrail, she toiled up the stairs to the top floor where Susan slept. And Rafael, too? 'Susan!'

She realized she couldn't be heard over the siren.

A swishing sound behind her, down below.

Thomas shouting.

Someone else shouting. Another man. Rafael?

Ellie stumbled on the top step and nearly fell. She pounded on the door of Susan's bedroom. 'Susan! Fire! Get up!'

More confused shouting from downstairs. There was a light on inside Susan's bedroom. Where was she?

Someone – a woman? – screamed.

Susan wasn't responding.

A pungent smell. Smoke was creeping up the stairs behind her? She'd heard that smoke can kill faster than flames.

Ellie burst into Susan's bedroom.

The bed was empty. What!

Ellie lunged for the other doors in the flat.

Her voice had gone. She tried to shout Susan's name, and failed. Croaked, rather. The rooms were all empty. Susan must have got out, somehow.

Someone was calling her name. 'Ellie! Are you all right?' Thomas was calling from down below. Urgently. On the verge of panic.

As suddenly as it had started, the siren ceased.

Silence banged her ears.

Back down the stairs she stumbled. People were on the landing, in their nightclothes. Diana holding little Evan, Kat putting a duvet around Diana's shoulders.

'What is it?'

'What's happened?'

Thomas! Where was Thomas?

'Ellie! Thank God you're all right!' Thomas, wrapping his arms around her.

She croaked, 'Susan!'

'Downstairs. She's safe.'

No flames. No bright flames.

Some smoke. Not much. A strong smell of burning.

Heaps of charred luggage and two figures in the hall, squirting red fire extinguishers around.

Susan in pyjamas. Rafael in jeans and a T-shirt. Both wearing shoes.

Rafael called up to them, 'Don't come down yet! Make sure you've got strong shoes on before you do. The floor's hot.'

Bleary-eyed, Trish came out on to the landing on the far side. 'What's happened?' She clutched at the banister and looked down at the charred floor below. 'Oh, my God!'

'Yes, quite!' said Thomas, making sure Ellie still had her arms and legs. 'Thank God!'

Ellie had a dreadful desire to giggle. 'Bless this house and all who sleep in her.' She told herself not to be frivolous. She was in shock, of course.

'The fire's out,' said Rafael, 'but we'd better call the fire brigade, just in case.'

Susan reached for the landline phone. 'I'll do that.'

The grandfather clock chimed. One, two, three.

Three o'clock? Three in the morning and all's well. Except that it wasn't.

Ellie said, 'Rafael! Fire extinguishers. You've got two. But I haven't. I mean, I did think about it, but I never got round to getting any.'

'I know. I saw. I got them for you this afternoon.'

'You didn't tell me.'

'I didn't want to frighten you. It might not have happened.'

She breathed deeply, inclined to be angry with him, but aware he'd saved all their lives by his forethought. 'Were you sleeping downstairs?'

'Yes. Just as well, eh? I was chatting to Susan for a while on the phone, then started watching a late-night film. Must have dropped off. Something woke me. A sharp clatter. I think it must have been the letter box snapping shut. I couldn't think what it was but then I smelt paraffin. Someone poured a bottle of the stuff through the letter box and tossed a match in after it. I heard it go whoosh and the fire alarm went off. I rang Susan to tell her to put some shoes on and get the hell out. I couldn't remember for the moment where I'd put the extinguishers, and then I did. They were under the staging in the conservatory. It could have been a lot worse. No one's hurt, right?'

Thomas said, 'For which I thank God, fasting.'

Ellie tried not to giggle. The idea of Thomas going without food was so ridiculous that it made her want to laugh uncontrollably. She told herself she was hysterical.

Susan talked into the landline phone. Her red-gold hair was all over the place, and she had dirty smears down her pyjamas, but she was awake and alive and functioning.

So was Rafael. 'I don't think there's all that much damage. We got on to it so quickly.'

Diana said, 'Someone is trying to kill me.' She sank to the floor. She was still holding little Evan, who was beginning to wake up and grumble.

'No, no,' said Kat, giving Diana a hug.

Ellie wanted to comfort her daughter but didn't know what to say. Was someone really after Diana?

Diana began to retch. She tried to get to her feet and didn't make it. Her colour was dreadful. She was going to be sick?

Kat took little Evan from his mother and helped Diana to her feet. 'Come along then, Diana. Just a few steps back to your room, and you can settle down again. I'll bring you a cup of mint tea.'

Diana resisted. 'I don't want to stay up here. Suppose there's another fire? It's not safe!'

Ellie tried to push her sluggish brain into action. 'It's safe enough, Diana. We don't need to use these stairs to the hall, remember? There's always the back stairs down to the kitchen.' Her eyes smarted.

Little Evan was waking up fast. He'd kept his father and his nanny awake the night before, he'd slept during the day so now he was raring to go. Was he going to howl the house down? Ellie cringed at the thought. She saw him fasten his eyes on some detail on Kat's elderly, high-necked nightgown, and become fascinated by it. Hurray!

Kat cooed at the little boy and, wide-eyed with speculation, he stared back at this strange woman who had come into his life only that day but who held him so securely. He banged her arm. 'Biccy!'

'In a minute, my sweetie pie,' said Kat. 'Let's get your mummy back to bed first.' She helped Diana back into her room and shut the door. Good for Kat.

Ellie found she was trembling. She told herself the danger was over. She tried to smile at Thomas, who understood that she was recovering from her shock, and let her stand on her own two feet again.

Rafael looked up at Ellie with narrowed eyes, asking a question without words. Did she know who had tried to burn the house down?

She shook her head. She didn't *know* who, and she didn't *know* why.

Susan put the phone down. 'The fire brigade are on their way. Do we tell the police as well?'

Rafael said, 'The fire brigade will do that. It's probably some kids. Vandals. Someone who likes setting fire to things.'

Ellie thought that he didn't believe that and neither did she, but it would serve as an excuse for the time being. The smell of burning paraffin filled her nostrils. Ugh!

Diana was right. Someone was out to kill . . . her? Or someone else?

If Rafael had not been sleeping downstairs! If he hadn't renewed the batteries in the alarms! If he hadn't bought the extinguishers!

Ellie shuddered. Now they were all up and out of bed, what was going to happen next? She said, 'Anyone like a cup of tea?'

Susan said, 'I'll put the kettle on,' and disappeared to the kitchen.

Thomas had his slippers on already and now inserted himself into his dressing gown. 'I could do with a cuppa. I'll make it. Ellie, you can go back to bed if you wish. I'll wait up with Rafael.'

Ellie shook her head. 'I can't sleep now.' She fetched her own dressing gown, found her slippers and tested the stairs. They seemed untouched. The fire hadn't reached them, thanks to Rafael's prompt action. She followed Thomas down to the hall.

Trish was ahead of them, going straight to her small pile of belongings which were still there. Rafael said, 'Don't touch anything yet,' but Trish couldn't resist trying to lift a carry-on bag and had to drop it because it was still too hot for comfort.

Thomas and Rafael went into a huddle about timings, wondering how long it would be before the fire brigade could get there and whether one of them should stay in the hall to make sure nothing burst into flames again.

Susan sang out, 'Tea's up!'

Ellie sleepwalked into the kitchen and slumped into a chair, trying to think. Her hands gripped the edge of the table.

Susan put a mug of tea in front of Ellie and bent down to catch her eye. 'What is it?'

Ellie said, 'I don't know. I'm afraid of . . . But no, surely not!'

Thomas and Rafael came in for their mugs of tea. Thomas took one look at Ellie and said, 'What's up? You're all right, aren't you?'

Ellie licked her lips. 'It would be ridiculous to phone someone up at half-past three in the morning, just to see if they're all right. Wouldn't it?'

Rafael caught his breath. 'What do you know, Mrs Quicke?'

'Barbie and Russet. I mean, if we rang them, they'd not hear it. Not in the middle of the night.'

Susan said, 'You think they might be targeted, too?'

'Yes. No. I don't know. I'm worried sick about them. Only, you can't go phoning people at this hour, can you?'

Rafael and Susan exchanged a long look. Those who are good friends as well as lovers can communicate without words.

Susan said, 'Would you like Rafael to go round there on his bike? If all is quiet, perhaps he could drop a note through their letter box asking them to ring us when they got up?'

Thomas put his mug down. 'Letter box. Someone poured paraffin through our letter box into the hall and set it alight. Ellie, do you really think someone might do it to them, too?'

Ellie wailed, 'I don't know!' And then, in a firmer tone, 'Yes!'

'I trust your instincts,' said Rafael. 'I'll go. Write a note and give me the address.'

The phone rang in the hall. Ellie stood up. 'It's too late for that.' She hurried to the phone. Was it going to be Russet or Barbie?

It was Barbie. In control, just. By the skin of her teeth. 'I'm so sorry to trouble you at this hour, Mrs Quicke. I would have waited but—'

'It's all right. We're all up. We've been fire-bombed—'

There was a gasp. Barbie said, 'Us, too. We're at the hospital. Russet is hurt but her brother's OK, sort of. He jumped from the bedroom window, got a sprained ankle and wrist and is moaning like mad but that's not important, is it?'

'Paraffin was poured in through the letter box and set alight?'

'Yes, the firemen said that's what it was.'

'The house is all right? Wait a minute, you said Russet has been hurt?'

'There's considerable damage to the property. To us, not so much. We could have been killed in our beds but luckily Russet got up for a drink and smelt something burning. She went out on to the landing and found the hall and staircase on fire. It's a modern house, all glass and metal. She touched the handrail. It was so hot that she burned her hand. She kept her head and woke me and her brother. I got us into the room farthest from the fire, shut the door and phoned the fire brigade. Russet's brother panicked. He wouldn't wait to be rescued and jumped from the window, which is how he got hurt. I got Russet's hand into cold water and we waited for the fire brigade to get us out. We've been at the hospital for ages, waiting for Russet's burns to be attended to.'

'When did it happen?'

'About two, maybe two thirty? I've lost count. What time is it now? I wanted to wait till morning to ring you, but Russet's in pieces and . . . I'm sorry . . . I'm not far off it, too. The thing is we're all in shock. And the house is . . . I don't know how badly damaged, but the firemen have turned off the electrics and the gas. We can't go back there. The firemen said one of their men would stay there overnight to make sure the flames didn't break out again. I was going to ring for a taxi to go to a hotel, but then I thought that you might . . .'

She started to laugh. There was a note of hysteria in her voice. And then, being Barbie, she controlled herself. 'We're in our nightwear and bedroom slippers. I snatched my handbag as we ran past the stairs to the end of the house. So I have cards and my phone. Russet has nothing. Neither has her brother.'

'I understand. The house is uninhabitable and you have nowhere to go,' said Ellie.

Thomas, Rafael and Susan were all crowding around her, wearing identical looks of shock. 'Come here, of course. All of you. Don't take any risks. Keep together, whatever you do. Don't let Russet go anywhere by herself. Or you. Get a taxi. If you haven't any money or cards, I'll pay at this end. Come straight away.'

Thomas signalled to her. She said, 'Wait! Thomas says he'll come and get you. Which hospital are you at, and where will you be?'

'Bless you,' said Barbie, and gave directions.

Thomas hurried up the stairs to put some outdoor clothes on.

At that moment the fire brigade arrived. Rafael said he'd deal with them.

Thomas left to fetch Barbie & Co from hospital.

The fire brigade inspected the hall inch by inch and said Rafael had done a good job, but that they would clear the floor to make sure that none of the baggage strewn around would burst into flames again.

Ellie retreated to the kitchen, trying to think where she could put three extra people to sleep.

Kat came downstairs, carrying little Evan, who was wide awake and red-faced. 'Biccy!'

Ellie got the biscuit tin out and told him to choose one. He took two, of course, and proceeded to stuff his mouth with them. Kat put the kettle on for a peppermint tea for Diana.

'Play!' said little Evan. 'Biccy!'

Of course. Little Evan's clock was out of kilter. It was now daytime for him.

Kat said, 'Now, now! One more biccy – only one, mind! Then we go play with toys, right?'

Ellie was grateful to Kat, but . . . 'No, Kat. I'll take him for a bit. You need your beauty sleep, too.'

'I manage OK,' said Kat, in her element. 'Back in two ticks.' She picked up the mug of mint tea and disappeared. Little Evan saw his new comforter disappear and opened his mouth to voice his displeasure. Ellie distracted him with the offer of another biscuit, which he accepted.

Susan sat down beside Ellie. 'I can take someone in upstairs. Perhaps two, if one of them doesn't mind sleeping on the settee.'

Ellie said, 'You're brilliant, Susan. And Rafael. We'd all have died in our beds tonight if he hadn't been looking after us so well.'

Susan dimpled. 'He likes you, Mrs Quicke.' A shadow crossed her face. 'I don't want him taking any more risks.'

'You think I'm risking a further attack by inviting Barbie and Co to stay here?'

Susan was silent. Her troubled expression told Ellie that that was exactly what she thought.

Ellie thought so herself. Somehow or other she had to get to the bottom of this tangled skein of motives, or someone else would die.

One of the firemen asked Ellie to join them in the hall, and she picked little Evan up to take him with her. The floor there had been cleared of all the burned and charred luggage that had been cluttering the place up for days. The front door was open. Ellie could see the women's belongings out in the driveway. It was starting to rain.

Trish was out in the drive, oblivious of the rain, trying to see what she could rescue of her things.

Ellie ached for these women. In the space of a couple of days they'd lost their husbands, their homes and now most of their possessions. Rafael stood by, eyes narrowed, ready to support Ellie if needed. Susan brought him a cuppa. He gave her a hug and drank the tea.

Little Evan gave the firemen a look of bewilderment and twisted round in Ellie's arms. 'Down. Play now.' The lure of his toy box was strong and, biscuit finished, he made his way into the sitting room to empty his toys out on to the floor again. It was daytime as far as he was concerned. The lights were all on, and there was a never-ending supply of biscuits in the kitchen. Business as usual.

The firemen addressed Ellie. 'Do you have any idea who might have wanted to set fire to your house?'

Ellie said, 'I suspect someone but have no proof. Will you be passing the case on to the police?'

Yes, they would do that.

Rafael gave Ellie a quizzical look. What did that mean? Did he know something that she didn't?

Ellie said, 'There's something else you should know. Earlier this morning another house was set alight in the same fashion, and a lot more damage was done. We know the people there. They ended up in hospital.'

A shrug. 'Not our fire. That's another crew.' Notebooks were flapped open. Details taken. They would pass details on to the police. The fire was completely out and the firemen would leave, provided they could be assured someone would stay awake and on guard. Rafael said he would.

They left.

Trish brought an armful of bits and pieces back into the house. Her face was streaked with rain and tears, her clothes sodden. 'Photographs . . . certificates . . .' The proof that she had been born, worked and married.

Ellie gave her a sympathetic hug, but it was Susan who swept Trish off to the kitchen to dry her and her belongings out.

Ellie looked hard at Rafael. 'What is it?'

Kat came downstairs, saying Diana was asleep. She wondered if she should heat up some hot milk for little Evan before trying to put him to bed again.

Ellie started to object, till Kat said, 'I sleep when I wish. I wish to look after little boy. He likes me. I like him. You leave us be.' She departed on her errand.

Rafael followed Ellie into the sitting room. The lights were on, and little Evan was sitting in a ring of toy Lego pieces.

Ellie said, 'Who was it who said time flies when you're having fun? It's nearly four o'clock. Thomas should be back from the hospital soon.'

Rafael grinned. 'You are embroiled in another mystery, aren't you, Mrs Quicke? Why didn't you tell the firemen what's been going on?'

'I suspect the two fires are connected, but I don't know who's behind them. Or who was responsible for Bunny's death. Or Walt's. I've tried to get the police interested but so far, no go. Yes, I'm sure they will get more involved soon. There have been two deaths already and there could have been more tonight. Let's hold off for a day. We are on our guard now, and I'm hoping it might be possible to save a couple of marriages before we get the police involved.'

Rafael raised his eyebrows.

Ellie sighed. 'Yes, I know. The prospect of these wives returning to their husbands is not one of unalleviated rapture, but these women have suffered greatly, and they should be given the choice.'

'There's no choice for Russet and Barbie.'

'There would be closure.' Little Evan knocked on her knees, trying to give her some pieces of Lego which he wanted her to fit together. She obliged. He was bright-eyed and bushy-tailed. In a moment he would ask for breakfast. It was going to be a long night.

She said, 'In the morning I'll ring around, try to get everyone round the table for a conference.'

It was indeed a long night. At half past four, Thomas brought an exhausted Barbie and Russet back to the house. Barbie looked more like Lauren Bacall than ever, her cheekbones sharply defined. She was wearing a housecoat over her nightdress and a decent pair of mules. She was also carrying her handbag.

Russet's left hand was bandaged, and she shivered under a hospital blanket, wearing nothing but a skimpy nightdress and hospital slippers. She was in a bad way, in considerable pain.

Barbie explained that Russet's brother had decided not to risk his skin by being around his sister and had phoned his wife to collect him and take him home.

Ellie nodded. There were certain people you could rely on when you were in trouble, and there were others whom you couldn't. Younger brothers did occasionally fall into the second category. Barbie was trying to tell Ellie that Russet didn't need to hear her brother criticized. Point taken.

By this time Ellie, Kat and Susan had worked out who should sleep in which bed. Ellie damped down hysteria, thinking, *Who's been sleeping in my bed? asked Mummy Bear.*

Kat said she would sleep on the settee in the sitting room as and when she could persuade little Evan to go upstairs to bed again.

Russet would occupy the end bedroom which had clean sheets on the bed. The refugees were dosed with sleeping pills and hot drinks where appropriate and sent off to bed.

Trish carried an armful of her reclaimed belongings upstairs with her. Ellie hoped none of Trish's paperwork was still capable of bursting into flames but was too weary to remonstrate.

Susan gave Rafael a hug and went upstairs to the top flat, taking Barbie with her.

Thomas and Rafael went into a huddle over how to protect the house. They decided that Thomas should take first watch and doss down in his reclining chair in the sitting room, while Rafael made do with the big chair in the kitchen for a couple of hours. Then Rafael would move to the sitting room and Thomas would join Ellie in bed.

Ellie objected. 'Thomas, you'll be fit for nothing tomorrow if you don't get more than a couple of hours' sleep. Remember, the magazine needs you!'

Thomas shook his head. 'I'm not taking any more chances. Bother the magazine. Keeping you all alive is more important.'

Rafael said, 'We're not arguing with the master of the house, Mrs Quicke, are we? Sleep tight and see you in the morning.'

Ellie trudged up the stairs, saying to herself, 'Please, Lord. Bless this house and all who sleep in it. I must make a list of who I have to ring tomorrow. Except that, oh dear, it is already tomorrow.'

Below her, little Evan stumped out into the hall. 'Biccy? I want Biccy!'

Kat toiled after him, saying, 'Hush!' But followed him into the kitchen to give him what he wanted.

Ellie decided to look in on Diana before she slid into bed herself. Diana was fast asleep, tears still glistening on her cheeks. She did not cry often. Ellie pulled the duvet over her daughter's thin shoulder and sighed out a prayer for her.

At last. Ellie got into her own bed and eased her aching back. She looked at the alarm clock which was inexorably working its way round to her usual getting-up time. Her brain was overactive. She knew she wouldn't sleep. She tried to pray and found herself saying, 'Bless this house,' over and over again.

She heard the cat Midge patter up the stairs. Would he decide to come in with Ellie or not? No, he skittered across the landing, chasing a moonbeam . . . or a mouse. The smell of burned paraffin still hung in her nostrils.

She knew she wouldn't sleep. She missed Thomas . . . *Dear Lord, bless this house and all who have taken shelter here.*

SIXTEEN

Wednesday morning.

Ellie half woke when Thomas joined her in bed but dropped quickly back into sleep and didn't wake again till the alarm went off. She flung out an arm, but Thomas was already up and in the shower.

She forced herself out of bed, followed him into the shower, pulled on some clothes any old how and stumped down the stairs feeling crotchety. She was just able to see Susan leaving the house at her usual time, and with a smile and a cheery wave of her hand.

Rafael and Thomas were in the kitchen, getting in one another's way. Ellie pushed them aside and cooked. As long as she was not asked to speak, she'd be all right. The men worked their way through everything she provided, also without speaking.

Midge appeared, and she fed him. At least he was easy to look after.

As soon as he was finished, Rafael shot off somewhere, saying he'd be back soon. Whatever that might mean.

Thomas helped himself to a fourth cup of coffee and cleared his throat. 'What would be the most helpful thing for me to do?'

'The magazine?' said Ellie.

'Forget it. This is more important. Our insurance is up to date, isn't it? Shall I get on to them about what happened last night? I assume we're covered for the damage to the hall floor. We may also be covered for the damage to our guests' property. The fire investigator will be round, I assume. He will have passed a note on to the police, won't he?'

'If you can deal with all that, it would be wonderful.'

'I'll start getting some quotes for resurfacing the hall floor, too.'

Ellie's mind was racing ahead. 'Russet's not going to be up to much for a while. If I can find out who her insurance company is, perhaps you could get a claim started for her house fire, as well?'

He reached for a pad and pencil. 'Poor woman. Will do. If the fire at Russet's was so bad that they couldn't get out of the house by using the stairs, perhaps they'll need someone to board up the ground floor to deter looters? Mm, hm.' Off he went to start on the phone calls.

Kat, singing a lullaby, carried a sleepy little Evan into the kitchen. 'He wants more "biccies". Is he meaning any food, or only biscuits?'

'That's a thought. I don't know,' said Ellie. 'You sit down and have some breakfast, Kat, while I try him on some proper food. He'll turn into a right pudding if he doesn't eat anything except biscuits and normally he eats some of whatever we're having. He's right out of his routine, isn't he? Turning night into day.' She boiled an egg and took little Evan on her lap to feed him while Kat rummaged for bread and cheese and tea for herself.

Little Evan demurred at first and murmured 'Biccy' several times, but finally accepted the egg and some bread and butter, followed by a hot milk drink.

Ellie said, 'You're very good with babies, Kat. Do you not want one of your own someday?'

'Rupert does not wish it.' Kat's hair was down around her shoulders, and she was showing the effects of a sleepless night, but she seemed to have reserves of energy.

Ellie said, 'Tell me, Kat. Did you sign a prenuptial agreement before you married Rupert?'

'I did. We went to the solicitors first, and then to registry office for the marriage.'

'Did any of his friends come to see you married?'

'No. I say we wait for my family to come, but he is in a hurry. I understand. His friends have money, and I have nothing. He say they will pity me. So he does not ask them. It was long time till I saw them, but they are very kind to me, Barbie and Russet most of all. They show me how to do things. I have great regard for them all.'

'Rupert was not very kind to you, was he?'

'When he is little boy, the family is very poor. His grandfather and father work very hard and they are lucky suddenly they are rich. He is afraid, always, that he will lose everything and be poor again.' She finished her tea, collected little Evan and bore him off upstairs.

Ellie looked at the clock and decided it was time to start ringing around.

She tried Monique's mobile first and got through. There were kitchen sounds in the background. A kettle shrilled. 'Yes?'

'Monique, you are back in your own home again? There's something you should know about. Last night . . .' Ellie reported what had happened.

Monique said, 'What?' In a shocked voice. 'Say that again.'

Ellie repeated what she'd said.

Monique hissed to herself. 'Where is this going to stop? I must sit down. I can't believe . . .! No, of course you wouldn't make it up. Who is doing this? It's not Evan. No, that I can't believe!'

'Well, it's not the wives. Barbie and Russet have lost even what they managed to salvage from their homes yesterday, and Russet has been badly burned and is in pain.'

'Well, that's awful. You think it's Terry or Rupert? No, surely not!'

'I don't know who it is.' Here Ellie crossed her fingers, because she thought she knew. Or suspected, anyway. 'The question is what happens next? The game is not over yet. I ask myself, who's next for burning alive? I want to get everyone round the table here this afternoon and see if we can work out exactly who is behind this nasty business.'

'You expect me to get the men to face their wives across a table? No way!'

'I expect you to repair some of the damage you've done. You took it on yourself to help the men get rid of their wives because you were playing off an old score against Diana. You amused yourself playing Musical Marital Chairs, but the name of the game has changed to Murder by Fire.'

'You can't hold me responsible for what's happened.'

'I don't. But if you hadn't taken a hand in the game, I doubt if the men would have been quite so quick to detach their wives from their homes. I can't see any of them orchestrating that operation, can you? Now someone has taken advantage of the situation to up the game and who can tell who's next for the chop? That includes the men. So, if you tell them what's happened and point out that one of them may be next, then they'll come to the table, won't they?'

'I don't know. I'll have to think about that.' The phone clicked off.

Ellie was fairly pleased with that conversation. What next?

Thomas erupted from his study at the end of the corridor, saying the fire investigator was ringing back soon to say when he'd be round, and the insurance people would be there some time later that day but couldn't say when. He'd had no joy with getting anyone to look at the parquet flooring but would carry on with that after he'd had another cup of coffee.

Hint, hint. Ellie made some more coffee, and Thomas retreated to his study.

Ellie lifted the phone to make her next call, only to be interrupted by Rafael rushing in with a laptop and an armful of files which he took straight through to the dining room.

She followed him. 'Rafael, I'm sure it's not necessary for you to stick around. I know you're a busy man.'

He grinned. 'Susan's very fond of you, you know. She told me she wasn't leaving the house unless I stayed. I didn't want her to miss classes, did I?'

She had to smile. 'Well, I'm grateful. I promise you that I am on the job. I'm setting up a conference in here this very afternoon. Perhaps you can move down to the library when people come?'

'I've brought some files I need to look at and can settle down wherever you wish. Any chance of a cup of coffee?'

Ellie made another cup of coffee and took it in to him. How many cups of coffee had she made that morning? Were they going to run out of milk?

Rafael set up his laptop on the table and began checking over some papers in the top file at his elbow. Ellie shuddered and withdrew, thankful that he didn't expect her to understand what he was doing.

What next? She found some painkillers, collected a lightweight dressing gown and, armed with a mug of tea, knocked on the door of the room in which Russet had been sleeping.

Not that it looked as if Russet had had a good night. She was awake, with a deep frown line between her eyebrows. The room stank of fire. Her bandaged hand had precluded her taking a shower or getting much sleep, but her manners were impeccable. She eased herself into a sitting position one-handed and attempted a smile.

'Mrs Quicke, you are so good, taking us all in like this. What a nuisance we're being.'

Ellie popped two painkillers out and placed them on Russet's undamaged palm. 'Don't talk. Get these down you and then rest till they take effect.'

'I ought to get up and take a shower. I stink of fire.' One side of her hair had been singed by the fire and she was in too much pain to relax. 'How is Barbie? Is she all right? She saved my life last night, you know. She came to help me and ended up losing even the little she had left.'

'Drink up. Do you have to go back to the hospital for your hand?'

'No. I have to see my local doctor.' Tears began to slide down her cheeks. 'Sorry, sorry. I'm not usually such a dreary person. I'll be all right. Of course I will. I keep telling myself that I'll survive, but I'm not sure I believe it.'

'Of course you will. I must find you something to wear until you can get to the shops.'

Again, Russet tried to smile. 'Oh, Mrs Quicke, I am so much taller than you that . . . Perhaps Trish might have something, even though she is broader across the shoulders than I. You are all so good to me. I keep thinking, what's it all about? First Walt threw me out, then he dies and then there was the fire last night. Barbie and Bro and I, we all nearly died. We were meant to die, weren't we? What on earth is going on?'

'That is indeed the question and we are going to deal with it. Meanwhile, could you bear to fill me in on how you got married to Walt? Did you sign a prenuptial agreement?'

'No. We never thought of it. It was a spur of the moment impulse to get married, you see. Not that I regretted it for a moment.' She almost laughed. 'You won't believe this, but we got married in Las Vegas. Walt had business in America and asked if I'd like to go along for the ride. We ended up dropping in to Vegas to see what the fuss was all about and Walt said, "Why not get married today?" and I said, "Why not?" So we did.'

'You'd known one another a long time? You knew his friends?'

'I'd known him about a year. We met in a busy restaurant. They'd double-booked a table and asked if we'd mind sharing. It went on from there. He was scared of trusting any woman again because his first wife had gone off with the man he thought was his best friend. I'd been married before as well. We were much too young. He drank and gambled. Ugh! Those experiences had scarred us both, but somehow . . . You know, we did laugh a lot. We really did. We had such good times.'

'I understand. So you didn't meet any of his friends before you were married?'

'No. You can understand why, can't you?'

'Did your family approve of your marrying Walt?'

'Except for Bro, my baby brother, who's always getting into fixes and expecting someone else to bail him out. He thought my getting married again meant I'd be less likely to help him out in future, and I suppose that is what's happened, but he did come to my rescue yesterday.'

And left again when the going got tough. But we won't mention that.

Ellie patted Russet's shoulder. 'I'm going to see how the others are getting on, and someone will be in shortly to help you bathe and get dressed. Meanwhile, Thomas has offered to go over to your house to see what needs doing. Can you remember who you're insured with?'

'How good of him. All the papers are in the desk in the study next to the kitchen at the back. Insurance? Let me think. It was done through Age Concern.'

'Which builder do you normally use?'

'The people in the Avenue. A small firm but good.'

'I know it.'

'Now, if the firemen will let Thomas get into the house, can he find my handbag because it's got my mobile phone, my keys and all my cards in it? I think I left it in the hall.'

'I'll see what can be done.'

Ellie went downstairs to tell Thomas what she'd learned from Russet. He said he'd be off there in a minute but he still hadn't found anyone to resurface their flooring.

Ellie said, 'Forget it for the moment. It's probably going to be an insurance job, and it's a small matter compared to what else needs doing.'

He nodded, collected his keys and left.

What next? Ah, yes. She had to ring Lesley at the police station. Ellie decided to get Lesley on her mobile as this was not going to be an official call. Ellie's call went to voicemail but, before Ellie could decide what to do next, Lesley rang back.

Ellie said, 'There's been some developments. Lesley, I know it's not possible for the police to move on the deaths for the moment, but last night Russet's house was torched. She and her brother and her friend were lucky to get away with their lives. Later, someone tried to torch this house as well. I don't know who is responsible. All I know is that certain people couldn't have done it. Maybe that will help.'

'I'm shocked.'

'So am I. Fire investigators are on to both incidents and I suppose reports will filter through to you eventually, but in the meantime I'm convening a meeting of interested parties here this afternoon. Even if you can't be here officially, I'm inviting you to join us. I hope to be able to clear up one or two misconceptions about this situation. Perhaps you can tape the proceedings?'

Lesley absorbed this slowly. 'You want me there, but not in an official capacity? It's unlikely the police will be informed about the fires until the investigators have produced their report, and that will take time. However, if you have suffered an incident I could, as a friend, drop in to see if you are all right. On the other hand, I can't tape proceedings without cautioning everyone first.'

Ellie grinned to herself. 'Just do it, right? Four o'clock. Tea and biscuits.' She killed the call. Now, what next? Was that the noise of a shower running up at the top of the house? Barbie had taken refuge up in Susan's flat, hadn't she?'

Barbie had arrived from the hospital in a dressing gown and

slippers over a flimsy nightie. Barbie could not go out on to the streets like that, and she was not as tall as Russet, so Ellie looked out a couple of T-shirts and some jogging trousers that she'd bought when she had resolved to take more exercise but had never worn. They'd be too large around the waist for Barbie, but perhaps a safety pin or two might make them fit, sort of?

Ellie toiled up the stairs to the top floor, carrying her clothes and yet another mug of tea. She knocked on the door of Susan's spare room and, on being given permission to enter, did so. Barbie was standing at the window, with a bath towel tied like a sarong around her breasts. She had showered and washed her hair and was trying to reduce her long bob to order.

'Oh, Mrs Quicke, how good of you. Susan looked after me beautifully last night. She said she'd be off early this morning and I didn't like to go into her kitchen though I was dying for a cuppa. Tell me, how is Russet?'

'She's as well as can be expected. She's worried about you. Drink your tea.'

'Bless you. Just what I need. I am truly grateful.' She sipped the tea and closed her eyes to enjoy the sensation. 'You know, Mrs Quicke, I was brought up in a churchgoing family, but I thought I'd grown out of all that. I haven't been to church for years. Now – can you believe it – I find myself praying. I thank the Lord that I was saved from the fire last night, and that Russet was, too. I am truly thankful that I have a comb and a lipstick and my credit cards. And for this excellent cup of tea.'

Barbie had lost everything but was putting a brave face on things. She was a thoroughbred.

Ellie said, 'I pray, too. I pray we may be shown how to defeat the evil mind which has been bent on destroying us.'

Barbie shot her a sharp look. 'Who do you think it is?'

'I don't like to say. How about you?'

'I know who I'd like it to be, but I've absolutely no proof.'

Were they both thinking of the same person?

Ellie said, 'I'm arranging a meeting this afternoon with the parties concerned. Perhaps we might get some idea of the truth then.'

'You are a brave woman, Mrs Quicke. Look what's happened

so far. Your house might have gone up in flames too if you hadn't a couple of men around to protect you.'

'True. I'm wondering if you have some protection yourself that you might have overlooked. Is your household insurance up to date, and will it cover your loss of personal goods outside your house?'

Barbie's legs gave way and she sat on the bed. 'I'm losing the plot. Why didn't I think of that? Yes, of course it would. Ah, but will that cow Fenella allow me to get at the paperwork, which is all in Bunny's study?'

'Your solicitor should be able to get you access.'

'He's not been terribly helpful so far. Bunny's family solicitor never cared for me because he's some kind of cousin of dear Fenella's. He could hardly hide his pleasure when I went to ask him about my husband's will. Bunny had told me he was drawing up a new will leaving me everything, but his solicitor said he hadn't got round to signing it, and therefore the earlier will, made when Sam was a little boy, must stand. It's true Fenella doesn't gain from it, but their wretched son gets the lot.'

'Was there a prenuptial agreement when you married?'

Barbie looked away. 'You know, don't you?'

Ellie sighed. 'I did wonder. You were never actually married to Bunny?'

'No, I wasn't. We met soon after he'd thrown Fenella out. I thought at first he was a funny little man but nice with it. I was taller than him, you see, and we did look odd together. But the more I got to know him, the more I found to admire. Do you know that bitch Fenella used to inflate all the bills and take a cut off each one? And the boy, who by all accounts was a sweet little lad, was so spoiled by Fenella that he developed into a bully who was constantly being asked to move schools. She said it was everyone's else fault and that Sam was an angel. Every time Bunny tried to correct the lad, Fenella said he was a sadist who should never be allowed near children. She dug away at his self-confidence, telling him how ridiculous he was and how nobody could possibly respect him. He was a successful businessman, he really was, and brilliant at sniffing out a bargain in the auction rooms. What she did to him was a crime in itself, wasn't it?'

'Yes, I rather think it was.'

'Bunny had a heart of gold, used to do all sorts of good in the community but kept quiet about it. If she ever found out he'd given someone a helping hand, she'd say he was a fool, that he was being conned, while all the time it was she who was the hustler. Don't take my word for it; Evan and Terry knew all about it, too. And Walt. It cost Bunny an arm and a leg to be rid of her, and after that he was wary of committing himself to another relationship. His friends accepted me as Bunny's partner when I moved in with him. We went away on holiday together and when we got back, everyone thought we'd actually done the deed and I wore a gold band on my ring finger and, well . . . that was it. It didn't seem to matter that we weren't married.'

'You began to think of regularizing the position when Bunny's health worsened?'

'Yes, we were going to have a quick visit to the registry office at the end of this month. Witnesses off the street, no fuss, no bother. That's when he said he'd make a new will in my favour. We had so many good years, you know. We worked well together and were careful of one another's failings. I can't say it was a great romance, but I miss him more than I can say.'

There was a tap on the door, and there stood Trish with an armful of clothing. 'Oh, Mrs Quicke. I can't remember; is it Russet in here, or Barbie?'

Barbie cried out, 'Come in!' And Trish came in.

Ellie looked at her watch, 'Barbie; Trish. Time's getting on. Can I quickly tell you what's been happening this morning, and what I have in mind to do to prevent this nightmare getting any worse?'

Trish put her hand to her mouth. 'It can get worse? I suppose you're right, but we don't know who's been doing this. Do we?'

Ellie was grim. 'I have an idea. This afternoon I want to get everyone round the table to talk about it. Meanwhile, can you two look after Russet? I've given her some painkillers but she can't wash herself or do her hair or dress without help. Put a plastic bag over her bandaged hand so that she can have a shower, but for the rest . . . Can you two help her look reasonable again? Clothes; Trish has brought some and so have I, but shoes are a problem. We might try some flip-flops? I have some I bought for the garden and never used.'

'Understood.' Barbie was on board. Trish would follow where Barbie led.

'Then,' said Ellie, 'you'll want some breakfast. Get yourselves downstairs for a light meal as soon as you can. Make out a list of what each of you need to buy. Just the essentials. One outfit each, shoes, night things, cosmetics, toiletries. I'll order a taxi to take you up to a department store. If you have cards, use those. If not, subsidize one another. Keep the bills. Have a light lunch out and be back here by half past three. The men are coming at four.'

Barbie's eyes narrowed. 'I get it. Trish, Russet and I are to stick together. If one goes to the toilet, the others must wait outside. We'll be safe in the department store because no one would expect us to be there. We order a taxi for the return journey.'

Trish said, 'I was going to drive up to my parents this afternoon, but I suppose I'd better stay for this. That is, if you don't mind, Mrs Quicke?'

'Of course you must all stay.'

Trish said, 'What about Kat and Diana?'

Ellie said, 'I'll see them in a minute. I'm hoping they'll pair off together. The main thing is can you look after Russet? If she can't manage all the shopping, would you send her back here in another taxi and I'll put her to bed till the men come? On the whole I'd say she's better taking painkillers and doing something positive than sitting around here worrying.'

'Understood. Throw those clothes over, Trish. Let's get the show on the road.'

Ellie made two more cups of tea. She took one into little Evan's room. Kat was lying on the bed and tucked up in his duvet beside her was little Evan, clutching his soft toy. Both were sound asleep. Ellie left one mug for Kat and took the other in to Diana.

Diana was also asleep, but less deeply. She stirred when Ellie drew back the curtains.

Diana started upright. 'Little Evan! Where is he?'

'Kat is looking after him. He's had some breakfast and now they're both asleep in his room across the corridor.'

Diana stretched, and sniffed. 'Pooh. What a stink of burning. Can't you open a window downstairs to get rid of the smell? And what about little Evan? He's usually awake by six at the latest. It was good of Kat to look after him last night for me, but we've got to get him back into his routine. If I wake him soon . . . Is it too late to take him to nursery this morning? I suppose it is. It seems strange not to have work to go to, but . . . Perhaps I should take him to the park? He enjoys that.'

Ellie remembered that Diana had gone to bed before Russet and Barbie had been collected from the hospital. 'Russet's house was firebombed last night. They got out in their nightwear and came back here to sleep for a few hours. Russet has a badly burned hand. She's in some pain but Barbie and Trish are looking after her. I thought they'd better go shopping for some clothes this morning. Do you want to go with them?'

Diana shook her head. She sat up, retched, but wasn't actually sick. She took a sip of tea and kept it down. 'I don't need to go shopping and I do need to look after little Evan. Poor Russet, poor Trish. Barbie can cope, and so will Russet, I suppose. I'll survive. I have my little boy to look after, I'll get another job and Evan will have to pay me some decent alimony or else! You know, I thought I'd reached some sort of stability in my life. We were getting along well enough. I'd got accustomed to his little ways. It doesn't take much to keep a man happy, does it? And he could be quite sweet at times. I've come to terms with the fact that he's too old to be a good father. He's more like a grandfather to our little boy. But that's what he is, and a little girl to come, too.'

'He's not a bad man,' said Ellie, crossing her fingers as she spoke.

A sigh. 'He's a product of his times, I suppose. Stiff upper lip and all that. I'll tell you something. He'd hate it to be known, but he sleeps with his bedroom door open and leaves a light on in the landing. It dates back to his childhood. His father used to frighten him with tales of ghosts lurking on the stairs. I hope he remembered to leave the light on and his door open last night. You'll say it's ridiculous to worry about him after the way he's treated me, but I do. Who's going to look after him now?'

Ellie said, 'That's something we need to discuss this afternoon. I've invited everyone to meet here at four.'

'You mean, Evan's coming here?' She considered the idea. It found favour. She ran her fingers back through her hair. 'He likes me to look feminine. Old Man's darling and all that. I need a wash and blow-dry. You say little Evan is still asleep? Could you watch him while I go to the shops, and maybe have a facial as well? Or would Kat look after him?'

'I'll ask her when she wakes.'

Diana was fretful. 'The police. Where are they at? Surely they should be taking some notice of what's happened? What are they doing about the arsonist? We could all have fried to death last night. Something ought to be done.'

'Yes, indeed. We need to eliminate the innocent and point the finger at the guilty. That's why we're meeting this afternoon.'

'Do the police still think I was responsible for Walt's death? What happened at the autopsy?'

'I've checked with my friend Lesley. She says the results of the autopsy are inconclusive. There was some bruising, but he was wearing a jacket and that padded him out. So far, no decision has been made about looking into either Bunny's or Walt's deaths. Breakfast downstairs when you are ready.'

Ellie left Diana to shower and dress. Uneasy laughter came down the corridor from where Barbie and Trish were helping Russet to face the day. Russet's door was ajar, and Ellie paused to listen to what Barbie was saying.

'I think we should aim for a look that says, *Don't mess with me!* We are three highly marketable commodities. Yes, Trish, that goes for you, too. We know how to dress and how to behave ourselves. We know how to keep house and how to look after a man. We want the men to appreciate what they're missing. We have a limited amount of time to make ourselves presentable. Let us organize the day like a military operation. When we get to the shops, what department do we hit first?'

As she descended the stairs, Ellie reflected that Barbie might give way to tears in private but would always put on a good show in public.

The phone rang, and Ellie scrambled to get it. The insurance man wanted to make an appointment for the following day but would ring again to confirm the time. The phone rang again. A concerned neighbour wanted to know if it really was a fire engine that she'd seen at Ellie's house the previous evening?

Ellie was on her way to the kitchen when the phone rang yet again. This time it was Thomas, to say that he was staying at Russet's house for a while. 'Her car's all right, not touched by the fire. I got hold of her builder and they're making the house secure by boarding up all the ground-floor windows at the front and fixing something temporary but solid over where the front door had been. He says it's going to take all day.'

Ellie said, 'Have you been able to get into the house?'

'Yes and no. The builder and I had a conference and I explained Russet had no keys or handbag and we agreed that the study window was so badly cracked that it had to be replaced with some boarding, so we climbed in there to see how bad the damage is. The door to the hall from the study had been left open so the furniture inside was charred though not burned through. We levered the desk drawer open and found the contents untouched. I rescued the insurance file. Russet's handbag had been left on the newel post at the bottom of the stairs and it's so badly burned it's almost unrecognizable, but I brought it out anyway.'

'The rest of the house?'

'Uninhabitable. The gas, electricity and water have been turned off. The kitchen's pretty well all right and so is a garden room at the back, but the two front reception rooms are badly affected and the stairs have gone. I asked if we could go up a ladder outside and get into the bedrooms that way, but the builder said to wait till the insurance people have been and done a survey of the damage. It's a sensible decision. I mean, if the floor's been burned through, anyone walking around upstairs might find himself dumped on the ground floor all of a sudden.'

'Russet will need to see for herself but she's very frail. I'm not sure she's up to looking at it today.'

'Tell her we're making it all safe, and that I'll get on to the insurance people for her. She doesn't have to make any decisions straight away. Between you and me, and judging from what the builder said, it would probably be best to pull down what's left and rebuild.'

Ellie kept that to herself while she went off to make breakfast for Trish, Barbie and Russet. The three made a reasonable stab at eating breakfast, helping Russet by cutting up her toast and so on. There was some hilarity caused by their being dressed in an odd assortment of clothes. Then they went off to raid the shops.

Diana came down, looking pale. She'd tried to wake little Evan and failed. She said she'd managed to wake Kat up enough to ask if she'd look after the boy that morning, and Kat had agreed to do so. Diana had a couple of dry biscuits and some water, and also left for the shops.

Rain threatened. Kat brought a fretful little boy down, fed him and said she'd take him for a walk to keep him awake for a while. Ellie couldn't find another front door key, so gave Kat hers so she could get back in when she'd had enough.

Ellie was exhausted. She told herself she hadn't done anything much that morning, but the fact was that she felt as tired as Russet looked. She left the breakfast things where they were and went down the corridor to sit in the Quiet Room for a while. She needed to regroup her forces for that afternoon. She needed to be quiet and talk to God.

What have I missed?

What have I left undone?

Please will you look after those poor women . . . please?

She drifted off to sleep.

SEVENTEEN

Wednesday afternoon.

Ellie woke with a start. What time was it? Rain had threatened that morning, but the day had brightened up after that. Someone barged into the Quiet Room, slamming the door back against the wall.

Little Evan had come to take a nap in this room, as he often did. He looked owlishly at Ellie, pulled his rug from the cupboard, laid it out and settled himself down to sleep.

Ellie looked at her watch. Horrors! It was half past three. The breakfast things hadn't been attended to. The men were coming to tea and they'd expect cake! And, there were noises off. Who else, apart from little Evan, might be in the house?

Then, she remembered. She bustled out to the kitchen, but everything was clean and tidy, and the dishwasher was working away. Kat had been busy. Where was she?

Ah, Kat was in Thomas's study at the end of the corridor, hoovering away while singing to herself. Kat was one happy bunny. Perhaps, thought Ellie, she was the one who had benefited most from being discarded by her husband, because she'd immediately dropped into housekeeping mode in someone else's house. What's more, she had lost the least in the move as she'd only had two suitcases with her when she arrived, and they were still present and correct.

If Rupert could be persuaded to take his wife back, would Kat return to him? Kat held strong views on the sanctity of marriage, didn't she? Perhaps she would.

There was no time to make a cake. Scones, perhaps?

Where was everyone? She'd called a meeting and no one had arrived.

Ellie dithered, and then realized there was no need to make cake, or scones. The meeting today was not going to be a social one. She went into the somewhat lifeless dining room which she only used for the weekly meetings of her charitable trust. The Victorian furniture looked good in the room; the long table and the chairs set around it shone with polish, and the claret-coloured, full-length velvet curtains were double-lined to keep out the cold.

Rafael had been working there that morning but had removed himself and his paraphernalia by this time.

Instead, Ellie found Lesley, her policewoman friend, who had set up a small table and chair for herself in a corner and was now unpacking a box of tricks. A machine?

Lesley said, 'If this is a scam, Ellie, I'll never speak to you again.'

'No scam, and I'm truly glad to see you.'

A taxi drew up outside and Ellie hastened to open the front door. From it, hung around with packages, came Barbie and Trish.

This was alarming. 'No Russet?'

Barbie said, 'We dropped her off at her house. Thomas rang

to ask her about something. He said he'd still be there for another hour as the builders hadn't finished. She wanted to see how bad it was for herself. It's all right – we delivered her into Thomas's hands and he said he'd bring her back in good time for the meeting. We've got the things she bought and will dump them in her room, if that's all right with you?'

Barbie was wearing a well-cut dress and jacket in a shade of grey to match her eyes, with medium-heeled court shoes. Her hair was as smooth as usual and she looked elegant, if a trifle tired.

Trish wore a stylish black and white pants suit which showed off her excellent figure. The youngest of the Orphans of the Storm, she had slept reasonably well and even in the harsh light of day she looked a million dollars. She said, 'Barbie chose this for me. I've never worn black before. It makes me feel, I don't know . . . grown up?'

They were both smiling, both pleased with themselves as they ferried the things they'd bought into the hall and up the stairs.

Before Ellie could close the door, a large, expensive car drew up. Monique got out, moving awkwardly and with her stick much in evidence.

A second car edged into the drive. Evan got out. He was looking frail. Perhaps he hadn't slept well, worrying about bogies and ghouls on the landing outside his bedroom? Ellie was amused by the thought and then told herself she ought not to laugh at other people's phobias.

Out of the passenger seat of Evan's car came Trish's husband, Terry, looking tousled as to hair and short as to temper. Last of all meek-looking, rat-faced Rupert emerged from the back. Trust him to get a lift, so that he didn't waste petrol driving to the meeting!

So Monique had managed to bring all the remaining husbands while Ellie was short of two on her side. Where was Diana? And how long was Russet going to be?

Ellie ushered Monique and the men into the fire-blackened hall and was grimly amused when they blenched and said 'Faugh!' or words to that effect.

'Yes,' she said, 'that's what the remains of a fire looks like, and we got off lightly. This way,' and she indicated they go into the dining room, while she called out to the women that the men had arrived.

Barbie and Trish came down the stairs together. They gave the impression of holding hands, even though they were not actually doing so. Kat cut short her hoovering and came, too.

Ellie put her head round the door into the sitting room to find Rafael doing something complicated on his laptop. He was abstracted, didn't take his eyes off the screen, but said, 'Leave the dining-room door open so I can hear if you call for help.'

She nodded and followed the others into the dining room.

As the mistress of ceremonies, Monique had taken the carver's chair at the head of the table, while the men occupied seats on her right. Barbie, Trish and Kat took seats opposite them. Men on one side and women on the other.

Trish and Terry tangled glances and looked away from one another. Terry smoothed his hair back and reddened. Trish looked down at her hands.

Lesley, in her corner, gave Ellie a narrow-eyed look and pressed buttons on her recording machine.

'Where's my wife, then?' Evan said, barking out his displeasure. 'Have you got us here under false pretences?'

A porcelain doll figure dressed in a flowered shift with a ruffled neckline appeared in the doorway, carrying a sleepy child in her arms. Her hair, usually cut severely short, had been fluffed out and waved into a becoming frame for artfully made-up eyes and lips. Ripe young motherhood in all its beauty.

'Great balls of fire!' Monique stared at the apparition. 'Hah!' She slapped the table in front of her. Monique recognized what Diana had done to herself and recorded a knock-out blow for the women's side.

Diana lowered her eyelids with an almost convincing show of modesty and took a seat next to Barbie.

Evan's mouth dropped open. Was this vision of motherhood really his businesswoman wife?

Terry gave vent to a whistle.

Rupert was bug-eyed.

Ellie coughed. 'Well, I think we should start. Russet has gone home to look at the damage. She'll be along soon, but we don't need her just yet.' Ellie took the chair at the end of the table opposite Monique. 'Are we all sitting comfortably? I'll serve tea later, when we've got over the business part of the meeting. I think we're all agreed that a series of events which may or may not have started out as a joke, has escalated to arson and murder. Marriages have been wrenched apart, three people nearly lost their lives in a fire last night, and Russet has suffered a nasty burn to her hand. I think it's time we ask ourselves why?'

The men paid close attention.

Monique said, 'Why? Well, the women disrespected the men.'

'No,' said Ellie. 'The men neglected the women. The men took them out to the golf club so that their peers could admire their choice of partner, and then left them strictly alone. The women took their revenge lightly. A murder weekend was coming up at the golf club, and th4ey amused themselves by suggesting how they might act if they took part in the make-believe.'

Terry glared at his wife. 'She suggested shagging me till I had a heart attack. She made fun of me by putting it on an email.'

'No, she didn't. That method of murder was Barbie's suggestion. You didn't read the emails properly, did you? The women made various suggestions, but they were purely hypothetical. In other words, they were not plotting the deaths of their spouses but taking part in a game.'

'Come off it! Bunny died in the way Diana proposed, and Trish's suggestion did for poor old Walt.'

'Let's deal with Walt's death first. Who was it who pushed him down the stairs? That is, if that is what actually happened. We don't even know that for sure.'

'Trish, of course.' Terry leered at his wife.

'Nonsense,' said Ellie. 'She was here all afternoon. As were Barbie, Russet and Kat. Diana was occupied elsewhere. You men are not thinking clearly. If the women didn't do it – and they didn't – then who did? Perhaps one of you men?'

'What!' Rupert gibbered.

Evan said, 'Oh, this is priceless!'

Terry sat back in his chair, looking bewildered. 'You can't put it on us. Why would we . . . No, that's ridiculous!'

'No more ridiculous than assuming that everything that has happened was done by one or other of your wives. Terry, I assume you have no alibi for yesterday afternoon when Walt died? No, I can see from your expression that you haven't. Well, your wives do have alibis. Another thing: last night Russet's house was torched. Russet, Barbie and Russet's brother narrowly escaped with their lives. This house was also attacked by an arsonist. The women didn't do it. They alibi one another. So who was responsible? One of you men?'

Monique rapped the table. 'All right. I get you. The women didn't do it. But the men didn't, either. Haven't you painted yourself into a corner?'

'I think someone, not anyone in this room, saw the emails and used them to his or her advantage. They wanted someone in this room dead. Or at the least, disgraced. So they took an opportunity to mix up Bunny's pills.'

The men's eyes swung to Barbie, who was gripping the table, hard. She said, 'You are thinking what I'm thinking?'

Ellie said, 'By great good fortune you've still got your handbag, which has accompanied you through fire and slaughter. I asked you to check your movements in the week before Bunny died, to see if anyone else had had an opportunity to meddle with Bunny's pills.'

Barbie licked her lips. 'Yes, I did start to check but got distracted.' She lifted her bag on to the table and extracted her smartphone. 'He was prescribed five different pills which he was supposed to take at different times of the day, some in the morning, some after lunch and some at night. He simplified matters by taking the lot together when he went to bed.

'I always filled his box on Monday morning and I did so the week he died. We went out together on Monday to have lunch with friends at a pub in the country. On Tuesday I went into town to meet an old friend for lunch and he played a round of golf. Wednesday I was out in the morning trying to find a suitable present for one of his old aunts' birthday and he had an appointment in town. I don't know who with. The name will be on his desk diary in his study and I don't have that. Wednesday afternoon a couple of people called. I know that because the hall and sitting room stank of a strong scent when I got back, and I had to open the window to get rid of it.'

Monique's eyebrows rose. 'Don't you use a perfume?'

'Yes, but not such a strong one. It was dense. Not floral.'

Monique said, 'A neighbour called. So what?'

'When I went upstairs I saw someone had thrown back the duvet on my neatly-made bed and tossed my nightdress on the floor. Also, they'd used the toilet in my bathroom and left the seat up. There was no trace of the perfume upstairs.'

Silence while everyone thought about that.

Monique said, 'Bunny might well have left the seat up.'

Barbie shook her head. 'No. He was good about such things. And don't say a neighbour might have done it. We have a perfectly good cloakroom downstairs for visitors. I mentioned it to Bunny. We were in a hurry, having a quick bite to eat before we went out to the theatre that evening – an amateur theatrical group, not bad. He said, "Typical! I'll tell you all about it tomorrow". Only tomorrow never came because he died that night.'

Barbie threw back her head. 'I had no reason to kill my husband. I swear it.'

Monique turned to Evan. 'You've known Bunny for ever. What do you think of Barbie's story?'

'I don't know. He didn't confide in me. I thought he and Barbie were getting on all right, but what do I know?'

Terry was frowning. 'Not long before he died, he did ask me if I'd made a will. I said no, that I thought I had a good few years in me yet.'

Barbie said, 'I suppose I have to explain. He made a will in favour of his first wife sometime after they got married. The divorce cancelled that will so he made another in favour of their son, Sam. But the boy grew up so twisted that . . . in fact, Bunny was beginning to doubt whether he was indeed his son and was going to ask for a DNA test to prove it one way or the other. Anyway, Bunny knew he was getting frail and he wanted to make sure I'd be all right after he went. We discussed his making a new will and I said I would do so, too.'

She choked, coughed and put her hand over her mouth, shaking her head. Mastering her emotion, she said, 'Can you believe, we joked about how much we'd each leave to charity? He said I'd been a good and faithful servant, and I said . . . Oh dear. Sorry. This is all a bit . . . You know?'

Ellie said, softly, 'I think what triggered Bunny's death was his resolve to change his will. When Barbie went to the family's solicitor after his death she was told that he hadn't signed a new will and that therefore the previous will, leaving everything to Sam, stood. He did *not* tell her that Bunny had instructed him to make a new will, but I do believe that that was exactly what had happened, probably when he'd had an appointment out early in the week that he died. Only he died before he could sign it.'

Terry pointed his finger at Ellie. 'If the solicitor can prove intent, then even if Bunny hadn't actually signed the new will, it has a good chance of being accepted.'

Barbie grimaced. 'It depends on the solicitor.'

Rupert chirped up. 'Ridiculous! The whole thing is ridiculous. I'm not going to stay to hear you spouting rubbish. Barbie killed him, following Diana's instructions.'

Diana gave him a look of melting innocence. 'Why would I want to kill Bunny?'

'Exactly,' said Monique, giving Rupert a dark look. 'Barbie didn't gain by his death, and neither did Diana.'

Ellie said, 'So who did gain from his death?'

Another silence. Everyone's eyes switched to and fro.

Terry turned his head to look at Rupert. He looked puzzled. 'Rupert?'

Rupert gobbled. He thrust back his chair. 'How dare you! I didn't have anything to do with it. I didn't know anything about it.'

'No,' said Ellie, 'all you did was put a match to the touch paper. You showed those emails to someone connected with the group. Fenella, wasn't it?'

Silence. Rupert folded his arms and shut his mouth tight.

Barbie sighed. 'Fenella is poison, and I'm not just referring to the strong perfume she wears. And her son is a spoilt brat who snorts anything he can lay his hands on.'

Rupert banged on the table. 'You have no proof! None! Fenella is a dear woman whom I've known for ever, and who has consented to be my wife when I'm free of my present entanglement. Yes, Fenella is concerned that Sam gets his rights. And yes, she is anxious about him. The young nowadays are exposed to all kinds of temptation. I admit he has had difficulty holding down a job, but that's because he has a problem, an irritation of the nervous system. He needs proper treatment, not the pills handed out automatically by the doctor, but some in-depth assessment and a course of therapy.'

Monique turned her beady eye on Rupert. 'You fell for that garbage? She saw you coming, didn't she? To her you're just a nice little earner, whom she can milk for your money, especially if she can lay her hands on Bunny's estate as well. I get it, now. It was you who told Fenella about the emails. You kept her informed about what was happening or not happening with the police? Rupert, don't you realize this makes you an accessory to arson and attempted murder?'

Rupert flinched. 'No, no! I never. You've got it all wrong.'

Ellie summed up. 'Barbie has been the target from the beginning. Her husband was going to change his will, so Fenella decided he had to die. She and her son visited Bunny while Barbie was out. It was her son who went upstairs and mixed up the pills. Barbie was supposed to take the rap for it but convinced the police of her innocence. So the emails were reeled out to incriminate her. That worked to a certain extent as Monique took a hand in the game and all the wives were thrown out of their homes. At that point Barbie might well have given up and left the field, but instead Diana organized her friends to come here and the women began to fight back.

'Barbie became their leader. Fenella decided that the police had to be given more incentive to suspect the women of murder, so Walt was pushed down the stairs to his death. Fenella was in a meeting with Rupert at the time so it would have been her son who did the deed. But the wives were all here that afternoon and had an alibi for that event, which meant the murderer was forced to think again . . .'

Except for Diana, but we don't need to mention that.

'This time she used another of the methods suggested in the emails and torched Russet's house with her and Barbie inside. And, because the arsonist couldn't be entirely sure that Barbie had moved in with Russet, this house was also attacked.'

Barbie lifted her hands and let them drop. 'Yes, but we have no proof.'

A phone rang. It was Barbie's. She answered it. 'What? Say that again? Russet, is that you?'

Someone screeched down the other end of the phone. Everyone looked at Barbie, who listened with an expression of shock and dismay.

Finally Barbie clicked her phone off and lurched to her feet. 'That was Russet. She says her house has gone up in flames again. She needs help. The fire brigade are on their way, but she's asking all her friends to help her rescue as much of her furniture and belongings as possible. I must go, straight away.' She would have started for the door, but Ellie caught her arm. 'Stop! Not you!'

'I'll go!' said Evan, who had finally decided which side of the fence he was on. 'I know Fenella and that ratbag of a son of hers. They're poison, though Rupert could never see it. Of course we must go and help Russet rescue her stuff. We'll take my car. Terry, are you with me?'

Diana, in a charming gesture, stood on tiptoe to kiss his cheek. 'My hero!'

Ellie subdued a quick impulse to be sick. Evan preened! He gave Diana a quick kiss and vied with Terry to get out of the room first.

Ellie turned to her police friend, Lesley, who had been sitting in the background all this while. Lesley, police instincts to the fore, was already on her own phone, ordering up reinforcements. And here came Rafael, who had been listening in from the hall, pulling on his jacket. He said, 'I'll help, too. Lesley, do you want to come with me? It will be quickest on the bike.'

Lesley, still talking on her phone, hurried out with Rafael.

And then there were only the women left in the room.

Barbie was indignant. 'Mrs Quicke, why did you stop me? I ought to be there.'

Ellie said, 'Use your head! That fire was well and truly out by this morning or the fire brigade would not have left the site. What's more, Thomas is there. Wouldn't he have rung us if the fire had started up again? It's a trap!'

Trish wailed, 'I don't understand!'

Ellie took out her own mobile and pressed Thomas's number. 'I'll check with Thomas. He said he'd bring Russet back here, so . . .'

They heard Thomas's phone ring and ring . . . and go to voicemail.

The landline in the hall woke to life.

Ellie hastened to answer it. 'Who is it?'

A man's voice spoke over her. 'Hell and fury, woman! Don't play games with me. Just don't! Is everyone on their way to help? Not Barbie, of course. But the others. You should come, too.'

He killed the call.

Ellie turned to face the others, who had crowded into the hall behind her. 'That was Thomas. On the surface he was making sure that everyone had gone off to Russet's house with the exception of Barbie. He even suggested that I go, too. But it was a coded message. Thomas never swears or orders me about. That message was given under duress. He said, '"Don't play games with me. Just don't!" In other words, don't do what he's asking me to do. Thomas is in trouble. He's trying to warn us.'

EIGHTEEN

Wednesday afternoon.

Barbie sank into a chair. She was wide-eyed with terror. 'You're right! They've decoyed the men away. There isn't another fire at Russet's place. They got Thomas to make that phone call. It means they're coming here!'

A car drew up outside.

The front door opened and someone called out, 'Just in time!'

But . . . who . . .?

'Rupert!' said Ellie. 'Where is he? I thought he'd gone with the others!'

Monique grinned. 'So now it's the women's team against the world. As usual.'

Diana juggled her sleeping son. 'Kat, do you think you could take the little one and hide him somewhere safe? In the cupboard in the Quiet Room, for instance. Stay there with him. Put a table under the doorknob.' She brushed her hands down her dress. The Little Woman act had disappeared and she was all business again.

Kat said, 'Understood. I will pray for you.' She disappeared with the boy.

Diana actually looked to Ellie for instructions. 'Now what?'

Ellie said, 'Diana, get behind the curtains. Trish, under the table. Put your mobile phones on. Call the police if you can do so quietly. Whether you knew it or not, my friend Lesley has been recording everything that's happened this afternoon. Her machine is still on and working so it should capture everything that's said from now on.'

They took her advice and hid.

Ellie looked at Barbie. 'You want to disappear upstairs?'

Barbie shook her head. 'It's me they're after.'

Ellie nodded. 'I'll try to divert them.' Crossing her fingers and toes. For how on earth could she deal with a pair of determined murderers?

'Come in, come in!' cried Rupert.

First came a young man with a laughing faun's face. Ellie shivered. She'd seen a sculpture of a boy looking like that once and had recognized it as evil.

The newcomer pulled a shambling figure in after him and thrust him against the wall. 'Stay!'

Ellie froze. She hardly recognized her burly husband. He was dishevelled, his eyes were almost closed and he didn't appear to know where he was.

Drugged? Concussed?

Russet stumbled into the room after them. She was wearing a black skirt and white top. She'd lost a shoe and lurched up and down on one high heel as she walked. The bandage on her hand was dirty, her hair a mess. Her eyes were wild, her mouth open. She tripped and fell to the floor, just missing a chair.

Barbie helped Russet up and into a chair. 'Oh, my dear, what have they done to you?'

'Who's still here?' A strong, heavy scent invaded the room. A woman with a stiffly lacquered blonde mop of hair stood in the doorway. Middle-aged. Corseted. Her face had been lifted and Botoxed; her eyebrows were arched in surprise. She cast a cold eye around the room.

Barbie blenched. 'I recognize that scent! So it was you who killed Bunny?'

The newcomer said, 'Not I.' The idea amused her. She turned to the rest of the women. 'Now, Monique I know of old. And this,' gesturing to Ellie, 'must be the old man's wife. Allie, isn't it?'

Ellie told herself to stop trembling. Was Thomas conscious? Barely. 'I'm Mrs Quicke, yes. Who, may I ask, are you? And what have you done to my husband?'

'I'm Fenella. First and only legitimate wife to the late Bunny. As for what I've done to your husband, I've done nothing. My son had to stop him making a nuisance of himself, that's all.'

Rat-faced Rupert hovered at Fenella's shoulder. He was barely as tall as her. He looked half worried and half elated. 'Sam is a naughty boy, isn't he? He shouldn't have done that, Fenella. Thomas is all right, really. He'll see reason, just as the others will. You have my word for it.'

'I don't take anyone else's word for it, Rupert. You should know that. Now, how many of them were left in the house when the men departed?'

'Well, they're all here . . . except . . . Oh! Where did they go?'

'Who?'

'Diana and Kat. And the boy. Diana was here, holding the boy on her lap a moment ago.'

'They've gone,' said Ellie, trying to think up a reasonable explanation. 'Out the back way. They went to help Russet.'

Rupert went to the window to peer out. He was standing next to the curtain behind which Diana was hiding. Oh, pray, *pray* he doesn't notice that that curtain isn't hanging as close to the wall as the others! He said, 'Her car's still in the drive.'

Ellie closed her eyes in prayer. *Don't let him discover Diana! Did she have time to ring the police? We're all going to die!*

Monique stirred herself to draw Rupert's attention away from the curtain. 'What do you know about it, you horrible little man? She went with her husband, of course.' Monique could have tried to flee, but she hadn't. Ellie worked out that from where Fenella was standing, Monique's bulk concealed Lesley's machine, which was still switched on and recording what was spoken. Monique was not going to move. Good for Monique.

Did the full-length curtains twitch? Ellie prayed that Diana would remain hidden. The situation was bad enough as it was, but if they discovered her . . . Ellie didn't like the thoughts that played through her brain.

And Thomas? What of him? He was still propped up against the wall, but a gleam from half-closed eyes told her he was still in the land of the living.

'Well?' Fenella demanded of Rupert. 'Could they have got out without your noticing?'

Rupert had his fingers in his mouth. He was so nervous and so excited that he couldn't keep still. 'I don't see how they could have gone past me in the hall. Trish was left behind, too. She was sitting next to Barbie.'

Fenella leaned over Barbie. 'So where are they?'

Barbie stared back at her. 'I suppose Rupert was looking out of the front door while they went out the back way. They are with their husbands. There's only us poor widows left behind.'

'I'm not sure I believe you,' said Fenella. She pulled out a chair and seated herself. 'But I suppose it doesn't matter very much if it's two corpses, or four or six or more found in a burned-out house. The result will be all the same.'

Russet began to sob. 'You can't!'

Barbie put her arm around Russet. 'Hush, now!'

'Of course I can,' said Fenella. 'Who's to stop me?'

Ellie said, 'I'm not sure I catch your meaning, Fenella. Why all this talk of corpses?'

Thomas had forced his eyelids open and was looking at her, hard. Was he biding his time to make a move?

Fenella twitched a smile. 'I like a good bonfire. So cleansing.'

Ellie said, 'And it was one of the methods of murder to be found in the emails.'

'True. I like to be consistent.'

'You expect us to accept our fate without defending ourselves?'

'Sam will see to it that you don't cause any trouble. Oh, you haven't been properly introduced to Sam, have you? Sam is my right hand. True, he has expensive tastes, but money is easy enough to come by, isn't it?' Here she poked Rupert, who was hovering at her shoulder. 'Isn't it, Rupert?'

'Well, yes. At least, I suppose. But I do think you have gone a little too far this time, my love. You've made sure Sam will get Bunny's estate and—'

'Ah, yes. That.' And she rounded on Barbie. 'I need the combination for the safe.'

Barbie laughed. 'You mean you haven't been able to open it yet? So my miniatures are still there? You really think I'm going to tell you? In your dreams, Fenella.'

'Sam is an expert at giving people bad dreams,' said Fenella. 'Believe me, you will be happy to give it to me before you die.'

Rupert began to perspire. He'd been fooling himself about Fenella, hadn't he? He'd been feeding her with information, yes, but he couldn't stomach murder. 'My love, I'm sure we can come to some arrangement. Barbie can sign her rights over to you and promise to disappear. Why not, eh?'

'Why not? *Why not?* Have you listened to yourself? Of course she's going to die, and so is that stupid friend of hers, Russet. I don't leave loose ends running about. They can trip you up and cause no end of problems.'

Ellie said, 'How exactly do you intend to kill so many of us?'

Yes, Thomas was definitely awake and thinking hard. As she was . . .

'Sam will see to that for me. You had a fire in this house last night. Unfortunately it will all start up again this evening when he and I are well away from here. This time there will be no one to put out the fire. I'll make sure of that.'

Ellie said, 'You forget my lodger and her fiancé.'

'I forget nothing. We will stick around till they return, and deal with them the same way.'

'What way is that?'

'Sam's way. With his sharp little needles and one of his speciality drugs. Designer drugs. I've never felt inclined to try anything like that, but he's a dab hand with them, aren't you, darling?'

Sam grinned, which made him look more like a pixie than ever. 'Who shall I do first?'

'Russet, of course. She's expendable, and Barbie needs to see we're in earnest.'

Russet cringed.

Sam drew a flat case out of his pocket and opened it. Syringes and needles glittered. He filled a syringe with liquid and held it up to expel a drop from the tip of the needle. He said to Russet, 'It won't hurt. Actually this drug is so powerful that it doesn't just put you into a coma but can sometimes go directly to your heart. Some people die from it straight away. You might be one of the lucky ones and not have to wait for the smoke to get you. Or you might just go to sleep. I promise you won't feel a thing.'

Was that a faint cry from the depths of the house?

Ellie's heartbeat went into overdrive. Was that little Evan yelling for attention?

She tried to think of something to say to cover any other noise he might make.

Too late.

'What was that?' Fenella got to her feet and looked around. 'Rupert, what did you say about Diana being here with her baby? Was that him, now? He hasn't left the house and neither has she!'

Barbie wrung her hands. 'For God's sake, what have they done to you? They haven't seen you. They don't know you're here. Let them go.'

Fenella wasn't taking any chances. 'Rupert, go and find them, and bring them here.'

There was no disguising the little boy's wails. They were getting louder with every second. Ellie started for the door, not thinking but reacting to little Evan's cry.

'Hold it right there!' Fenella caught Ellie's arm. 'One wrong move and I'll have Sam deal with your husband first. If you are very, very good, and behave yourself I might let him live.'

Ellie froze. She realized how clever Fenella was. Each one of them could be neutralized by the hope that Sam might let one of them live.

Rupert came back into the room with Kat, who was holding a red-cheeked little boy in her arms. 'He woke up. He wants Mummy.'

'Biccy!' howled little Evan. 'Mummy! Biccy!'

Sam said, 'Shut him up. He's doing my head in.'

Fenella laughed. 'Well, ducky. You have the remedy in your hand. Give him a shot.'

The curtain swayed and Diana ran out. 'Don't you dare!' She snatched the boy from Kat's arms. Little Evan switched from rage to reassurance, putting his arms round her neck and almost cooing in delight. 'Mummy, Mummy. Biccy?'

'Yes. Biccy. In a minute.' Diana jiggled him in her arms, fixing Fenella with her eye. 'You don't dare kill a child. Not even you would do that.'

'Wrong,' said Fenella. 'In fact, I won't need to, as he can't testify against me or Sam. I shall let him go. He will be found wandering the streets tomorrow morning, crying for his mother. That is, if you all behave yourselves and cause me no further problems. Do you understand?'

Diana flushed with anger and fear. 'You want us to accept death for ourselves so that my darling boy has a chance of life?'

'Nicely put.'

'What you don't realize is that I am carrying another child now. You can't kill that child as well.'

'Wrong again. Go and sit down. Yes, everyone sit down at the table. You, Kat: you're Rupert's wife, aren't you? Come and sit here by me. Pull your chair right in under the table, so you can't get out easily. That's right. The rest of you, do the same. Rupert, take the child from Diana. Go and feed his face with something in the kitchen. I know you're a little squeamish, so you don't need to see what's going to happen next. Sam, are you ready? Leave Barbie till last so that she can give us the combination of the safe before she passes out.'

Sam waved his syringe around. 'I'm ready, willing and able.'

Monique stirred herself. 'Are you sure, young man? You don't look to me as if you know what you're doing. Have you ever tried to inject anyone but yourself? I bet you make a hash of it. You've never been any good, have you? A great disappointment to poor Bunny, who spent so much time and money on you. Look at you now! Reduced to being your mother's lapdog.'

Sam advanced on her. 'Just for that, you can be first, you—'

Monique brought up her stick and caught him on his forearm. He screamed but held on to the syringe.

Somebody swiped at his legs from under the table.

He stumbled, mouth agape.

Trish scrambled out, clinging to one of his legs.

Fenella screamed.

Thomas lurched from where he'd been propping up the wall

and fell on Sam . . . Who tried to stab him with the syringe . . . Only to have Barbie grab his wrist and, exerting all her strength, force it away from Thomas . . .

Barbie was thrown off Sam. She skidded across the floor.

Russet screamed.

Somehow Sam managed to free himself from beneath Thomas's weight and got to his feet. He was groggy, but still waving the syringe.

Trish launched herself at him from behind so that he fell towards Thomas . . .

Who was still on the floor and helpless.

Ellie picked up a chair, swung it high, and with all her might clocked Sam one over his shoulders.

He staggered, off balance.

Thomas kicked up at Sam, catching him in exactly the right place.

Barbie flailed around. She caught Sam's right arm and drove it down and down.

Sam folded down on to the floor, the syringe embedded in his thigh.

Fenella screamed again.

Everyone was breathing hard.

Rupert stood in the doorway, wringing his hands. Tears spurting. 'Oh, no!'

Little Evan toddled into the room. Hungry. Miserable. 'Mummy! Biccy!'

Both Diana and Kat dived for him. Diana got there first and scooped him up. 'Come on, Kat. This is no fit place for us. Let's go and find something for my little love to eat, right?'

They disappeared.

The front door crashed open. Rafael appeared in the doorway with Lesley at his shoulder. 'Are you all OK? It was a hoax! No sign of Russet or Thomas! No fresh outbreak of fire, either.'

Ellie, breathing hard, waved a hand towards Sam on the floor.

Rafael got out his phone. 'You need the police, right?'

Lesley was already on her phone. 'Yes, yes! At Mrs Quicke's! Now!'

A police car drew up outside. Two large men emerged, talking into the equipment on their shoulders.

Trish, panting, helped herself up on to a chair. 'I texted the police. Is that them?'

Russet put her head in her hands. 'Is it over?'

Barbie said, 'Can I have hysterics now?'

Chaos ruled, OK. Ellie felt unreal.

Time compacted. More police arrived.

Lesley flexed her muscles to take command.

Sam lay on the floor, snoring. Not dead. The syringe had fallen off his thigh on to the carpet.

Thomas hugged Ellie. 'Thank God you're safe.'

Ellie hugged Thomas back. 'My hero.'

Fenella gabbled, 'It's all a lie. I'm leaving, now, and don't you dare stop me!' She tried to waltz round a burly female police officer who was standing between her and the door. The police officer, unsure what to do, looked to Lesley for orders.

Ellie realized that Lesley didn't know who Fenella was or Sam, or how they'd intended to commit mass murder. Lesley hadn't yet listened to her recording machine, which would enlighten her as to what had happened after she left in response to the fake call for help from Russet. That material would probably not be admissible as evidence but would be helpful to guide the police when they questioned the suspects.

So Ellie said, 'Don't let her go! I want her to understand that she's killed two people and torched a couple of houses for nothing! The law prevents criminals gaining from their crimes, and Barbie will inherit as Bunny intended she should.'

'That's not true!' Fenella was in shock. She thrust the police officer aside.

The police officer said, in a conciliatory voice, 'Now, now! No need for that.'

Stupidly, Fenella lost her temper. She yelled, 'How dare you!' and swung her handbag at the woman, who rocked on her feet but didn't give way.

Lesley said to the officer, 'Charge her with assault for starters.'

Exit Fenella, whisked away by said policewoman and a colleague.

Sam struggled back into consciousness. He hadn't taken enough of the drug to knock him out for good.

Ellie tried not to panic. 'Lesley, take care! That's Sam, Fenella's son. He's dangerous. Please, get someone to take those needles away from him before he does any more damage.'

Sam was already reaching for the syringe, but the police were trained to know how to deal with men brandishing syringes. Sam's arm was caught and held up behind him. The syringe dropped to the floor.

Sam wept. 'It's not my fault!'

Ellie explained, 'Lesley, Fenella is Bunny's long-divorced wife. Bunny made a will leaving everything to Sam when he was a child. Sam hasn't turned out too well. Bunny was going to make a new will in Barbie's favour. Fenella wanted to stop him doing that. Fenella and Sam visited Bunny the day he died. Fenella told Sam what to do and he did it. It was he who rearranged Bunny's pills while his mother talked to Bunny downstairs. They thought they could frame Barbie for Bunny's death. When that didn't happen, they tried all sorts of ways to get at her. It was Sam who set the fires here and at Russet's. I suppose he killed Walt, too. Today he's assaulted Thomas and Russet and threatened to kill us all. With any luck everything that he and his mother said will be recorded on your tape. Fenella was the mastermind; he happily fulfilled her orders. He's got some drug or other in that syringe which was supposed to knock us all out so that we would conveniently die in yet another fire. Would you please remove him?'

Lesley cut her eyes to her machine. 'Everything's recorded?'

'Yes,' said Ellie. She gestured at Rupert. 'Take him away, too. He helped Fenella by feeding her all the information she needed to murder anyone who stood in her way.' She gulped air. Fenella's strong scent was making her brain fuzzy. 'I hope I'm making sense. It's been a very trying day.'

Rupert wrung his hands. 'No, no! I didn't understand. I trusted Fenella – she's such an old friend. I had no idea what she was up to.'

Lesley was sharp. 'You knew about Bunny's pills?'

Rupert said, 'No, no. Well, I know she and Sam went to see Bunny that day, but it would have been Sam who actually mixed the pills up, wouldn't it? I mean, she did ask me once about how many pills Bunny was on, but I didn't think . . . It never occurred to me . . . I suppose it does make sense because Sam always hated Barbie, and so did Fenella, although really, I know nothing. I really don't. I'm anxious to cooperate with the police if . . . I'm so distressed, I had no idea.'

Ellie said, 'Excuse me, I've got to open a window to get rid of Fenella's scent.' She tried to wrestle the window open, but it stuck. Thomas came to help her. He put his arm around her and they stood there, breathing deeply, while Sam and Rupert were removed and Lesley made arrangements to take statements from everyone.

People came and went. There was a lot of tidying up to do. Statements were taken one by one.

All Ellie could think of was how many would there be for supper? Every time she counted, she got a different result.

First things first: she went to the kitchen to make a pot of tea.

Thomas made himself a giant sandwich, saying, 'Russet asked me to check that the back door was locked after the builder had gone. This young man came round the side of the house holding a cricket bat and knocked me out. When I came round, he was holding a syringe to Russet's neck, threatening to kill her unless I rang you to say the house was on fire again and I needed help. I did, hoping you'd realize I'd been forced to make the call.'

Ellie nodded. 'I understood.'

He set to work on his sandwich with gusto.

Monique appeared, walking with some difficulty. 'I'm off now. I'm stiff. I need a good lie down on my own bed or I'll be back to the physio first thing tomorrow. I've had Evan and Terry on the phone, wanting to know why there was no fire at Russet's place. I put them in the picture so no doubt they'll be round here soon. I expect you can cope.' And then she was gone.

Ellie took cups of tea into Barbie and Russet in the sitting room.

Russet said, 'I can't believe it's really over. Mrs Quicke, Barbie is trying to persuade me to join her in renting a two-bedroom furnished flat for a while. I do realize my house is uninhabitable for the time being so it makes sense. On the one hand, it was my home for so many years . . . But then Walt died and there was the fire. I'm not sure I can face moving back there again.'

Barbie said, 'That's it exactly. I don't much want to go back to my place, either, but I realize that in time I may think differently. If we rent somewhere else for the time being, it would give us time to consider what we want to do in the long run.'

Ellie recognized this as her cue. 'I think you're right, Barbie. Give yourselves a breathing space. Barbie, let me give you my solicitor's phone number. If anyone can, he'll see you get your rights. In law, Sam can't profit from his crimes and, as Bunny's intention to change his will has been established, you should be able to claim his estate and regain your house. As for your finding somewhere to live temporarily, young Rafael is doing up a block of flats locally and might be able to find you something suitable. Or Diana, of course.'

Barbie didn't even bother to exchange glances with Russet before saying, 'Thank you. Yes, we'll certainly have a word with Rafael.'

No sooner had Ellie regained the hall than Rafael passed her, going out. He said he was off to collect Susan and he'd be back in a tick. Did that mean they'd be joining the party for supper?

Would Lesley be through taking statements in time to join them or not? No, probably not.

Ellie went back to the kitchen to find Diana and Kat there. Kat bounced little Evan on her knee. He loved it. 'Rrrrrr . . .! More!'

Ellie counted on her fingers. She made it nine for supper. Could that be right? Was there anything in the freezer, possibly under those packs of vegetables at the back, which might do? Or what about the food that had been delivered from the supermarket?

Ellie investigated and unearthed a frozen fish pie and some cooked apples. Oh, joy! But, what about vegetables?

Trish wandered in, saying, 'That was Terry on the phone. Monique's been putting him straight about what happened. He's apologized for doubting me and wants me back.'

Ellie willed the girl to say she'd refused . . . and then hoped she hadn't.

Thomas suspended operations on his second sandwich in mid-bite. Everyone looked at Trish. Ought she to return to a wife-beater? Probably not. On the other hand, she'd discovered that she could give as good as she got, so perhaps her relationship with Terry had moved into a different phase.

Trish sighed. 'I told him I was going to stay with my parents for a week. I said that if, by the time I return, he's enrolled in an anger management course, he could take me out to lunch and we'd talk about it.'

That was sensible. Ellie resumed her search for some frozen peas to go with the fresh broccoli which had been delivered from the supermarket.

Someone rang the front doorbell. Trish went to answer it and brought in Evan, looking sheepish. He said, 'Monique's been on the phone, explaining what's happened. What a thing, what!'

Little Evan held up his arms and cried, 'Dada! Up, up!' He was taken from Diana's arms and thrown into the air, father and son enjoying the moment.

Evan cradled his son as to the manner born. 'Hrrumph! Well, that's all very well, but . . . Diana?'

Diana exchanged a long look with Kat. She pushed back her chair and went to her husband. 'I know I've been a bad little wifey of late. I was so wound up with business that I neglected my darling husband.'

Ellie told herself she couldn't believe her ears. Had Diana been taking lessons in how to captivate an older husband?

Diana took her husband's free hand and placed it just under her heart. 'Can you feel the heartbeat? I don't know if it's a boy or girl yet. Do you have any preference?'

'Hurrumph! Well, Monique did say that you . . . It's all very well, Diana, but you did play that stupid game about killing your husband.'

'Yes, it was stupid. I was feeling neglected myself, but I shouldn't have done it. Will you ever forgive me?'

Ellie blinked. Diana was really laying it on with a trowel. Everyone else round the table was goggle-eyed, waiting to see if Evan would go for it.

Evan preened. Yes, he really did. 'Well, if you promise me it won't happen again.' He transferred his son over to Diana.

'Of course not. I've realized I need some help in the house. I'm wondering, do you think it would be a good idea to ask Kat to come and live with us? She's a wonderful housekeeper, she loves little Evan and he loves her. Then we can get rid of the new nanny, whom our little boy doesn't like. It would take such a load off my shoulders.'

Kat nodded, smiling. She'd been plotting this with Diana, hadn't she?

'Hurrumph!' said Evan again. 'I'll have to think about that.'

It was Trish who intervened. 'Kat, you don't have to go out to work in someone else's house again. You can divorce Rupert and get enough to live on comfortably.'

Kat shook her head. 'Divorce is not for me. I know Rupert has been a bad man, but it is that woman who has made him like that and in time perhaps he will want his wife again.'

Trish said, 'But Kat, he may well go to prison for what he's done.'

'Then I wait for him. When he is dead and I am old, maybe I will go back home to my own country, or maybe I will find someone else here who likes my cooking. For now, I am going to look after my little Evan, who loves me, and I will cook for Diana and her husband and we will be a family together.'

Evan looked as if he wasn't sure he liked this plan but as they all watched in fascination, they saw him decide that there were more pros than cons to the idea. 'Well, well,' he said. 'I suppose you must have it your own way. Now, are you all packed up, you two? You have your car outside and so have I. Let me have some of your things so that you can have the boy and Kat in your car, right? Chop, chop, now. Time is money.'

Diana said, 'Kat can get her things ready in a trice, and it won't take me long to pack up again. Thomas will help put our things in the cars, won't you?'

Yes, Thomas would. He finished his mouthful, sent a look to Ellie full of amazement at Diana's tactics and offered to start straight away.

Ellie relaxed. And then started to worry again. Strike Kat, Diana and little Evan off the list. Add Susan and Rafael, perhaps? So how many would there be for supper? Did it still make seven . . . or eight?